BEYOND THE BIG WOODS

BEYOND THE BIG WOODS

THE CONTINUING STORY OF THE BOYD FAMILY

AL LAMANDA

THORNDIKE PRESS
A part of Gale, a Cengage Company

Copyright © 2023 by Al Lamanda.
The Big Woods #2.
Thorndike Press, a part of Gale, a Cengage Company.

Thorndike Press® Large Print Softcover Western.
The text of this Large Print edition is unabridged.
Set in 16 pt. Plantin.

LIBRARY OF CONGRESS CIP DATA ON FILE.
CATALOGUING IN PUBLICATION FOR THIS BOOK
IS AVAILABLE FROM THE LIBRARY OF CONGRESS.

ISBN-13: 979-8-88579-971-3 (softcover alk. paper)

Published in 2024 by arrangement with Alfred John Lamanda.

BEYOND THE BIG WOODS

CHAPTER ONE:
1874

Every time he rode on the railroad, U.S. Marshal Emmet Boyd was reminded of the years he spent as head of the railroad police with the Transcontinental line when it was constructed between 1866 and 1869.

Born to a farmer in a place called The Big Woods in Wisconsin, it was his brother Ellis, who hated the farm and wanted to see the world and it was Emmet who left the farm and did the traveling.

First as a soldier in the war under Grant, then Grant appointed him to head the railroad police during the construction. He met his first wife, Eva in sixty-seven. She was a madam with the brothel that traveled with the railroad and they struck up a friendship that eventually led to marriage.

Eva loved him more than he loved her, but they were a good match even if he never really forgot Rose. Wounded in sixty-three in battle, Emmet was sent to a Washington hospital to recover. Rose was his nurse, a striking looking woman, two years older than he and she stole his heart completely.

Rose's husband was killed in battle, or so it was believed. Emmet asked Rose to marry him and she agreed and they made plans to marry after the war.

At the war's end, Emmet, a junior lieutenant by that time, returned to Washington to face the bad news. Rose's husband wasn't dead but a prisoner of war and he had returned to her a sickly, beaten man but still alive.

Emmet was devastated and returned to Grant's Army where he took the assignment with the railroad and later met Eva. They were good for each other. Eva was outgoing and friendly and he was somewhat shy and reserved. Together they were a formidable team.

At the railroad's conclusion, Grant called upon Emmet again. He appointed him the marshal for Cheyenne, Wyoming for one year. Cheyenne, built by the railroad in sixty-seven was a booming, lawless cattle town in desperate need of law and order.

Emmet and Eva moved to Cheyenne, where he hired deputies and calmed the wildness that ran through the streets. While Emmet did that, Eva used her savings to open the most popular saloon in town.

After a year, Cheyenne was tame and Grant called upon Emmet one last time, recruiting him for the newly formed Secret Service. Emmet and Eva moved to Washington, DC where Emmet began his new duties.

One of which was to go undercover in the south to infiltrate the rise of the Ku Klux Klan. The assignment took months and worried about Eva living alone, he sent her to live with his parents on their farm near Stockton in California.

While living with Emmet's parents, Eva discovered she was pregnant. Ellis, his wife Bettina and Eva took a buggy ride to Stockton to see the local doctor. On the way, three drifters who once worked for the railroad, recognized Eva as the railroad madam. They shot Ellis, beat Bettina and raped and murdered Eva.

Once Emmet got word of Eva's murder, he resigned his position and returned to Stockton. After Eva's funeral, Emmet began a year-long manhunt for the three men responsible. He knew the men from his days with the railroad and found the first two after months of hunting.

Over the winter, Emmet traveled to Washington to request a favor from Grant. He wanted to be reinstated as a marshal so he could pursue the final murderer, a man named Suggs and legally arrest him.

Grant agreed, but with one catch. He would reinstate Emmet but wanted five years in return. Emmet agreed and set out to find Suggs. The task took months and when Emmet finally caught up to Suggs, he was with his two brothers. Emmet killed the brothers and wounded Suggs, but not before one of them shot Emmet in the lower abdomen.

The nearest doctor was forty miles away in Fort Laramie Hospital and Emmet made the trip with Suggs in tow. Suggs didn't survive and by the time Emmet reached the hospital, he was close to death.

When he woke up in a hospital bed, for the second time in his life, the nurse was Rose. Her husband died of natural causes and she moved away from Washington and settled at Fort Laramie Hospital.

Emmet owed Grant five years and allowed Emmet and Rose to move to California where they settled in Sacramento where it was just a short hour by train to his family in Stockton.

As the U.S. Marshal for California, Emmet employed thirty deputies to cover the enormous state of one hundred and sixty-three thousand square miles and most of the time thirty seemed hardly enough.

Between the boom towns and mountains and deserts, California was a dream hideout for outlaws, which was the reason Emmet and one deputy were on a train to Omaha, transporting three prisoners on a warrant.

The three outlaws were wanted for bank robbery and murder in Omaha and sought refuge in the old town of San Diego, where they thought they would disappear in a sea of outlaws. Mail was slow, wanted posters were even slower, but eventually the law caught up with them in San Diego, where they hid out under assumed names.

The local sheriff recognized their faces from wanted posters and wired Emmet in Sacramento. Emmet arrived with six deputies and together with the sheriff, found the three outlaws living in a cabin in the mountains with three prostitutes.

There was a shootout and two of the outlaws were wounded and one prostitute was killed when she attacked a deputy with an ax as she proclaimed her love for one of the outlaws.

The ride from Sacramento to Omaha took thirty hours. Once the three outlaws were secured in the prisoner transport car, Emmet and his deputy were free to do as they liked, but except for reading, eating, playing cards in the gentlemen car and sleeping, there wasn't much to do besides watch the scenery roll by outside a window.

Emmet was anxious to return home. Rose was five months pregnant with their first child and he tried to be away as little as possible.

Emmet looked at his watch. "Time to feed the prisoners dinner," he said to his deputy, a man named Chase.

"I'd let them starve," Chase said.

"We might as well eat, too," Emmet said.

They went to the dining car and ordered steaks for the prisoners. When the steaks were ready and placed on a serving tray, they carried the tray to the prisoner car.

The prisoner car had a jail cell built into the car, where the three outlaws were behind the bars.

"Got supper for you fellows," Emmet said.

The three outlaws stood up from their bunks.

"Face the wall, hands behind your head," Emmet said as he drew his Colt Peacemaker and cocked it.

The three prisoners went to the wall and placed their hands behind their heads. Chase used a key to unlock the cell door, placed the tray on the floor, then locked the cell door again.

"We'll be back directly to pick up the tray," Emmet said.

Emmet and Chase returned to the dining car and ordered steaks.

"We reach Omaha at two in the afternoon," Emmet said. "But our return train isn't until ten o'clock the following morning."

"I'm a single man, but it must be rough on your wife when you're away from home, especially being pregnant and all," Chase said.

"She stays with my folks," Emmet said.

John and Sarah Boyd came from humble beginnings in The Big Woods of Wisconsin where they had a small farm. They survived frigid winters and drought-ridden summers, the Civil War and other hardships. They had two fine sons and twin daughters and life took a sharp turn for the better when Ellis convinced the family to move to California to the fertile land near Stockton.

With the money raised from selling the farm in Wisconsin and their life savings, they were able to buy five hundred acres of good farm land. They grew all types of melons, then expanded to orange groves, of which they had one hundred trees. Ellis built a separate house for his wife and two children on the property, but Sunday dinner was always held in John and Sarah's house at the long table in the dining room.

John sat at the head of the table, with Sarah to his right. Then came the twins, Anna and Emma, followed by Robert Olson, the boy they recently took in after their mother, Beth passed away.

On John's left were Ellis, his wife Bettina, their two children and Rose.

Supper was a plump turkey with all the trimmings. John did the carving, Ellis did the passing of the plates.

"How long will Emmet be gone this trip?" John said to Rose.

"Four days," Rose said.

"I wish he'd give up being a marshal and settle down on the farm," John said. "There is room for a third house and . . ."

"John, Emmet gave his word he would give five years to President Grant," Sarah said. "You don't really think our son is going to break his word to the President, do you?"

"No, I don't," John said.

"Mr. Boyd, I would like to ask a favor," Rose said.

"No favors unless you start calling me John and my wife Sarah," John said. "All this mister and missus stuff is for Boston people and that's one thing we're not."

Rose smiled. "Alright, John," she said. "I'm due for a checkup with my doctor at the hospital in Sacramento. Could I impose on you and . . ."

"Sarah and I will take you tomorrow," John said.

"Can we go?" Anna said.

"Please," Emma said.

"John?" Sarah said.

"Only if you two do all the dirty dishes tonight," John said.

"Deal," Anna said.

After dinner, John and Sarah took coffee on the front porch.

"They only want to go to Sacramento to look for boys," John said.

"They're seventeen now, John," Sarah said.

"Young men just aren't respectful like in our day," John said. "This generation is . . ."

"No different than ours," Sarah said.

"When I was seventeen . . ."

"You were on me like an octopus," Sarah said.

John looked at her. Sarah smiled and they laughed together.

Rose joined them and took a chair. "I

would love nothing more than for Emmet to give up being a marshal, but he did give his word," she said. "And besides, he's too good at his job and the country needs men like him. That second time I treated him in the hospital, he rode forty miles with a bullet in his stomach and still delivered his prisoner."

"He never tells us these things," John said.

"No, he wouldn't," Rose said.

Ellis came out to the porch with two cups of coffee and gave one to Rose. "Pa, you don't know your own son," he said. "Emmet is about the most dangerous man there is walking the earth."

"Don't say that about your brother," Sarah said.

"Ma, I've seen him do things in Cheyenne I wouldn't believe," Ellis said.

"Sarah, Emmet is a lawman and I've accepted that about him," Rose said. "The truth is we all sleep better knowing men like him are out there protecting us and like Ellis said, he's about the best there is."

"He'd be a good farmer, though," John said, which made everybody laugh.

"What?" John said.

After doing the dishes, Anna and Emma boiled water to take a bath. The tub was large and they weren't, so they often shared the tub.

As twins often were, they were not shy about being naked around each other. Often, especially at bath time, they inspected each other's bodies and talked about their good points and their flaws.

As they soaked and scrubbed and washed their hair, they talked about Sacramento and meeting boys.

"Pa gets so upset when we talk about boys, but Ma understands," Anna said.

"We're almost women now, we have needs," Emma said.

"Like what?" Anna said.

"Like boys and kissing," Emma said.

"That could get us in a lot of trouble with Pa," Anna said. "Remember that talk we had with Ma when we turned fourteen?"

"I remember, but we're not fourteen anymore," Emma said. "We have to see for ourselves sometime, right?"

"Right, but when is that sometime?" Anna said.

"I'm not sure, but we can't ask Ma. She'd slap us silly for sure," Emma said. "Maybe we can talk to Bettina or Rose."

"Wash my hair and then I'll do yours," Anna said.

■ ■ ■ ■

Emmet and Chase led the three outlaws off the platform to the streets of Omaha. The heavy chains clanked as the three outlaws walked.

"Hold up," Emmet said. "Let's get a taxi to the sheriff's office."

"That's a waste of money," Chase said.

"Maybe so, but I don't want every person in town gawking at us walking them through the streets," Emmet said. "Go to the taxi stand in front of the depot and get us a taxi for six."

Thirty minutes later, Emmet and Chase were in Sheriff Jenner's office after locking the three outlaws in a jail cell.

"They give you any trouble, Marshal?" Jenner said.

"Two of them have gunshot wounds and the third is a coward," Emmet said.

"Will you be staying for the trial?" Jenner said.

"No need," Emmet said. "My report covers it all."

"You have a hotel?" Jenner said.

"Not yet," Emmet said.

"Try the Hotel Omaha on Front Street," Jenner said. "They have the best steak in town."

"Why don't you join us for dinner, say around seven?" Emmet said.

"I'll do that," Jenner said.

The buggy ride to Stockton to the railroad depot took about as long as the train ride to Sacramento. At the Sacramento depot, John, Sarah, Rose and the twins took a taxi to the hospital where Rose worked as a nurse.

"Ma, Pa, can we look around while Rose sees the doctor?" Emma said.

Before John could veto the idea, Sarah said, "Stay together at all times and be back here in one hour."

"Yes, Ma," Emma said.

Anna and Emma walked along the street in front of the hospital, taking in the sights, sounds and smells of the big city.

To them it was overwhelming to see so many people and carriages all in one place. Stockton was small in comparison and far less exciting.

Young men dressed in suits and ties seemed to be everywhere. Young women dressed fashionably in clothes their father would never allow walked the streets freely.

"How old was Ma when she married Pa?" Emma said.

"Eighteen, I think," Anna said.

"We're seventeen and don't even have beaus," Emma said. "No one even calls on us and do you know why?

"Why?"

"Because we're farm girls," Emma said.

"What's wrong with that?" Anna said.

"I didn't say anything was wrong with it," Emma said. "Look at these men in their suits and hats and these girls in their dresses and shoes. They're what you call sophisticated."

"And we're not."

"No."

"Well, how do we get sophisticated?" Anna said.

"I don't know," Emma said.

"We could ask Ma."

"Ma won't know," Emma said. "She's a farm girl just like us. So is Bettina."

"Rose isn't," Anna said.

"Yeah, we'll ask Rose," Emma said.

Emmet and Chase ordered baths after getting a shave by the hotel barber, then dressed and met Jenner for dinner in the lobby restaurant.

"Five years ago, Omaha had two thousand people," Jenner said. "Today we're approaching twenty-five thousand. I have twelve deputies and it's not nearly enough when cowboys come to town after a drive."

"If I can make a suggestion?" Emmet said.

"Of course," Jenner said.

"What we did in Cheyenne was hire part-time deputies to use when a cattle drive came to town," Emmet said. "Trained men held in reserve to be called up on those occasions. Find yourself some good men and swear them in as reserve deputies."

"It will take some convincing the mayor and the town council to spend the extra money," Jenner said.

"Ask them how much they like their town shot up on every cattle drive?" Emmet said.

"Expect to deliver in two months," Doctor Slocomb said. "I know it's your first, but you're healthy and strong and you should have no complications."

"Will you deliver?" Rose said.

"I'd be pleased to," Slocomb said.

"When do you want to see me again?" Rose said.

"Two weeks," Slocomb said. "Get dressed. I'd like to talk to you in my office."

After dressing, Rose met Slocomb in his office. He served tea and she sat in the chair opposite his desk.

"Rose, how long have you been a surgical

nurse?" Slocomb said.

"Since sixty-two," Rose said. "Why?"

"I think you would make a fine doctor," Slocomb said. "Hell, you know as much or more as most of us. All you need is two years in school and your degree."

"Doctor Slocomb, there isn't one female doctor in this hospital, nor in Washington or anywhere else I have been a nurse, including the Civil War," Rose said.

"So?" Slocomb said.

"So . . . do you think I can do it?" Rose said.

"I know you can," Slocomb said. "You can do your studies right here at the hospital."

"And my baby?" Rose said.

"Are you forgetting the hospital has a nursery?" Slocomb said.

Ellis, Bettina, Anna and Emma walked through the grove of orange trees and sampled a few oranges from various trees.

"We start picking tomorrow," Ellis said. "With the four of us, Ma and Pa and Rip, we can have them to market in three days."

"Seven of us to pick fifteen thousand oranges?" Bettina said.

"We did it last year," Ellis said.

"And what do we do next year when the fifty new trees grow an additional seven thousand oranges?" Bettina said.

"I guess we'll need to have more kids," Ellis said.

"Sure, if you carry them for nine months," Bettina said.

"We could get some kids from school and pay them two cents an orange?" Anna said.

"Do it," Bettina said and walked away.

Ellis looked at Anna and Emma. "Best do as she says, girls," he said.

"I thought the man was in charge," Emma said.

"Yeah, who told you that?" Ellis said.

Anna and Emma knocked on the bedroom door where Rose was staying while Emmet was away. Rose was at the chair before the vanity, brushing her hair.

"Come in," Rose said.

Anna and Emma entered the bedroom and closed the door.

"Rose, can we talk to you?" Anna said.

"Of course, girls," Rose said.

"You're a sophisticated woman of the world, so we thought you'd know best," Emma said.

Rose held back her laughter. "Didn't your mother talk to you about the birds and the bees?"

"We grew up on a farm," Emma said. "We

know all about that."

"What we want to know is when," Anna said.

"When as in . . . ?" Rose said.

"We're supposed to do it," Emma said. "We figured you would know because you're a sophisticated woman from the city."

Rose set her brush aside and looked at them. "Girls, a woman doesn't give away free samples," she said. "Men lose respect for a woman who does."

"But you're from the big city," Emma said.

"It's the same everywhere all over the world," Rose said. "Women are expected to act a certain way and men are supposed to respect that. Now why don't you tell me what's really on your mind?"

"The truth?" Emma said.

"Yes, of course," Rose said.

"I want to do it with a boy," Emma said.

"Do you know what the word regret means?" Rose said.

"When you do something you wish you hadn't," Anna said.

"The both of you think on that tonight and we'll talk more tomorrow," Rose said.

Ellis drove Rose to the railroad depot in Stockton to meet Emmet at four o'clock in the afternoon. The train was on time and Emmet walked along the platform with his satchel and greeted Rose with a kiss.

"How was your trip?" Ellis said.

"Uneventful," Emmet said.

"That, knowing you, could mean anything," Rose said.

"Let's get home, Ma is cooking dinner for us," Ellis said.

As Emmet shaved in a wash basin in his room, Rose watched him and said, "You have a problem with your sisters."

"The girls? What?" Emmet said.

"Boys."

Emmet grinned. "They're seventeen."

"No, this is different," Rose said.

"How?"

"They don't just want beaus," Rose said. "They want to give away free milk, especially Emma."

"They told you this?"

"Yes, but in strict confidence, so . . ."

"I'll ring their necks," Emmet said. "I'll . . ."

"Do nothing of the sort," Rose said. "It's bad enough I violated their confidence, but to have big brother step in would only make it worse."

Emmet sat on the bed and looked at the

floor for a moment.

"What is it?" Rose said.

"Ma has to handle this," Emmet said.

"How without telling tales out of school?" Rose said. "They'll never speak to me or you again, much less trust us."

Emmet sighed. "I won't allow them to become Beth," he said.

"Who?"

"In Wisconsin where I grew up," Emmet said. "Her folks had a small farm next to ours. She hated the farm. One day she up and ran off with a drifter named Rip when she was nineteen. I don't want my sisters doing anything like that."

"Rip? As in Robert?" Rose said.

Emmet nodded. "They got lucky and found gold," Emmet said. "But that's not the point. After Beth ran off, she didn't send word to her parents for five years. Something like that would kill my parents."

"I'm supposed to talk to them tomorrow, I'll see what I can do," Rose said.

"Please," Emmet said.

"I have something of my own to tell you," Rose said. "After seeing Doctor Slocomb today, I decided to return to medical school and become a doctor."

Emmet stared at Rose for a moment. "I think that's wonderful, honey, but what about the baby?" he said.

"I'll be studying at the hospital and it has a full nursery," Rose said. "I'll just bring the baby with me."

"After seeing what you done for me twice, I think you'd make a fine doctor, honey," Emmet said.

"There aren't many woman doctors," Rose said.

"I've never seen one," Emmet said.

"Are you sure it's okay with you?" Rose said.

"I'm sure. Why?"

"I was a bit worried you would be against it?"

"Rose, I'm not the kind of man to stand in his wife's way of what she wants to accomplish," Emmet said.

"Most would."

"I'm not most," Emmet said. "Besides, who better to take care of me in my old age than the doctor I'm married to?"

Rose smiled. "You are a good man, Emmet. A truly good man."

"Right now I'm a hungry man," Emmet said.

"Well, let's go eat supper."

At the dinner table, Ellis said, "Emmet, do

you have to return to Sacramento tomor-row?"

Emmet looked across the dinner table at his brother. "Sacramento will still be there if I don't. Why?" he said.

"We have fifteen thousand oranges to pick," Anna said.

"Now Ellis, you can't expect a United States Marshal to spend his time picking oranges, do you?" John said.

"The pay is two cents an orange," Emma said.

"That much, huh?" Emmet said. "Well, with a baby on the way, I expect I could use the extra money."

Emmet put on the specially designed apron that was built to hold thirty oranges at a time and then climbed a ladder.

Rose stood nearby with Sarah and laughed at the sight of her tougher than nails, marshal of a husband as he started picking oranges.

Ellis, Anna, Emma, Bettina, John and even Rip scaled ladders to pick oranges.

"Come on, dear," Sarah said to Rose. "They'll be expecting a good lunch."

"Have you thought about what I said yester-day?" Rose said.

She was in Anna and Emma's room after supper.

"I have," Anna said.

"And?" Rose said.

"I wouldn't want to do anything that Ma and Pa would be ashamed of me," Anna said.

"Emma?" Rose said.

"I guess so," Emma said.

"You don't sound too convinced," Rose said.

"It's just that it's not fair men get to have all the fun and we have to act so prissy," Emma said.

Rose slapped Emma, stinging her face and shocking Anna.

"Fun?" Rose said. "Do you see Ellis and your father breaking their backs plowing fields twelve hours a day to keep you in dresses and put food on the table. Emmet has been shot twice in the line of duty by outlaws, do you think that's fun? Because if you do, you are one spoiled child."

Emma touched her face and said, "I'm sorry. I didn't mean the way it sounded."

"I know," Rose said. "It's difficult to make sense of it all. Just act like the young woman that you are and never let your parents down and you'll be fine."

■ ■ ■ ■

Ellis drove Emmet and Rose to the railroad depot in Stockton. "Thank you, big brother," Ellis said as he helped Rose down from the buggy.

"For what?" Emmet said.

"For getting me out of picking oranges this morning," Ellis said.

"I'll see you later, little brother," Emmet said.

The ride to Sacramento was just one hour and ten minutes. On the ride, Emmet read the newspaper. "Look at this," he said to Rose. "There's a man in Boston named Bell who claims he will invent a working telephone within a year."

"What's a telephone?" Rose said.

"No idea, but he says he's going to invent one," Emmet said.

"I talked to your sisters again last night," Rose said. "I don't think Anna will be a problem."

"But Emma will?" Emmet said.

"I'm not saying that," Rose said. "I'm just saying she'll need to be watched a bit more carefully."

"Who is going to watch her if nobody is made aware?" Emmet said.

"Anna," Rose said.

"The cat protecting the mouse, huh?" Emmet said.

"One more month," Rose said as she served Emmet breakfast.

"You shouldn't be up doing things," Emmet said.

"I'm fine," Rose said. "I am a nurse, you know. I've delivered a hundred babies or more."

"Yeah, well, shooting someone is not the same as being shot," Emmet said.

"Eat your breakfast and go to work, I have studying to do at the hospital," Rose said.

"Yes sir, doctor," Emmet said.

"Not yet, but I will be," Rose said.

"Come on, Ellis, or we'll be late for the meeting," John said.

Ellis came out of his house and climbed aboard John's wagon and John drove them to Stockton for the monthly meeting of the Grange.

The meeting was held once a month in the Town Hall building. The Grange was an agricultural organization with a countrywide membership. As an organization, the group helped get lower shipping rates for farmers and even lobbied to Washington.

Women and teens as young as fourteen were allowed to take part as long as they were behind a plow.

In order to keep railroad spies out of meetings, they often used secret passwords to gain entrance to a meeting.

Farmers came from all over California to voice their opinions and vote on various issues.

When John parked his buggy, there were fifty other buggies already parked outside the Town Hall.

Coffee and doughnuts were on a table in the lobby and John and Ellis grabbed one of each on the way in. At least a hundred farmers were assembling in the meeting hall.

Meetings always began exactly at noon.

The first order of business was the rising cost of shipping by railroad. Since the railroad was part of the Federal Government, a trip to Washington was in order. By one-thirty, all open discussions were concluded but one.

"Members of the California Chapter of the Grange, I would like to make nomination on whom to send to Washington to speak on our behalf," the Chairman said. "I nominate John and Ellis Boyd. All in favor say yeah. All apposed say nay."

The vote was unanimously in favor.

John went to the podium to reject the vote. "Now folks, you all know me," he said. "You know how much I hate crowds and public speaking."

"That's why Ellis is going with you," the Chairman said and everybody laughed.

Emmet was in his office with deputy Chase when Rose stopped by around one o'clock.

"Mrs. Boyd, nice to see you," Chase said.

"May I steal my husband for an hour for lunch?" Rose said.

"What are you even doing out in your condition?" Emmet said.

"The baby isn't due for a month yet and I'm hungry," Rose said.

"Watch the store, I'll be back," Emmet said.

They walked to a café near the office and ordered lunch.

"How are you feeling?" Emmet said.

"Hungry," Rose said. "Would you relax. I'm fine."

"How do we know when the baby is ready to . . . ?" Emmet said.

"Pop out?" Rose said.

"I'm sure there's a technical term," Emmet said.

"I'm sure there is," Rose said. "So I'm

working only half the time now while I study and I won't be working at all after the baby comes for months."

"I know," Emmet said.

"Do we need the money, because if we do . . . ?

"I make three hundred a month and have twenty-seven thousand in the Bank of Sacramento, don't give it a thought," Emmet said.

"Did I tell you you're a good man?" Rose said.

"At breakfast."

"I may want more than one," Rose said.

"Lunch?"

"Babies."

"Oh."

"Sunday, when we go to dinner at your parents, I'll work it out with Sarah about coming to help out," Rose said.

"I seem to remember cleaning and powdering the twins, I'm not helpless," Emmet said.

"Did you carry the weight of a Marshal's badge when you were doing all that powdering?" Rose said.

"After lunch, I'll walk you back to the hospital," Emmet said.

"After lunch, I'll let you," Rose said.

"I can't wear this suit to Washington," John said. "It's at least fifteen years old."

"You bought that suit to wear to church when the twins were baptized," Sarah said. "Seventeen years ago."

John sighed. "I guess it's time for a new one," he said.

"And Ellis," Sarah said. "We'll all take a trip to town tomorrow now that the oranges have been shipped."

"Alright, but no fancy dude suit," John said.

"John, no matter what you wear, no one will ever mistake you for a dude," Sarah said.

Emmet was reading the latest batch of warrants issued by the courts from California and several other surrounding states.

Chase was at his desk, writing reports.

"Have a look at this," Emmet said.

Chase came to Emmet's desk and took the wanted poster Emmet handed him. "Joseph Pike, wanted for bank robbery and murder in Arizona. Reward posted of one thousand dollars dead or alive," Chase said.

"Now take a look at the warrant," Emmet said.

Chase read the warrant. "Believed to be hiding out in the region known as Yosemite," he said. "Along with his three brothers and one cousin."

"We'll have to smoke him out," Emmet said.

"That's in the mountains, Emmet," Chase said. "We're talking weeks, maybe months away from home."

"I know."

"You got a baby due," Chase said. "I'll take five deputies and we'll go."

"No married men, otherwise, pick who you want," Emmet said. "I'll ride over to Fort Baker tomorrow and request a tracker."

"I feel ridiculous," John said. "And what kind of a hat is this?"

"It's called a derby and you look fine," Sarah said.

"We've never seen you so dressed up, Pa," Anna said.

"Never you mind. Where's Ellis?" John said.

Ellis stepped out from the back room wearing a new suit and a derby hat. Anna, Emma and even Bettina looked at him and laughed.

"That tears it," John said. "Ellis, let's get these monkey suits off."

"John, Ellis, you look fine," Sarah said and laughed.

"I think they look silly," Rip said.

"I agree," John said.

"You look like gentlemen," Sarah said. "Did you expect to go to Washington and meet with the Secretary of Agriculture wearing your overalls?"

"Let's go to the café and get some lunch," John said.

"Now you're talking," Rip said.

Emmet loaded his horse on the boxcar of the train that took him to San Francisco, an enormous city of a hundred and fifty thousand residents, then rode his horse to Fort Baker, located ten miles to the north.

Fort Baker was home to two hundred soldiers, four junior officers and Colonel West, the commanding officer.

Emmet had sent a telegram and was expected. He was received in Colonel West's office.

Over coffee, Emmet told West what he needed to track Joseph Pike and his brothers and cousin in Yosemite.

"That's hard country, Marshal," West said. "It requires a scout of the highest order. I have just such a man, Joseph Takes His Horse. He's a full Lakota and has been with me since I was stationed in North Dakota eight years ago. He's the best tracker and scout I've ever seen."

"Sounds like the man for the job," Emmet said.

John took the entire family for lunch at the café just a few blocks from the clothing store.

"We'll pick up the suits after lunch," John said.

"Now that we have the clothes, Pa, what are we supposed to tell them in Washington?" Ellis said.

"We have two weeks to work on that, son," John said.

"Ma, is it okay if me and Anna go to the general store when you pick up the suits?" Emma said.

"I suppose, but don't take too long," Sarah said.

After lunch, Anna and Emma went to the general store where a cowboy was out front, loading supplies into his saddlebags. He was around twenty or so, handsome, and he smiled at Emma as she and Anna entered the store.

Emma felt herself blush as she made eye

contact with the cowboy. As she and Anna entered the store, they went to the section with combs, brushes and perfume.

They were sampling perfumes when the cowboy approached them from behind.

"Howdy, miss," he said to Emma.

Anna and Emma turned and looked at the cowboy. He was as tall as Ellis and handsome with a well-tanned face and a nice smile.

"Hello," Emma said.

"I couldn't help notice you outside," the cowboy said.

Anna glared at the cowboy. "What do you want?" she said.

"You're sisters, aren't you?" the cowboy said.

"We're twins and you didn't answer my question, what do you want?" Anna said.

"Why, I would like to talk to your sister for a few minutes is all," the cowboy said.

"Before you decide to talk to my sister, you should know that our big brother is the U.S. Marshal for all of California and if you do anything disrespectful, you'll have to deal with him," Anna said. "And that wouldn't be very pleasant for you."

"Anna, please," Emma said.

"I'm just letting him know in case he has any ideas," Anna said.

"Believe me, miss, my intention is just to talk," the cowboy said.

"I'll be right outside, Anna," Emma said.

Emma and the cowboy left the store and stood beside his horse.

"My name is Paden. Josh Paden."

"Emma Boyd."

"Do you live in town," Paden said.

Emma shook her head. "On a farm about ten miles from here. Are you a cowboy?"

"I am," Paden said. "I'm top hand on the Welding ranch about twelve miles to the west."

"So what did you want to talk to me about?" Emma said.

"I think you're the prettiest girl I've ever seen," Paden said.

"Thank you, Josh," Emma said.

"I feel kind of silly," Josh said.

"Me too."

"Do your folks let you have a beau?" Josh said.

"I don't know," Emma said. "I could ask them."

"Please do."

"Do you want to be my beau?"

"I think I would like that very much," Paden said.

"You'd have to ask my Pa," Emma said.

"Is that true about your brother being the

marshal?" Paden said.

"It's true," Emma said. "And if you hurt me he will hunt you like a bloodhound and it wouldn't end well for you."

"Why would I hurt you?" Paden said. "I would never hurt a girl."

"I'm talking about my virtue," Emma said.

"Your . . . oh," Paden said. "Well, like I told your sister, my intentions are just to talk and get to know you better."

"How often do you get to town?" Emma said.

"Saturday and Sunday belongs to me unless there's a drive on," Paden said.

"Come to our house on Saturday and talk to my Pa," Emma said. "If he doesn't shoot you, we can take a buggy ride."

"Alright. What time?"

"Noon."

"Wait. Where's your farm?" Paden said.

"Ten miles to the east," Emma said. "You can't miss it."

"I'll be there," Paden said. He mounted his horse, touched the brim of his hat and rode away.

Anna came out of the general store. "What happened?"

"He's coming to the house on Saturday to ask Pa if he can court me," Emma said.

"Pa will shoot him on sight," Anna said.

Emma laughed. "Probably," she said.

"And that's nothing compared to what Emmet would do to him," Anna said.

Chase, five Deputy Marshal's and scout James Takes His Horse met in Emmet's office before leaving for Yosemite.

Emmet had a map of the area on the meeting table.

"The train will take you to Stockton where you get another train to Modesto," Emmet said. "From there you ride to Yosemite. Scout Joseph, how well do you know that area?"

"I've scouted there before," Joseph said. "It's a harsh area if you're unfamiliar or a tenderfoot. It may be still summer down here, but in those mountains it's cold at night."

"The only information we have on Joe Pike, his brothers and cousin is they're possibly hiding out somewhere in Yosemite. The information comes from one of his men who was wounded by a bank guard before the guard was killed. In exchange for a reduction of sentence, he gave up the information on where Pike likes to hide out after a job. Joseph, what do we need to track them?"

"Five good horses, two mules, a hundred pounds of food, two tents, a Winchester for each man, a hundred rounds of ammunition per man and a medical supply kit," Joseph said.

"Chase, I'll give you the money to buy what you need," Emmet said. "Joseph, when can you be ready to leave?"

"As soon as we have the supplies," Joseph said.

"Do you have a place to stay tonight?" Emmet said.

"I got a room at the boarding house near the railroad," Joseph said. "It's not bad."

"We'll get you everything you need tomorrow," Emmet said.

At the dining room table in John and Sarah's house, John and Ellis worked on their presentation to the Secretary of Agriculture.

"I don't think simple dollars and cents is going to sway them, son," John said. "The railroad is government owned, but also in business to make a profit. By asking them to reduce their shipping costs we're asking them to cut their profits. We need another way."

"What if we threatened a boycott?" Ellis said.

"A boycott?"

"There's only a handful of states and territories that grow year-round," Ellis said. "If we threatened to ship by freight wagon locally and eliminated the railroad entirely, how much shipping business would they lose?"

John looked at Ellis as he thought for a moment.

"They either lower their cost five percent or lose a hundred percent," John said. "I think that might be the solution, son."

Emma entered the dining room with two cups of coffee and set them down on the table. "Ma thought you might like some coffee," she said.

"Thank you, sweetheart and thank your ma," John said.

"Pa, can I talk to you for a minute?" Emma said.

"Is it important?" John said.

"It is to me."

"Have a seat," John said.

Emma took the chair between John and Ellis.

"What is it, honey?" John said.

"Would it be alright if a boy came over on Saturday to ask your permission to court me?" Emma said.

John stared at Emma.

"Pa?" Emma said.

"Who is he, what does he do and where does he do it?" John said.

"His name is Josh Paden and he works as a cowboy at the Welding Ranch," Emma said. "And he's very nice."

John looked at Ellis. "Sooner or later, Pa," Ellis said.

"What time will he be here?" John said.

"Noon."

"I'll see him at noon then."

"Thank you, Pa," Emma said.

"I should be going with you men," Emmet said.

"Now Emmet, we'll be gone a month or more and your baby is due in three weeks," Chase said. "You want to miss your own baby being born."

Chase mounted his horse. "Joseph, let's get to the railroad," he said.

Emmet stood on the sidewalk and watched his six deputies and Joseph ride to the railroad.

John looked out the window at the front porch. He turned and looked at Sarah. "Make sure she stays in her room," he said. "Anna, too."

John watched through the window as Josh

dismounted, tied his horse to the post and walked up the steps.

Josh knocked and John opened the door.

"Hello, sir, my name is Josh Paden," Josh said.

"I'm John Boyd, Emma's father," John said.

Josh offered his right hand. "Pleased to meet you, sir," Josh said as they shook.

"Let's sit on the porch," John said.

John and Josh took chairs on the porch.

"My daughter tells me you're here for permission to court her," John said.

"Yes sir," Josh said.

"Emma is seventeen, how old are you?" John said.

"Twenty."

"And you're a cowboy at the Welding Ranch?"

"Going on three years," Josh said.

"Where are you from?"

"Wyoming."

"Your folks still there?"

"They died when I was fifteen," Josh said. "I've been on my own since."

"We're from Wisconsin," John said.

"Yes sir."

"So Josh, I need to know your intentions?" John said.

"Strictly honorable, sir," Josh said. "I

would like to get to know Emma better and the only way to do that is if you give me permission to call on her."

"And if I don't?"

"I'll respect your decision, sir."

"You have my permission," John said. "You may take a buggy ride with Emma provided her brother rides behind you on his horse."

"The Marshal?"

"I would not inflict that upon you," John said. "Ellis, her other brother."

Josh smiled. "When, sir?"

"Right now if you'd like," John said. "Wait here while I go talk to Emma."

John entered the house where Sarah was standing by the staircase. "Could you get Emma, hon?" he said.

"I heard," Emma said as she came running down the stairs.

"You're supposed to be in your room," John said.

"Well, what did he say?" Emma said.

"You can take a buggy ride provided Ellis rides behind you," John said.

"Ma, do I look alright? How is my hair?" Emma said.

"You look fine," Sarah said.

"I'll get the buggy and your brother," John said.

■ ■ ■ ■

John, Sarah, Anna, and Rip watched as Josh and Emma, followed by Ellis, rode away in the buggy.

John looked at Sarah. "How is it you just happened to have a fully packed picnic basket ready to go?" he said.

"What's the big deal?" Rip said. He looked at Anna. "Want to go fishing?"

"Sure," Anna said.

Josh held the reins and drove the buggy at a slow pace. Ellis rode a hundred feet behind them, close enough to intervene if need be, too far away to hear them talking.

"Do you like being a cowboy?" Emma said.

"I love horses, so I guess so," Josh said. "What about you?"

"I was born on a farm, I know farming," Ella said. "I know how to plow and grow orange trees."

"You know how to plow?" Josh said.

"Since I'm twelve," Emma said.

"What's in this basket here?" Josh said.

"Fried chicken, bread, cheese, milk and apple pie," Emma said. "And we should find a nice spot to eat it before it gets too cold."

"How about under that big tree over there?" Josh said.

While Emma and Josh sat on a blanket and ate their picnic lunch, Ellis stayed well back and ate some jerked beef with water.

Emmet paced his office for what seemed like hours but was really just minutes. He ought to have gone with Chase, but Rose would have skinned him alive if he missed the baby's arrival.

He went to the post office for the mail, of which there was a stack and returned to the office to read through it for something to do other than worry.

There were wanted posters and warrants from outside of California and requests for help with citizen's disputes and a host of other things.

He made some coffee at the woodstove and sat down at his desk to see what he would tackle first when an aide to Judge Thomas came to see him.

"Marshal, Judge Thomas would like to see you at the courthouse," the aide said.

Emmet grabbed his hat and walked with the aide to the courthouse four blocks away.

Judge Thomas saw Emmet in his chambers. "Fresh pot, Emmet, pour us a cup," he said.

Emmet filled two cups from the coffee pot resting on a small table and brought them to the desk, set them down and took a seat.

"Emmet, have you heard of the Kitchen brothers?" Thomas said.

"I've seen posters on them," Emmet said. "They're from Texas. Three brothers. They like to rob stage coaches."

"Their real name is Blunt," Thomas said. "They've operated for ten years in Texas, Arkansas, Oklahoma, Colorado and Kansas, but they're really from Corbin Canyon in the Santa Monica Mountains."

Emmet sipped coffee and waited for Thomas to continue.

"Judge Oppenheimer in Topeka sent me a detailed report on a stagecoach robbery that went bad," Thomas said. "A stage coach carrying six passengers and a shipment of railroad payroll and scheduled to travel from Topeka to Kansas City was held up by the three brothers. What they didn't know was that besides the shotgun rider, two of the passengers were railroad detectives there to protect the payroll."

"How many were killed?" Emmet said.

"The two detectives, the driver, the shot-gun rider and one passenger," Thomas said. "One of the Kitchen brothers was wounded. How badly we don't know."

"How large a payroll?" Emmet said.

"Forty thousand."

"That's a tidy sum," Emmet said. "And you think they're headed to Corbin Canyon?"

"According to the remaining witnesses of the robbery, the oldest brother names James remarked they better lay low in the canyon for a while," Thomas said.

"When was the robbery?" Emmet said.

"Three weeks ago to the day."

"Write out the warrants," Emmet said. "I'll head out on Tuesday."

"Any word from your deputy?" Thomas said.

"Not yet, but I expect Chase to wire when he can," Emmet said.

"Your baby is due pretty soon, isn't it?"

"Three weeks and a few days," Emmet said. "Plenty of time."

John, Sarah and Anna greeted Emma and Josh from the porch when they returned from the buggy ride.

Josh helped Emma down from the buggy and they went up to the porch. Ellis took his horse and the buggy to the barn.

"The picnic lunch was wonderful, ma'am," Josh said.

"Would you like coffee before you go?"

Sarah said.

"I don't wish to bother anyone, ma'am," Josh said.

"It's fresh made," Sarah said. "Girls, bring us all a cup."

Anna and Emma went inside for the coffee.

"Please sit down," Sarah said.

John, Sarah and Josh took chairs. Anna and Emma returned with three cups of coffee.

"Thank you," Josh said.

Ellis returned from the barn. "Pa, a problem with my horse. I think his right front leg is sore," he said.

"Let's have a look," John said.

Everybody went to the barn where Ellis walked his horse a few steps. "I noticed it the last hundred yards," he said.

"Let me take a look," Josh said. He took the horse by the reins and walked him outside and noticed the horse favored the right leg. John lifted the leg and inspected it. "The shoe is cracked, his leg is sore."

"We best change it out," John said.

"May I?" Josh said.

John nodded.

Josh entered the barn and removed the small sack from his saddlebags and returned to Ellis's house. He removed a small bottle of liniment and rubbed the leg with it near the joint, then removed a wrap and expertly wrapped the leg.

"He'll be sore for a couple, three days, but it's not serious," Josh said. "I'll take him in the barn and change out the shoe."

After changing the shoe, Josh walked his horse to the porch. "I best be getting back to the ranch before dark," he said.

Emma tugged Sarah's elbow.

"Josh, do you go to church?" Sarah said.

"I used to back home, ma'am," Josh said. "I haven't in a while, I'm afraid."

"If you meet us at church tomorrow, you can ride back with us for Sunday supper," Sarah said. "On Sunday we eat at four."

"I'm afraid I don't really have any church going clothes," Josh said.

"I'm sure God doesn't care about the clothes on a man's back," Sarah said.

Josh smiled. "I'll see you in church," he said.

After Josh left, everybody except John went into the house. He sat in his chair and shook his head. "What just happened?" he said aloud.

"I'll be gone four days, Rose, don't be upset," Emmet said.

After a year of being married, Emmet

discovered and learned not to tangle with Rose's Irish temper. Get on her bad side and she went off like a keg of black powder.

Brushing her hair, Rose turned and looked at Emmet. "I'm not upset," she said. "But if you miss the birth of your child, don't come home."

"Aw, honey," Emmet said.

"Don't aw honey me, Marshal Boyd," Rose said. "Just make sure when I go into labor it's you taking me to the hospital. Let's go or we'll be late."

Ellis waited for Emmet and Rose at the railroad depot with a buggy. As they walked to the buggy, Emmet held a large satchel.

"Staying over?" Ellis said.

"No, but Rose is for a few days," Emmet said. "I have to go to Corbin Canyon on business," Emmet said.

Ellis knew better than to ask for details. He took the satchel and tossed it into the back as Emmet helped Rose into the seat. Once all were aboard, Ellis tugged the reins and they headed to church.

"Emmet, there's going to be a new addition at church today," Ellis said.

"Somebody have a baby?" Emmet said.

"Emma met a boy," Ellis said.

Emmet looked at Ellis.

"Now don't give me that look," Ellis said.

Rose turned her face to hide her grin.

"A boy?" Emmet said.

"He's a nice kid, Emmet. A cowboy and . . ."

"A cowboy? Jesus Christ, Ellis," Emmet said.

Rose tried to hide her laughter but couldn't.

"Oh you think it's funny?" Emmet said. "My little sister being taken advantage of by a cowboy."

"No, Marshal," Rose said.

Ellis looked at Rose and they both grinned.

They arrived at the church and Ellis parked the buggy. John, Sarah, the twins, Rip, Bettina and the two children and Josh waited in front of the church.

"Is that the cowboy?" Emmet said as he hopped out of the buggy.

Emmet started for the church. "Emmet," Rose said.

Emmet turned and took her hand and helped her down. Emmet started to walk away and Rose took his arm.

"Emmet," Ellis said. "He's a cowboy, not an outlaw."

In front of the church, Emma said, "Pa, Emmet looks mad. Like really mad."

"Is that the Marshal?" Josh said.

"Wait here," John said and walked to Emmet.

"I see what your pa meant when he said inflict," Josh said to Emma.

John reached Emmet. "A moment, son," he said.

Ellis took Rose's arm and they walked to the church.

"I see that look, Emmet," John said. "He's a nice boy."

"He's a cowboy, Pa," Emmet said.

"Emmet, cool off," John said. "He's smart and polite and has a good head on his shoulders. Give him a chance."

"To do what?" Emmet said.

"Not a good attitude right before church, son," John said. "Come on."

John and Emmet walked to the church. "Emmet, this is Josh Paden," John said.

Josh looked up at Emmet's towering height and barndoor shoulders and offered his right hand. Emmet took it and Josh's hand all but vanished inside Emmet's.

Emmet leaned in close and whispered in Josh's ear. "Dishonor my sister and your body will never be found," Emmet said.

"Let's go to church," John said.

Before supper, Emma took Josh for a walk

56

through the orange grove. They didn't hold hands or touch for fear Emmet might see them.

"Your brother the Marshal, he looks like he could eat nails," Josh said.

"You don't know the half of it," Emma said. "He fought with General Grant, then worked for him on the railroad, then with the Secret Service and finally as the U.S. Marshal for California."

"He makes a man feel kind of small just being a cowboy," Josh said.

"Don't talk like that," Emma said. "Emmet was born on a farm same as me and cowboys are important."

"I've never seen trees as pretty as these orange trees," Josh said.

"They've been recently picked," Emma said. "When they're in full bloom you can smell the oranges clear to the house."

"Ma's going to ring the dinner bell in a few minutes," Emma said.

"Do we have time to check on the horse?" Josh said.

"Sure."

They went to the barn where Josh checked Ellis's horse. He bent the leg, checked for soreness and stiffness, then walked him forward and backward.

"He's coming along fine," Josh said.

Outside the barn, the dinner bell rang.

"Let's go, I'm starving," Emma said.

At the dinner table, Ellis said, "How's my horse coming along, Josh?"

"Coming along fine," Josh said. "Keep that bandage on him another two days and then walk him in the corral. He'll tell you when he's ready to ride."

"I have horses, lots of them," Rip said. "At least a hundred."

"Rip is heir to the Beth Olson ranch and farm," John said.

"No kidding," Rip said. "Mr. Welding buys horses from them."

"Can we take a ride to the farm and show the horses to Josh, Grandpa?" Rip said.

"I don't see why not?" John said. "Josh?"

"It would have to be on Saturday," Josh said.

"Meet us here and we'll ride over Saturday morning," John said.

"Emmet, where you off to?" Sarah said.

"Corbin Canyon for a few days," Emmet said.

Sarah looked at Rose. "You know, Emmet," she said.

"I'll be back in plenty of time," Emmet said.

"See that you are," Sarah said.

"Yes, Ma," Emmet said.

After dinner, Ellis, Emma and Josh went to the barn to check Ellis's horse.

Josh took the reins and walked the horse out of the barn. "His gait is close to normal. Two days and he'll tell you to ride him," Josh said.

Ellis patted his horse. "My brother can be very frightening," he said.

"Sure can," Josh said.

"Don't let him bother you none," Ellis said. "Emmet is afraid of Ma just like the rest of us."

Josh looked at Emma.

"The one thing Emmet won't tangle with is Ma," Emma said.

Josh walked the horse back into the barn. He returned with his horse and said, "I best say goodbye to everyone and get going."

"See you next Saturday?" Emma said.

"Sure will," Josh said.

"I don't like it, Pa," Emmet said. "She's just a kid."

John and Emmet were on the porch having coffee.

"The twins are seventeen, Emmet," John said. "I married your mother when she was seventeen."

"Things were different back then, Pa," Emmet said.

"Boys are boys and girls are girls no matter what year it is," John said. "Don't let anybody ever tell you different."

Emmet sipped coffee and looked at John.

"Besides, Emmet, she's my daughter to raise," John said. "You'll have your hands full soon enough."

"I suppose," Emmet said. "Just keep an eye on her is all I'm saying."

"When have I not?" John said.

Rose, Anna, Emma and Sarah watched Emmet ride away after breakfast.

Rose put her arm around Anna. "Don't ever marry a lawman, honey," she said.

John rushed out to the porch. "Rip had an accident washing dishes," he said. "He cut his arm with a knife."

"Sarah, get my medical bag from the bedroom," Rose said.

Rose and the twins, John and Sarah went to the kitchen where Rip was sitting in a chair with a bloody towel on his left forearm.

"Let me see," Rose said.

She removed the towel and looked at the ugly, jiggered gash on the left side of Rip's forearm. It immediately started bleeding and Rose replaced the towel. "Hold it tight," she said.

Sarah entered the kitchen with Rose's bag.

"Robert, what I'm going to do is going to hurt," Rose said. "I'm telling you so you can take the pain like a man. Understand?"

"Yes," Rip said.

Rose removed a bottle of antiseptic from her bag and a clean cloth. She poured some antiseptic onto the cloth, removed the towel from Rip's arm and cleaned the wound.

"Hold the cloth on the cut," Rose said.

Rip held the cloth on the cut.

Rose removed a stitching needle and a spool of white sutures. She threaded the needle and looked at Rip. "Ready?" she said.

Rip nodded.

"It helps to look away," Rose said.

Rose dipped the needle into the bottle of antiseptic and then went to work stitching the deep cut in Rip's forearm.

Rip didn't look away. He clenched his jaw tight and his eyes watered, but he didn't cry.

Rose made eleven continuous stitches that closed the wound. Then she cut the thread and tied it off and dabbed antiseptic over the stitches.

"I'm going to cover it with a clean wrap

that can't get wet," Rose said. "And don't use that arm for a few days or the stitches might pop."

"I feel a little dizzy," Rip said.

"I'll bet you do," Rose said. "A combination of blood loss and pain. Go lie down for a while and we'll fix you a steak later."

Sarah took Rip by the right hand. "Come on, honey, let's put you to bed."

Sarah and Rose took coffee on the porch after Sarah put Rip to bed.

"We can't thank you enough," Sarah said.

"He'll have a slight scar, but it will fade as he grows," Rose said. "Fortunately the cut wasn't on the fleshy side of the arm."

Anna came out to the porch. "Rose, can I talk to you for a minute?" she said.

"I'll go check on Robert," Sarah said.

After Sarah went inside, Anna took her chair. "Rose, what you did with Rip was amazing," she said. "I mean you just went to it, no questions asked. I've never seen anything like it."

"I've been a nurse for quite a while, Anna. Sewing people up is part of what I do," Rose said.

"You're studying to be a doctor now," Anna said.

"Better late than never," Rose said.

"I want to do what you do," Anna said.

"Be a nurse?"

"Yes."

"You just decided this?"

"Watching you I did," Anna said. "It just hit me like a . . . a . . ."

"A calling?"

"Yes. What's a calling?"

"A feeling that you were meant to do something," Rose said.

"Yes, that's it," Anna said. "I had this feeling that I want to do what you do. That's the best I can explain it."

"You finished school?"

"Me and Emma graduated top students," Anna said.

"Sleep on it," Rose said. "If you still feel this way in the morning, I'll speak to John and Sarah."

"Thank you, Rose," Anna said. "Thank you."

"I better check on my patient," Rose said. "Want to help?"

Emmet went straight to his office when he arrived in Sacramento. Deputy Marshal Max Cody was on duty in the office.

"Afternoon, Emmet," Cody said.

"Any word from Chase?" Emmet said.

"Telegram came this morning."

"Let me see."

Cody handed Emmet the telegram. "This is from three days ago," Emmet said.

"Their lines were down," Cody said. "It just came in."

"By now they're in the mountains," Emmet said.

"No point in sending a return," Cody said.

"No. Send a wire to Parker in Los Angeles," Emmet said. "Tell him I need three deputies in full gear and ready to go day after tomorrow."

"I'll go," Cody said.

"I need you here," Emmet said. "I'm going home to pack. I'll stop by in the morning after I see Judge Thomas."

"That's a big steak," Rip said.

"To feed your blood," Rose said.

"How does that work?" Rip said.

"You lost a good amount of blood," Rose said. "Blood has iron in it. Steak feeds your blood by replacing the lost iron, so eat up."

"You heard her, eat up," John said.

"Yes sir," Rip said.

"Oh boy," Rose said. "The baby is kicking."

"In your stomach?" Emma said.

"Close enough," Rose said. "Would you

like to hear it's heartbeat?"

"I would," Emma said.

"Get my bag from the bedroom."

Emma dashed off and returned a minute later with Rose's bag.

"Pull up a chair close," Rose said as she dug out her stethoscope. She placed the ear-pieces into Emma's ears. "Now listen," she said and placed the bell over her stomach. "And tell me when you hear the baby's heartbeat.

Emma listened carefully. Then her face lit up. "I hear it," she said.

"Let me try," Anna said.

They switched places and Anna smiled. "I hear it," she said.

"Okay, that's enough," Rose said. "The baby is kicking up a storm and I need to lie down for a bit."

Emmet packed his gear for the trip, selecting warmer shirts, long underwear and a heavy jacket. Late summer was different in the mountains than on low ground. Sixty-five degrees and sunny often meant thirty-five and windy in the mountains.

After packing his gear, Emmet cleaned his Colt Peacemaker and Winchester rifle. He added two boxes of ammunition for each to his saddlebags.

Then he boiled water, shaved and took a bath.

He owed Grant four more years. That wasn't a lifetime, but it was long enough for a man to get killed in the line of duty.

Or worse. To become so hard and callous he lost all feeling for what was good and kind around him.

He saw it in career soldiers and lawmen who spent too much time on the job. Their bark became so hardened even their families couldn't penetrate it.

As he soaked in the tub, Emmet wondered if that was happening to him. Since he was nineteen, he was in the service of the government in one form or another as soldier, railroad police, Secret Service and marshal and every one of those jobs required killing at one time or another.

In four more years, would he be able to turn off what had become ingrained in him over time?

Emmet had seen the results of staying too long on the job. Broken marriages, children who barely knew their fathers, bitter, angry, old men who wished they got out when they had the chance.

By God, that was not going to happen to him.

"A nurse?" John said. "When did you decide this?"

"When Rose was fixing Rip's arm," Anna said. "It just hit me this is what I want to do."

"Sarah?" John said.

"We can't expect the girls to stay on the farm forever, John," Sarah said.

"She'll have to go to school," John said. "Where?"

"Sacramento at the hospital where I work," Rose said. "Our house has three bedrooms and she can stay with us. She has to be eighteen, but she can enroll early."

"Pa, please," Anna said.

John looked at Sarah and Sarah nodded. "I think it's fine, honey," John said.

Anna hugged John. "Thank you, Pa, thank you, Ma," Anna said.

"When Emmet returns, you can go back with us and enroll," Rose said.

Anna smiled. "I'm going to be a nurse," she said.

The two o'clock train from Sacramento arrived in Los Angeles at seven in the morning. Before boarding the train, Emmet stopped by Judge Thomas's office to pick up the warrants for the Kitchen brothers.

The warrants were issued in their real name of Blunt. Henry, sometimes called Hank was the oldest at forty-one. Roger was next at thirty-nine. Tony was the baby of the group at twenty-seven.

The wanted posters were made up of eyewitness sketches compiled over the years. No known photographs of the three existed.

Reports claimed they had robbed more than twenty stagecoaches, three banks and several private citizens noted to be carrying large sums of money. Six murders were attributed to the three brothers, but it was probably higher.

Emmet passed the time reading a newspaper and then a book. *Les Misérables* by Victor Hugo. The book was a slow read and took up most of the afternoon into early evening. At seven o'clock, he went to the dining car for supper.

Emmet ordered a steak and continued reading the book. He looked up when a woman said, "Excuse me, Marshal, but may I sit at your table. I am traveling alone and I'd feel safer if I could."

Emmet stood and pulled out the chair for her to sit.

"Thank you," she said as Emmet took his seat.

"My name is Alice Russell of Chicago," she said.

"You a long way from home, Miss Russell," Emmet said.

"I'm going to San Diego to join my father," Alice said. "He lives there."

"San Diego is a beautiful town," Emmet said.

"You've been there?"

"Yes."

"Of course, you're a U.S. Marshal," Alice said.

"One of the benefits of the job is free travel," Emmet said.

Alice laughed. "I see by your ring that you're married," she said.

"Yes," Emmet said. "Going on a year."

"And how does your wife feel about you being a Marshal?" Alice said.

"She doesn't like it," Emmet said.

"I would imagine she doesn't," Alice said. "Why don't you do something else?"

"I will, when my five-year contract is up in another four years," Emmet said.

"I see," Alice said. "I sort of know the feeling. You see, my father owns a successful imports company in Chicago and recently opened stores in Philadelphia and San

Diego. I'm to run the shop in San Diego."

"You don't sound too happy about it," Emmet said.

"I'm twenty-eight, have no husband or prospects for one and all I do is work for my father," Alice said. "So we're not too different you and I in that regard."

"You have a long way to go, Alice, and you never know what's around the next corner," Emmet said.

Alice grinned. "Maybe there is hope for us yet, Marshal," she said. "And I thank you for letting me share your table."

Los Angeles was a port town of six thousand residents and a major railroad stop because of its port. Deputy Marshal Parker kept law and order along with two other junior deputies.

Parker waited on the platform while Emmet retrieved his horse and walked to him.

"Deputy Parker, how are things in Los Angeles?" Emmet said.

"Keeping me busy, Emmet," Parker said.

"Let's go over to the office," Emmet said.

They walked through muddy, busy streets to Parker's office, which was next door to the Sheriff's office.

"Coffee's fresh made," Parker said.

Emmet filled two cups and handed one to Parker. The door opened and Sheriff Dean entered.

"Marshal Boyd, it's been a while," Dean said.

"Thanks for coming over," Emmet said.

"You need two deputies?" Dean said.

"Do you know who the Kitchen brothers are?" Emmet said.

"I've seen their posters," Dean said. "Is that why you're here?"

"They robbed a stagecoach carrying Army payroll and killed the driver, shotgunner and a passenger in Kansas," Emmet said. "One of them was wounded, how badly we don't know. They headed for Corbin Canyon."

"In the Monica mountains?" Dean said. "Why?"

"Their real name is Blunt and they come from the canyon area," Emmet said. "Probably have family there somewhere. We're going to have to smoke them out."

"I can go and take one deputy," Dean said.

"I'll take Deputy Swisher," Parker said.

"That makes us five," Emmet said. "Get your gear and supplies and we'll leave after breakfast."

After Rose removed the bandage from Rip's

left arm, she checked the stitches and for signs of infection. There were none. She applied more antiseptic and covered the arm with a fresh bandage.

"Now we can eat breakfast," Rose said.

At the table, John said, "Ellis and I are leaving for Washington next week. We were wondering if the girls and Rip would like to go?"

"Ma, can we?" Anna said.

"We've never seen Washington," Emma said.

"John, Washington is a large city," Sarah said. "A hundred and fifty thousand people or more."

"I lived in Washington for years when I worked at the hospital," Rose said. "It's a wonderful city with many exciting things for the girls to see. Please let them go."

"Ma?" Anna said.

"Please," Emma said.

"John, someone has to watch these two, so I'll be coming along," Sarah said.

"I never thought otherwise," John said.

"We need clothes," Anna said.

"Yes we do," Emma said.

"Let's go make a list of what we need," Anna said.

"Right."

Anna and Emma went to their room.

"Girls are a lot of trouble," Rip said.

"Yeah," John said.

By noon, Emmet, Parker, Dean, Swisher and Parker's deputy Talbert were in the Santa Monica Mountains.

Parker and Dean knew the mountains and rode point.

"That tall mountain there in the distance is Sandstone Peak," Parker said. "Just over three thousand feet high."

"And Corbin Canyon?" Emmet said.

"Maybe an hour from here," Parker said.

An hour later they rode into the canyon where rivers and streams flowed down into a basin where groups of panhandlers were panning for gold.

Emmet and the group dismounted.

"I'm U.S. Marshal Emmet Boyd," Emmet said. "We're after three outlaws known as the Kitchen brothers we believe are hiding in the mountains."

"Kitchen brothers?" a man said. "That's a stupid name, Marshal."

"I can't say as I disagree with you on that point, but that's the name they go by," Emmet said. "Their real name is Blunt and they supposedly hail from these parts somewhere."

"Most folks around here are prospectors

like us and live in tents," a man said. "There's a settlement in the flats about a mile from here where we cash in and buy supplies. You might ask them."

"Thanks," Emmet said.

Emmet and his posse rode to the settlement located in a flat valley nestled between Sandstone Peak and another mountain.

The settlement consisted of a small general store, a saloon/restaurant, a government gold trading station and a livery that boarded and sold horses.

"We might as well get a hot lunch," Emmet said.

"Five lawmen in the same place is never good news," a woman about sixty years old said when Emmet and the posse entered the saloon/restaurant.

"You run this establishment?" Emmet said to the woman.

"Name is Ma. You here to eat or to practice you profession," Ma said.

"What's on the menu?" Emmet said.

"Beef stew," Ma said.

"Bring us five bowls," Emmet said. "And bread."

"Sit yourselves," Ma said.

Emmet and the posse took a table. At the bar, a few men were drinking and smoking cigars.

Ma carried a large tray to the table and gave each man a bowl of stew, crusty bread and a whiskey glass and placed a bottle of whiskey on the table.

"Two dollars a man," she said.

Emmet gave Ma twelve dollars. "You're a tipping man I see," Ma said.

"You could earn a much bigger tip if you sit down and talk to me," Emmet said.

"How much and about what?" Ma said.

"A thousand dollars and the Kitchen brothers," Emmet said.

"I never liked them sons a bitches," Ma said. "Evil bastards the three of them."

"Can you help us?" Emmet said. "I'll pay you one hundred just to talk to us."

"Not in here," Ma said. "When you is done eating, pay a visit to the shitter house out back."

Ma left the table.

"How's the stew boys?" Emmet said.

"Not too bad," Parker said.

"Pour us a glass of that bourbon," Dean said.

Parker filled each glass with bourbon. They sipped as they ate and when lunch was finished, Emmet said, "Stay and have another drink, boys, while I visit the out-house."

Emmet went out the back door and

walked fifty feet to the outhouse and stood behind it. Five minutes passed before Ma came out and joined Emmet.

"Do you know the Kitchen brothers?" Emmet said.

"I know them," Ma said. "Scum of the earth. Came here in forty-nine with the rest of us fools looking for gold. Kilt my husband, my two sons and kilt their pa. Real name is Blunt."

"Why the name Kitchen?" Emmet said.

"They claim back home in Missouri they were so poor they was born on the kitchen floor," Ma said.

"Can you read?" Emmet said.

"Better than most."

"Read this," Emmet said and showed the wanted poster to Ma.

"One thousand dollars reward for information that leads to the capture of the Kitchen brothers," Ma said.

"I'm going to sign the back of this with my promise of the reward over to you," Emmet said and wrote in pencil on the back of the poster. He handed the pencil to Ma. "Write your name below mine and keep the poster."

Ma wrote her name and returned the pencil.

"Now where can I find them?" Emmet said.

"Five miles due west they have a cabin built by their father back in fifty," Ma said. "Their mother still lives there. They come home whenever they feel the law on their backs."

"What's the mother's name?" Emmet said.

"They call her Eddie," Ma said. "Real name is Edith."

Emmet took out his wallet and counted one hundred dollars in bills and gave them to Ma. "We'll be back this way," he said. "Wait until we leave before going inside."

Emmet met Parker, Dean, Swisher and Talbert in front of the saloon/tavern where several men were standing by, watching them.

"They're going to follow us," Parker said.

"Yup," Emmet said.

Emmet walked to where the two men were standing. "Help you, gents?" Emmet said.

The two men, surprised, looked at Emmet.

"Got mud in your ears?" Emmet said. "What's your interest in me?"

"Just surprised to see so many lawmen all at once," one of the men said.

"What you doing here anyway?" the other

man said.

"When it concerns you, I'll let you know," Emmet said.

Emmet returned to the posse. "The Kitchen place is five miles west," he said. "We'll ride north a bit and double back on these two."

Emmet and the posse mounted up and rode north away from the settlement.

"Give them an hour and then we'll circle back and come up behind them," Emmet said.

They rode three miles and then circled back to the west and south and waited behind a hill for the two men to arrive. They watched them come and go and Emmet said, "Who can rope?"

"I'm a fair hand," Parker said.

"Me too," Dean said.

"Get your rope, we'll hit them from behind," Emmet said. "Ride hard."

Emmet led the chase and by the time the two men realized they were being pursued, three ropes had yanked them from the saddle.

"Parker, you men put your Winchesters on them," Emmet said.

Emmet dismounted and walked to the two fallen men. He took their six-guns and tossed them to Parker.

"You men get up right now," Emmet said.

The two men slowly stood up. "What did you do that for, Marshal?" one of them said.

"You don't talk, you listen," Emmet said. "We're going to tie you up so you can't follow us and thank your lucky stars we don't bring you in on charges. We'll cut you lose on the way back."

"We ain't done nothing," one of the men said.

"And you won't," Emmet said.

"Parker, you men tie these two hoople-heads to that tree yonder and gag them good," Emmet said.

After the two men were securely tied to a tree, Emmet and the posse rode west. After an hour, they sat atop their horses on a hill that overlooked a cabin, barn and corral.

"Four horses in the corral, fire in the chimney," Emmet said. "Looks like Ma was telling the truth."

"If their mother is home, how do we get them out without hurting her?" Parker said.

"Burn the house," Emmet said. "They'll come out."

"We'd have to get close to do that," Parker said.

"You men ride down on the left side of the house," Emmet said. "Stop about a hundred feet away and wait for me."

"What are you gonna do, Emmet?" Parker said.

"Let me have that whiskey you got in your saddlebags," Emmet said to Dean.

After the posse rode down to the left side of the house, Emmet went through his gear for an extra undershirt, dismounted and found a stick and wrapped the shirt around it. He mounted up and poured whiskey on the cloth, struck a match and lit it.

Emmet rode down the hill on the right side of the cabin and tossed the torch onto the roof, then rode around to the left and joined the posse.

The dry roof ignited quickly and spread rapidly. From inside, windows broke and one of the Kitchen brothers yelled, "Who's out there?"

"The law, you idiot," Emmet said.

"Our ma's in here," the brother said.

"Send her out," Emmet said.

The fire spread to the walls and front.

"Dean, Talbert, go around back," Emmet said.

Dean and Talbert rode to the rear of the house.

"Now you men come out with hands in the air and surrender right now," Emmet said.

The roof began to collapse and the front

door opened and the Kitchen brothers ran outside and fell to the ground in a fit of coughing.

Emmet, Parker and Swisher rode to them with Winchesters drawn.

"Where's your ma?" Emmet said.

Dean and Talbert walked Edith Blunt to the front of the burning house. "We got her, Emmet," Dean said.

"You had no call to burn the cabin," Henry Kitchen said. "Our ma lives here."

"Would you rather a shootout and her get hit?" Emmet said.

"You miserable coward," Henry said. "A man would fight me fair."

Emmet dismounted and walked to Henry. "Get off your knees," he said.

Henry looked at Emmet.

"I said get up," Emmet said.

Henry slowly got to his feet.

"You wanted a fair fight, I'm giving you one," Emmet said.

"You, Marshal?" Henry said.

"You're wearing a gun, use it," Emmet said.

"You'd like that, wouldn't you?" Henry said. "Have your deputies gun me down like a dog in the street."

"My men won't interfere, you have my word," Emmet said. "So are you having any or do you only shoot unarmed stagecoach passengers?"

"Alright, Marshal, let's do it," Henry said.

"Anytime you're ready," Emmet said.

Henry grinned, reached for his gun and Emmet cleared his Colt, cocked it and aimed before Henry cleared his holster.

"Drop it or die," Emmet said.

Henry dropped his gun to the dirt.

"You two," Emmet said to Roger and Tony. "Drop your guns and the three of you go to the corral and saddle your horses."

"What about me?" Edith said. "You burned my cabin."

"Call it a small price to pay for harboring three wanted killers," Emmet said. "Now where did you hide the railroad money?"

"Why should we tell you a damn thing?" Henry said.

"Because returning the money voluntarily is the difference between a noose and life in prison," Emmet said.

"In the barn under the empty rain barrel," Henry said.

"Parker, go get it," Emmet said.

Parker went to the barn.

"You're a hard man, Marshal," Henry said.

"It's a hard country," Emmet said.

Parker returned with a bank sack and

handed it to Emmet.

"How much did you spend?" Emmet said.

"Couple thousand," Henry said.

"Mrs. Blunt, you'll ride with us to the settlement," Emmet said. He removed three thousand dollars from the sack and gave it to Edith. "This should get you started again."

"Ma, I'm leaving Mrs. Blunt in your care for the time being," Emmet said. "Mrs. Blunt, say goodbye to your boys."

"You're no good the three of you, but your mine and I love you," Edith said. "Goodbye, boys."

"Ma, a moment out back," Emmet said.

Emmet and Ma went out the back door where Emmet gave Ma one thousand dollars. "I'll take my poster as a receipt," Emmet said.

Sarah was shucking corn and beans on the porch when she spotted dust rising on the road. She stood, squinted into the sun and then went to the screen door. "Rose, come out here," she said.

Rose, followed by the twins and Rip, came out to the porch.

They waited until Emmet arrived and then Rose stepped off the porch to greet him. Emmet dismounted and they hugged and kissed.

"How did it go?" Rose said.

"The usual," Emmet said.

They linked arms and walked up to the porch. "Hi, Ma," Emmet said and kissed Sarah's cheek.

"You'll stay for supper and leave in the morning," Sarah said.

"Ma, I have to get back to . . ." Emmet said.

"You'll stay for supper and leave in the morning," Sarah said.

"Yes, Ma," Emmet said.

Rose had to look away to hide her grin.

At the dinner table, John said, "We have much to talk about, Emmet."

"I'm going to nursing school in Sacramento and Rose is helping me," Anna said.

"Well, that's one of the things," John said.

"I can live with you while I go to school," Anna said to Emmet.

"That's another one of the things," John said.

"Please say it's alright," Anna said.

"That third bedroom is just going to waste," Emmet said.

Anna looked at Rose. "You were right, he's mush on the inside," she said.

Emmet looked at Rose.

"Oops," Anna said.

"Never mind oops," Sarah said. "You're on dishwashing duty tonight. You too, Emma."

"I didn't say anything," Emma said.

"For just in case," Sarah said.

"Emmet, I'm taking the whole family to Washington next week for the Grange meeting," John said. "The girls have never seen it and come to think of it, neither have I."

"I'll send Grant a wire," Emmet said. "Maybe if he's not too busy you can have dinner with him."

Rose looked at Emmet. "Just like that, huh?" she said. "The President of the United States."

"We go back a ways," Emmet said.

"I'll get coffee and dessert," Sarah said.

"I'll help," Rose said.

Emmet, John and Rip looked at each other.

"Girls sure make a fuss about everything," Rip said.

"The whole point of the trip is to represent the grange to the railroad and convince them to lower the shipping cost or farmers will go under," John said.

"I know these people, Pa," Emmet said. "The way to convince them is through their pocketbooks. Tell them you'll only ship locally by freight wagon if they don't comply. California is becoming the number one producer of produce and grain, they'll listen."

"That's what we figure," John said. "Hopefully they'll listen. The thing is, son, greed is a powerful devil hard to shake once it bites you."

"That's why they'll listen," Emmet said. "Greed. They'll calculate what they lose from a boycott compared to what they'll lose from a reduction of rates. Point out to them how much they'll lose compared to their profits made over time."

"Maybe you should go instead of me," John said.

"Can't, Pa," Emmet said. "I'm a federal employee, same as the railroad. You and Ellis are on your own."

Sarah returned with the coffee pot. "Apple pie fresh from the oven," she said.

"We need a bed and a dresser for Anna," Rose said as she and Emmet stood in the empty bedroom.

"We could bring hers from her room or buy her new?" Emmet said.

"Emmet, are you sure you don't mind?" Rose said.

"Mind my own sister? Of course not," Emmet said. "Now I have to go to the office. I'll be back for supper."

Emmet left Rose with a kiss and rode his horse to the office where Cody was behind the desk. "Any word from Chase?" Emmet said.

"Nothing yet," Cody said.

Emmet grabbed a cup of coffee from the pot on the wood stove and looked out the window.

"Emmet, you can't be everywhere and handle every situation yourself," Cody said. "That's why you have deputies."

"I have to send a telegram," Emmet said.

Emmet left the office and walked several blocks to the telegraph office. "Morning, Marshal," the clerk said.

"Morning," Emmet said as he took a paper and pencil and wrote out the telegram. Finished, he handed the paper to the clerk. "Send this as soon as you can and put it on my account."

The clerk glanced at the paper. "President Grant?" he said.

Josh arrived in time for breakfast and joined the family at the table.

"We'll take the wagon and the buggy,"

John said. "Rip, you ride with Emma and Josh."

After breakfast, Ellis met them out front and rode with John. Anna, Sarah and Bettina stayed behind. Rip tethered his horse behind the wagon.

The ride to Beth Olson's ranch took about two hours. They arrived around eleven and met Beth's parents on the porch. Since Beth's death a year ago, her parents took care of the orange groves and the horses and her interest in the gold mine she owned in the mountains.

"Morning, John. Everyone," Mr. Olson said.

"This young fellow is Josh," John said. "He's a cowboy at the Welding Ranch."

"We've sold Mr. Welding horses several times," Mr. Olson said. "There's twenty horses on the range the Army wants to buy but I'm having a hard time getting cowboys."

"I can get them for you, Mr. Olson," Josh said.

"Alone?" Mr. Olson said.

Josh stepped down from the buggy and helped Emma out of the buggy.

"Mr. Olson, where are the horses right now?" Josh said.

"A mile west is the range," Mr. Olson said.

"Be back directly," Josh said. "When you see me, open the corral."

Josh untied his horse from the wagon and mounted the saddle. "Let's go, boy, we have a job to do."

Emma, John, Ellis, Rip and Mr. Olson went to the corral as Josh rode west.

Josh rode to the west range where twenty horses were grazing. A large stallion looked at him and snorted.

"So you're the boss, huh," Josh said. He opened a saddlebag and removed a twelve-foot-long whip. "We'll see about that," he said.

Josh used his horse as a barrier to prevent the herd from running. Using the crack of the whip to guide the herd, Josh herded the twenty horses into a group and slowly got them moving east. With his horse acting as the alpha, Josh got the herd running.

At the corral, Emma stood on the bottom rung. "I see him," she said.

"Ellis, open the gate," John said.

Ellis opened the gate and they waited, and Josh guided the twenty horses into the corral, then Ellis closed the gate.

"That was a fine show of horsemanship, young man," Mr. Olson said.

"Thank you, sir," Josh said as he dismounted.

"Josh, want to see what a real orange grove looks like?" John said.

John, Ellis, Rip, Emma and Josh took a walk to the groves.

"Five hundred trees," John said. "Mr. Olson hires a crew to take care of them. Same for the wheat and the gold mine his daughter owned."

"They must be very wealthy," Josh said.

"Actually, young Rip owns it all," John said. "Or will when he turns eighteen."

"Josh, can you teach me to be a cowboy?" Rip said.

"With all this, why would you want to be a cowboy?" Josh said.

"Grandpa says we have over a hundred horses out there," Rip said. "Someone has to take care of them."

"Cowboying is hard work," Josh said. "Seems to me a wealthy boy like yourself would be better served managing his businesses."

Rip held up his hands and showed Josh his callouses. "I've been pitching hay and watering trees since I was nine," he said.

"Rip, that's a subject for a later date," John said.

"Where are the rest of the horses?" Josh said.

"On the range," John said. "They're all

branded but without working cowboys they could be anywhere."

"Maybe we should ride over and take a look?" Josh said.

They returned to the house where Mr. and Mrs. Olson were on the porch with a pot of coffee and glasses of lemonade for Rip.

"We thought we'd take a ride and see the rest of the horses," John said.

"Have coffee first," Mrs. Olson said. "I made cookies."

After coffee, Mr. Olson rode in the wagon with John, while Ellis rode with Emma and Rip, Josh rode his horse.

The range was several miles to the south at the edge of Beth's property. It was fenced at the border to keep the horses from wandering.

A hundred or more horses were grazing on tall grass. A dozen foals galloped around their mothers.

Josh rode to the herd and some of them nervously moved away. "No one is gonna hurt you," Josh said.

A large stallion looked at Josh. "Are you in charge?" he said.

The stallion held his ground and glared at Josh. "Yeah, you're the boss," Josh said.

Josh rode back to the buddies. "Mr.

Olson, you have a lot of fine animals in that bunch. Besides those foals, you got a dozen more on the way."

"Where can I get some good cowboys to look after things?" Mr. Olson said.

"There's hardly enough ranches in California for cowboys to work," Josh said. "Most are in Colorado, Nebraska, Kansas and Wyoming. I can ask around for you though."

"I'd appreciate it," Mr. Olson said. "John, stay for lunch. It's a nice day to eat in the backyard."

At the lunch table, Mr. Olson said, "John, I was coming to show you the quarterly report next week but as long as you're here, we might as well review them before you go."

After lunch, John and Mr. Olson went to the study to review the account books. On the ride home, John said, "Rip, when you turn eighteen, you're going to be one wealthy young man."

"I want to be a cowboy, sir," Rip said.

"You got plenty of time to think about it," John said.

When they returned home, it was still early enough for Emma and Josh to take a walk through the orange grove.

"I was very impressed with your skill at

riding today," Emma said.

"It was nothing, really," Josh said. "Just something I do every day."

"That's the point," Emma said. "It's a skill you have that most don't. You should be proud of your skill. I am."

Josh stared at Emma for a moment. "The only thing stopping me from stealing a kiss is the thought of your brother the Marshal."

"My brother the Marshal isn't here and I won't tell him," Emma said.

"I don't like it," Emmet said as he looked out the window of his office. "Too much time has passed without word."

"Let me take six men and a guide and go after them," Cody said.

"I should . . ." Emmet said.

"Miss the birth of your first child," Cody said. "Rose deserves better than that, Emmet."

"If they're not back after the baby comes, I'm going after them," Emmet said.

"Let me take a ride to Modesto and check things out," Cody said. "I'll be back in a few days one way or the other."

"Go tomorrow," Emmet said. "Wire me when you get there."

The train ride from Stockton to Washington,

DC took fifty-six hours and was scheduled to arrive at six PM.

John, Sarah and Rip shared a large sleeping car, while Ellis, Bettina and their two children also shared a large car. Anna and Emma were in a car for two.

Rip, Anna and Emma were excited about the long journey. To everybody else, time spent traveling was dull and slow.

John and Ellis rehearsed their speeches, Sarah and Bettina knitted and took care of the children and every stop was a welcome relief.

As he sat down to breakfast, Rose suddenly stood up from the table. "Emmet, get the buggy," she said.

Emmet looked at her.

"Emmet, it's time," Rose said.

"The baby isn't due for two weeks," Emmet said.

"The baby doesn't have a calendar," Rose said. "Get the buggy."

Emmet got the buggy and raced it through the streets of Sacramento to the hospital. As part of the staff, Rose knew every doctor and nurse and she was immediately admitted and whisked away to the ward reserved for pregnant woman.

Emmet was told to stay in the waiting area

until called.

Hours passed without news. Emmet paced the room, talked to several other expectant fathers, went to the hospital cafeteria for coffee, read a newspaper and paced some more. Finally a nurse came to get one of the other men and Emmet asked her for news.

"Rose hasn't gone into labor yet," the nurse said. "Please be patient, Marshal."

Shortly after noon, the nurse returned and told Emmet that Rose had gone into labor. She told him it would be a long wait and suggested he go home for a while.

Emmet returned to the cafeteria and had lunch and read a newspaper. He went back to the waiting area and asked a nurse for news and was told to be patient.

Sick of sitting in the waiting area, Emmet left the hospital and walked over to the courthouse to see Judge Thomas.

"Rose is in labor," Emmet said.

"Then what the hell are you doing here?" Thomas said.

"They said it would be a long wait," Emmet said.

Thomas opened a desk drawer and produced a bottle of whiskey and two glasses. He splashed an ounce into each glass and gave one to Emmet.

"I sent Cody to Modesto to check on this

Pike business," Emmet said. "I have a bad feeling something's gone wrong."

"You're in the gone wrong business, Marshal," Thomas said. "I know you were appointed by Grant and I know you the best Marshal we got, but if I were you I would think about another career choice."

Emmet sipped whiskey and nodded.

"In a way you're about to become a father for the second time, Emmet," Thomas said. "You bring a child into the world, raise it, teach it as best you know how and then trust that some of what you taught stuck. It's the same with the men you pick as your deputies. But sometimes, no matter how much we teach and guide them, things go wrong. You just have to trust in what you taught."

Emmet nodded. "I better get back to the hospital," he said.

As he walked the streets, he realized he never told Cody, who was probably wondering where he was. Cody was at the desk and jumped to his feet when Emmet entered the office.

"Emmet, where you been?" Cody said. "I stopped by your house. I was going to Modesto, remember?"

"Rose went into labor this morning," Emmet said.

"What the hell are you doing here?" Cody said.

"Waiting," Emmet said. "They said it was going to take a while and I forgot to check in."

"Modesto can wait until tomorrow," Cody said.

"Is that coffee fresh?" Emmet said.

Cody filled a cup and gave it to Emmet. Emmet sipped and looked at the stack of mail on the desk. "Anything?" Emmet said.

"Nothing from Chase if that's what you mean," Cody said. "A few warrants, but nothing that needs taking care of today."

"Go to Modesto tomorrow and find out what the hell happened," Emmet said. "I'm going back to the hospital."

At the hospital, Emmet sat alone in the waiting area for several hours. Around five o'clock in the afternoon, a man about forty, dressed in a suit entered the area and took a seat.

"First one, Marshal Boyd?" the man said.

"Do I know you?" Emmet said.

"Probably not," the man said. "But everybody in Sacramento knows you. And sleeps better for it, I might add. So is this number one?"

"It is," Emmet said.

"Six for me," the man said. "And my wife

wants more, God help me."

Emmet grinned. "How do you afford that?" he said.

"I'm the president of the First Bank of Sacramento," the man said.

"You're Herbert Novack, I recognize you now," Emmet said.

"Well, Marshal, how about we go to the cafeteria and see what we can have for supper?" Novack said.

"They might call us?" Emmet said.

"Your first takes a while," Novack said. "By the sixth, you haven't missed anything."

They went to the cafeteria and ordered the beef stew and carried trays to a table. "I must confess, I envy you, Marshal," Novack said.

"Me?" Emmet said.

"You're a man of adventure, Marshal," Novack said. "Of action. All I do is sit at a desk."

"People depend on your bank, Mr. Novack," Emmet said. "Farmers, business people, a great many people rely on you."

"A great many people rely on the dentist as well, but nobody is ever really happy to see one," Novack said.

"You could say the same for a Marshal," Emmet said.

"There is where you are wrong," Novack

said. "Only the criminal and outlaw is not happy you're around. Everybody else sleeps better knowing the law is around to watch over them."

"Never looked at it that way," Emmet said.

"Only way to look at it," Novack said. "Let's get back to waiting."

Around seven o'clock, a nurse came to the waiting area to tell Novack he had a new baby boy. "After five girls, finally a boy," Novack said. "Good luck, Marshal," he said and shook Emmet's hand.

Another hour passed and the nurse returned. "Marshal, you have a daughter."

Emmet jumped to his feet. "A girl?"

"Most daughters are," the nurse said.

"My wife?"

"Rose is fine. Exhausted and sleeping," the nurse said. "Come take a peek at your daughter and then go home."

Emmet followed the nurse to the nursery where six babies were in cribs behind a glass wall. Two nurses were inside with the babies, tending to them.

"Which one is mine?" Emmet said.

"Number six," the nurse said.

Emmet looked at the baby in crib six. "She's so small," he said. "And wrinkled."

"She'll smooth out in a few days and she's

normal size and weight," the nurse said. "Now go home, Marshal. You can visit Rose in the morning."

Emmet left the hospital and walked the dark streets to the telegraph office. The night clerk was on duty, mostly to receive telegrams. "Marshal, what are you doing here this hour?" he said.

"I need to send a telegram," Emmet said. "To Washington, DC."

After dinner in the Washington Hotel restaurant, John stopped by the front desk to check for messages. There were two. He took both to his room without opening them.

Sarah was seated at the dresser, already in her nightgown and brushing her hair.

"Rip in his room?" John said.

"Yes, and thank God the Grange is paying for all this," Sarah said.

"Got two telegrams," John said.

"From?"

"I left my reading specs in the room," John said and handed them to Sarah.

"This one is from President Grant," Sarah said. "We're invited to have lunch with him after your meeting."

"I have a feeling Emmet had something to do with that," John said.

"The second one is . . . John, go get everybody and bring them to our room right now," Sarah said.

"What is . . . ?"

"Hurry."

Ten minutes later, Ellis, Bettina, their two children, the twins and Rip were assembled in John and Sarah's room.

"Rose had a baby girl," Sarah said.

"I thought it wasn't due for weeks," Ellis said.

"Babies come when they want to come," Sarah said.

"Did they pick a name?" Ellis said.

"He doesn't say," Sarah said.

"I can't wait to see the big, bad Marshal change a diaper," Ellis said.

"Boys don't change diapers," Rip said.

"They do if they want to eat," Ellis said and looked at Bettina.

"John, go down to the desk and send Emmet a telegram congratulating him and Rose," Sarah said.

"I'll go with you, Pa," Ellis said.

John and Ellis went down to the desk and send a telegram to Emmet in care of the Marshal's office in Sacramento.

"How do you think Emmet will do?" Ellis said.

"As a father?" John said. "Just like us, he'll

do what his wife tells him."

The baby was with Rose when Emmet entered the hospital room.

"Emmet, she's beautiful," Rose said. "Look at your daughter."

Emmet sat in the chair beside the bed and looked at his daughter. "She looks like a piece of beef jerky," he said.

"Oh Emmet," Rose said. "Here, hold her."

"I don't . . ." Emmet said as Rose handed him the baby.

Emmet held her in his hands and felt powerless at the sight of his newborn daughter. Her eyes were closed and her tiny right hand gripped his pinky. Then she started making sucking noises with her mouth.

"She's hungry," Emmet said.

"Let me have her," Rose said.

Emmet gently returned her to Rose and Rose lifted her gown and nursed the baby.

"I remember the same noise my sisters made when they were hungry," Emmet said.

"We need to pick a name," Rose said.

"We do," Emmet said.

John and Ellis met with the Secretary of the Interior, Columbus Delano and the Chief Executive Officer of the railroad, Sidney Dillion and a committee of senators in a meeting room in the halls of Congress.

"The railroad appreciates your position, Mr. Boyd, but do you know the cost of operating the freight lines?" Dillion said. "The Grange can't expect us to operate at a loss."

"And you can't expect the farmers to put themselves out of business with such high shipping costs," John said.

"Every year for the past three years, the railroad has raised its shipping rates," Ellis said. "We're at the break-even point. Another few years and we all go under."

"I suggest you raise your prices to the retailers," Dillion said.

"I have another suggestion," John said. "We don't use the railroad and ship locally by freight wagon."

"Now see here, Mr. Boyd," Dillion said. "I don't like threats."

"That wasn't a threat," John said. "Just a suggestion of what we might be forced to do if your rates keep going up."

Delano cleared his throat, took a sip of water and said, "Mr. Dillion, the California Grange isn't the only chapter to raise concerns about rising costs."

"The Grange doesn't answer to stockholders, Mr. Secretary," Dillion said. "I do."

The door to the room opened and Grant

stepped inside. Everybody stood.

"Sit down," Grant said.

Everybody sat.

Grant stood. "Mr. Dillion, I heard that last remark before I entered," he said. "And while it's true that you do have to answer to stockholders, I don't."

"Mr. President . . ." Dillion said.

"Shut up while I'm talking," Grant said. "Now despite what you might think, Mr. Dillion, the farmers and ranchers are the backbone of this country. If your greed puts them under, I will put the railroad under."

"You can't . . ." Dillion said.

"I can," Grant said. "The railroad is federal and I can slow it down, speed it up or stop it. Now I'm going to my office. I expect you to work out a fair deal or the trains won't roll tomorrow. How would your stakeholders react to that, I wonder?"

Grant left the room.

"Well, gentlemen, shall we work this out," Delano said.

"When will you be coming home?" Emmet said.

"They usually keep a mother and baby five days, but I'll see what I can do," Rose said.

"I need to get to the office," Emmet said

and kissed Rose. "I'll see you later."

Emmet walked to the door.

"Emmet?" Rose said.

Emmet looked back. "We did good," Rose said.

"Sure did," Emmet said.

He left the hospital and walked to the office. A telegram from Cody was waiting for him in the mail slot in the locked office door. He unlocked the door, grabbed the telegram and put it on the desk.

Before reading the telegram, Emmet made a fire in the woodstove and put on a pot of coffee to boil. When it was ready, he took a cup to the desk and read the telegram.

It was from Cody and sent from Modesto.

Emmet, please come to Modesto as soon as possible. Chase is seriously wounded and others. Situation is bad.

Emmet dropped the telegram to the desk and stood up and left the office.

John, Sarah, Ellis and Bettina were escorted to the White House dining room for lunch by one of Grant's aides.

"Where are the children?" Grant said.

"Our daughters are watching our grandchildren at the hotel," John said. "We're staying an extra day to sightsee."

"And Emmet?" Grant said.

"His wife had a baby girl last night," John said.

"Well, congratulations to them both," Grant said. "I'll send them a telegram."

The White House chef entered the dining room. "We'll start with the soup," Grant said.

The chef nodded and left the room.

"Emmet deserves all the happiness he can get," Grant said. "I realize it must be hard on his wife and family, but men like Emmet are all that stand between lawlessness and a country. He's worth more to this country than all the politicians in Washington."

"We agree, but it's difficult to watch our son in harm's way all the time," Sarah said.

"I share that very feeling," Grant said. "In the war I commanded millions of men and had that very thought each time I sent them into battle. If there is a better way to enforce the law, I just don't know it."

"You haven't asked how the meeting concluded," John said.

"I was leading up to that," Grant said.

"Mr. Dillion agreed to a five percent reduction on all freight," John said. "I guess he figured ninety-five percent of something is better than a hundred percent of nothing."

"That five percent reduction will be made

up by a rise in stock, which will happen when more freight is shipped cross-country," Grant said.

The chef returned with a serving trolly.

"Well everybody, let's eat," Grant said.

Emmet showed the telegram to Judge Thomas. "I'll be going to Modesto early tomorrow morning," Emmet said.

"Your wife just had a baby, Emmet," Thomas said.

"I'll be back in time for dinner," Emmet said.

Thomas read the telegram. He sighed. "Somebody is dead," he said.

"That's why Cody didn't specify," Emmet said. "All telegraph operators aren't honest and most are nosey."

"Report back to me as soon as you return," Thomas said.

"I will."

Emmet left the courthouse and walked to the hospital. Rose was seated in a chair beside the bed, breastfeeding the baby.

"She's gained six ounces already," Rose said.

"I have to go to Modesto in the morning," Emmet said. "I'll be back around six."

"Something bad happened?" Rose said.

"Yes."

107

"Emmet, can't you quit before you get hurt or killed?" Rose said.

"Would you rather be married to a man who gave his word to the President of the United States and then broke it?" Emmet said.

"Just be careful," Rose said.

"How about some lunch?" Emmet said. "The hospital cafeteria has some decent food."

"Are you asking me for a date?"

"Yes."

"I accept," Rose said. "We can take the baby to the nursery on the way down."

"We have the entire day tomorrow, what would you like to do?" John said.

"See the Washington Monument and the park near the White House," Anna said.

"That's a start," John said.

"There's a whole bunch of museums listed in this book we got at the desk," Emma said.

"Well, we're going to have a busy day then," John said.

Emmet caught the eight o'clock train that arrived in Modesto at ten-fifteen. Cody met him at the depot and they walked to the sheriff's office together.

"Chase isn't going to make it, Emmet," Cody said. "Three deputies are dead and Scout Joseph is recovering from a bullet at the doctor's office."

"Do you have any details?" Emmet said.

"It's better the deputies tell you," Cody said.

Sheriff Rich and Emmet's two deputies, Cale and Wes were in Rich's office when Emmet and Cody entered.

"Marshal Boyd, I'm Sheriff Rich," Rich said.

"Sheriff," Emmet said. "Cale, Wes, what happened?"

"We rode into an ambush, Emmet," Cale said. "Joe Pike, his three brothers and cousin and four other men had lookouts in Yosemite. They opened up on us before we even reached their hideout."

"The shooting lasted two days," Wes said. "We got Pike's brothers and cousins before Pike and the others ran off."

"They killed Gates and Willis, shot Joseph and maybe killed Cody," Cale said.

"We were lucky to make it back," Wes said.

"Where are Joseph and Cody?" Emmet said.

"At the doc's," Rich said.

The doctor's office was actually a mini hospital with six beds, an operating room and a recovery room.

Scout Joseph Takes His Horse was recovering from a bullet to the left shoulder in one of the recovery rooms.

Joseph sat up in bed when Emmet and Cody entered his room.

"How are you, Joseph?" Emmet said.

"The doc says I'll be fit to travel in a few days," Joseph said.

"What happened?" Emmet said.

"Pike had extra men at this hideout in Yosemite," Joseph said. "They had lookouts. I tracked them into the hills and then the shooting started. They had us pinned down in the rocks. Two days later, three deputies were dead, I was shot and I don't know if Chase will make it or not."

"Let's find out," Emmet said.

Emmet and Cody went to Chase's room where the doctor and a nurse were examining Chase.

"Doctor?" Emmet said.

"He's hanging on," the doctor said. "Don't ask me how, but he is."

"His chances?" Emmet said.

"Twenty percent he'll make it," the doctor said. "But he has a strong will to live and that counts for a lot."

"Thanks, doctor," Emmet said.

Emmet and Cody returned to Joseph's

room. "Joseph, I'll be back tomorrow," Emmet said. "Cody, you stay here. Tell Cale and Wes to go home."

"Alright, Emmet," Cody said.

When Emmet entered Rose's hospital room, she was in the chair, breastfeeding the baby.

"You look like you had a tough day," Rose said.

Emmet kissed Rose, then sat in the second chair. "Nothing like two train rides in the same day," Emmet said.

"Look on the dresser," Rose said.

Emmet turned to the dresser where a vase of flowers rested.

"There's a telegram," Rose said.

Emmet stood and walked to the dresser and read the telegram. It was from Grant, congratulating them on the birth of their baby.

"Not many can say they received a telegram from the president on the birth of their child," Rose said.

"I haven't eaten since breakfast," Emmet said. "Let's go to the cafeteria and get some dinner."

After bringing the baby to the nursery, they went to the cafeteria where they ordered bowls of soup, followed by steaks.

"I didn't realize I was so hungry," Rose said.

"We have to think about a name," Emmet said.

"Sarah, after your mother and Ann after mine," Rose said. "Sarah Ann Boyd. What do you think?"

"I think it's perfect," Emmet said. "When are you coming home?"

"Tomorrow at eleven," Rose said.

"Good," Emmet said.

"Why Marshal Boyd, I do believe you miss me," Rose said.

"Would you think it unmanly of me if I said I did?" Emmet said.

"I think it's the most manly thing you've ever said to me," Rose said.

Emmet picked Rose and the baby up at eleven o'clock, then turned around and caught the one o'clock train to Modesto.

Chase had passed away during the night.

"His body just shut down is the best way I can describe it," the doctor said. "I'm so sorry, Marshal."

"Send his body to Sacramento for burial," Emmet said.

Scout Joseph was up and walking around in his room. "I'm sorry about Chase," Joseph said. "He was a good man."

"Do you feel up to returning to Fort Baker?" Emmet said.

"The doctor said I can leave tomorrow," Joseph said.

"Deputy Cody, I want you to travel with Joseph to Fort Baker tomorrow," Emmet said.

"Yes sir," Cody said.

Emmet caught the five o'clock train to Sacramento and when he walked through his front door at seven-thirty, his entire family was having dinner with Rose at the table.

"She's beautiful, Emmet," Sarah said.

"Congratulations, son," John said.

"Emmet, I'll be staying for a week to help out," Sarah said.

"Pull up a chair, son, have some dinner," John said.

Emmet sat beside Rose. "How did it go in Washington?" he said.

"We got what we wanted, but we'll talk about that later," John said. "Right now is a time to eat and enjoy."

"He'll turn up, Emmet," Judge Thomas said. "Sooner or later, men like Joe Pike always turns up and when they do, the law is always there."

Emmet and Thomas were having a drink in Thomas's chambers.

"The bodies of Chase and the other deputies will arrive tomorrow," Emmet said. "They will get a full Marshal's burial. I'd like you to attend."

"I'll be there," Thomas said.

"Thank you," Emmet said. "Right now I'm going home and enjoy my daughter."

CHAPTER TWO:
1875

"Emmet, we're leaving now," Rose said.

Emmet was in the water closet, shaving. "Okay," he said. "I'll see you tonight."

Rose held the baby while Anna drove the buggy to the hospital. Rose worked three shifts a week as a surgical nurse and took classes two days a week as she studied to become a doctor.

Since turning eighteen earlier in the year, Anna took nursing classes five days a week.

Sarah Ann was placed in the nursery while Rose worked or took classes.

Rose and Anna had grown as close as sisters, even though Rose was fifteen years older than Anna, who had matured into a bright, young woman who was dedicated to her studies.

On breaks between classes and work, Rose and Anna would take coffee together in the hospital cafeteria.

"Rose, don't you ever get afraid for Emmet?" Emma said as they drank coffee.

"Only every minute of every day," Rose said.

"He's very tough and smart," Emma said.

"He is that," Rose said. "But I still fear for him every time he leaves the house."

"Can't you make him quit?" Emma said.

"Emmet gave his word to President Grant he would give him five years as a U.S. Marshal," Rose said. "Do you think your brother would ever go back on his word once given?"

"I think he would die first," Anna said.

"Let's get back to class," Rose said.

The chairman of the Grange stood at the podium and looked at the standing room only crowd and cleared his throat.

"Members of the Grange, my term as chairman is just about up," the chairman said. "As you're all aware, we have had just about the most profitable season in our history, mostly due to good weather and the reduced cost of shipping."

The chairman paused while everybody clapped and cheered.

"We all know who is responsible for the reduction of railroad shipping costs and I would like to nominate that man as your next chairman," the chairman said. "Mr.

John Boyd."

The clapping and cheering was deafening.

"Now hold on," John yelled. "I don't want . . . I didn't ask . . ."

"John, come up here," the chairman said.

"Go on, Pa. You can't fight it," Ellis said.

Reluctantly, John went to the stage and stood next to the chairman.

"By a show of hands, is John Boyd our next chairman," the chairman said.

"You doublecheck your saddle?" Josh said.

"I did," Rip said.

"So we get to riding and your saddle falls off and takes you with it, whose fault is it?" Josh said.

"I'll check it again," Rip said.

Josh looked at Emma.

"I'll check mine, too," Emma said.

After checking the saddles, Josh, Emma and Rip mounted up and rode from the corral to the path beside the orange groves.

"Race you to the creek," Rip said.

"Let's not," Josh said.

"Why not?" Rip said.

"Because if you fall and break your neck, your brother the Marshal will break mine," Josh said.

"Are you afraid of Emmet?" Rip said.

"Everybody's afraid of Emmet, Rip,"

Emma said.

"Even Ma?" Rip said.

"A mother is never afraid of her child, but everybody else is," Emma said. "And when did you start calling her Ma?"

"That's how I think of her," Rip said. "Is that okay?"

"It's fine," Emma said. "How do you think of me?"

"My sister," Rip said. "Is that wrong?"

"No, it's fine, too," Emma said.

They reached the creek and dismounted.

"What do we do first?" Josh said. "Rip?"

"Remove the saddles to give the horses a rest," Rip said.

"Good man," Josh said.

After the saddles were removed, the horses grazed on grass. Emma, Josh and Rip dug for worms beside the creek and then cast in their lines.

"We need a dozen or more for a fish fry tonight," Rip said.

"Catch the most and I'll teach you to rope," Josh said.

"Me too?" Emma said.

"Girls don't rope," Rip said.

"Why not?" Emma said.

"I've seen some girls who could rope as good as men," Josh said. "Shoot, too."

"Shoot?" Rip said.

"Maybe not a large six gun, but with a Winchester rifle," Josh said.

"Are we going to talk or fish?" Emma said.

An hour later, the wicker basket had fifteen fish in it.

"Let's take a break and eat the lunch your sister packed for us," Josh said.

The picnic basket contained fried chicken, fresh bread, apple pie and cold bottles of milk.

"Josh, I want to be a cowboy like you," Rip said.

"Rip, you're a wealthy boy who will be a wealthy man one day, why do you want to be a cowboy?" Rip said.

"I like horses and I like to ride," Rip said. "Why can't I be wealthy and be a cowboy, too?"

Josh looked at Emma.

"I don't see why he can't be what he loves," Emma said.

"Teach me to be a cowboy, Josh?" Rip said.

"After church tomorrow," Josh said. "Right now, let's eat some apple pie and catch more fish for tonight."

Emmet entered the house to the smell of bread baking in the oven. Rose was on the sofa with the baby, Anna was in the kitchen.

Emmet sat beside Rose, kissed her and then the baby.

Anna came in from the kitchen, apron over her dress and said, "Fried chicken, potatoes and corn and fresh bread for supper," she said.

"Good, I'm starved," Emmet said.

"Wash your hands, first," Anna said.

"You sound like Ma," Emmet said.

"And proud of it," Anna said. "Go wash your hands."

"Yes ma'am," Emmet said.

At the dinner table, Anna said, "Tomorrow is Sunday, we have to get the eight o'clock train in order to make church. Ma will skin us if we miss it."

Emmet grinned.

"What?" Anna said.

"I remember changing your diapers and here you are barking orders at me," Emmet said. "When did you grow up?"

Anna smiled. "Am I that bad?"

"One woman ordering me around is bad enough, but two?" Emmet said.

The baby started to cry in her crib.

"She needs to be changed," Rose said and looked at Emmet.

Emmet sighed and stood up. "Make that three women," he said.

Rose and Anna looked at each other

and grinned.

Ellis met Emmet, Rose and Anna at the train station and drove them to church in his buggy. Anna held the baby on the ride.

John, Sarah, Emma, Josh, Rip, Bettina and her two children waited in front of the church. Once Ellis arrived and parked the buggy, the entire family entered the church.

After church, the family rode to the farm where Anna and Emma took charge of the Sunday dinner.

Sarah, Rose and Bettina took coffee in the parlor. "It appears we've been replaced," Sarah said.

John, Ellis, Emmet, Rip and Josh went to the corral where Josh gave lessons on roping to Rip.

In the corral was a rocking horse that John built for Emmet and Ellis nearly thirty years ago that Anna and Emma played with and now Ellis's two children played with.

Josh made handling the rope and tossing the lasso seem effortless. After a dozen throws, Rip managed to rope the rocking horse around the neck.

"How do you rope from a horse?" Rip said.

"Go saddle mine and I'll show you," Josh said.

Rip grabbed Josh's saddle from the corral fence and managed to carry it to Josh's horse and secure the saddle under Josh's watchful eye.

"Boy's learning," John said.

Josh checked the saddle after Rip was finished. "Nice job," he said and mounted up. "Now give me your rope and stand back."

Josh rode his horse to the rocking horse and roped it around the neck, then used Rip's rope to lasso it around the tail.

"First you rope the neck and then the back legs," Josh said. "That makes it easier to apply a brand without getting kicked."

From the house, the dinner bell rang.

"We best go eat," John said.

After dinner, John, Emmet, Ellis and Josh took coffee on the porch.

"Rip's learned a great deal from you, Josh," John said.

"He's a very smart boy," Josh said.

Emmet looked at Josh. "You been seeing Emma six months now, it's time you state your intentions," Emmet said.

"God, Emmet," Ellis said.

"Is her honor intact?" Emmet said.

"You've gone too far, son," John said.

Emmet stood up and glared at Josh. "He

can speak for himself," he said.

"Of course her honor is intact," Josh said.

"It better be," Emmet said and walked off the porch to the corral.

"Pa," Ellis said.

"I know," John said. "Josh, before he kills you I suggest you go have a talk with Emmet, just the two of you."

"Right now?" Josh said.

"Pa, Emmet will . . ." Ellis said.

"Right now," John said.

Josh stood up. "I would like a Christian burial," he said and walked off the porch.

"Pa," Ellis said.

"It will be alright, son," John said.

Josh walked to the corral where Emmet was looking at the horses.

"May I speak with you," Josh said.

"Speak," Emmet said.

"I know you don't like me," Josh said.

"I never said that," Emmet said.

"You act it," Josh said.

"Emma is my baby sister, what do you expect?" Emmet said.

"At the risk of getting beat to death, Emma is not a baby," Josh said. "She's eighteen and a woman. You asked my intentions, so I'll tell you. I plan to marry her."

"On the twenty-five a month a cowboy makes?" Emmet said.

"I have plans," Josh said. "I save every penny I can. I have a thousand dollars in the bank. I'm going to have my own spread one day."

"One day," Emmet said. "In the mean-time, you sleep in a bunkhouse on a cow-boy's wage."

"You're a hard man, Emmet," Josh said. "I was hoping we could be friends, but I guess you can't be everybody's friend."

Josh turned and started back to the house.

"Hold on," Emmet said.

Josh turned and looked at Emmet. "Emma is my sister and it's hard for me to think of her as a woman," Emmet said. "But I guess she is and knows her own mind. Just don't ever disrespect her."

"I won't," Josh said. "You have my word."

"Let's go see what we got for dessert," Emmet said.

Ellis drove Emmet, Rose, Anna and the baby to the train station in Stockton. It was an hour before sunset and the streets were congested with people.

As they neared the station, two men were arguing in the street.

"I warned you to stay away from Ellie," one man said.

"Ellie didn't tell me to stay away," the

other man said.

"One of us ain't leaving here alive," the first man said.

"Suits me," the second man said.

"Stop," Emmet said.

Ellis stopped the buggy and Emmet jumped down.

"Emmet," Anna said.

"Let him go," Rose said.

Emmet walked to the two men. "You men want to fight," he said. "Fight me."

The two men turned to Emmet.

"Now, Marshal, we got no . . ." the first man said.

"Fight me," Emmet said.

Neither man moved.

"You're so anxious to die, come on then," Emmet said. "I'll oblige you."

"We draw on you and you'll kill us," the second man said.

"Damn right I will," Emmet said.

"I don't even like her anyway," the second man said, turned and walked away.

"You know what, me either," the first man said and walked away.

"Christ sake, Emmet," Ellis said when Emmet returned to the buggy.

Rose and Anna were silent for most of the train ride back to Sacramento. About ten minutes away from Sacramento, Anna said,

"Were you really going to kill those two men in Stockton?"

"If I had to," Emmet said.

Anna stared at Emmet.

"If those two started shooting at each other, across the street was a woman with a baby and a dozen other people," Emmet said. "Those two idiots could have hit and killed any number of people, including that baby."

"I'm glad you're the Marshal," Anna said. "One time I overhead Ellis tell Pa that you had balls of iron."

"Anna," Rose snapped.

"Well, it's true," Anna said. "You saw it yourself today."

"Yes, it's true, but young, professional women don't speak that way," Rose said.

"How would you say it?" Anna said.

"Emmet is a man of courage, conviction and valor," Rose said.

"Balls of iron sounds better," Anna said.

"I can't fault you that," Rose said. "Emmet, what do you say, courage and valor or balls of iron?"

"This is our stop," Emmet said.

Rose and Anna looked at each other and laughed.

John and Ellis walked through the orange

grove and inspected the trees and fruit. "Those fifty new trees will be ready to fruit the next growing cycle," John said.

"The melons will be ready in a few weeks," Ellis said. "I'll go to town next week and hire pickers."

"Why wait?" John said. "All the best pickers will be taken by then. It's only an hour to town, let's hitch the team and post our ad."

"I'll get the team," Ellis said.

After hitching the buggy, Ellis and John rode to Stockton to the meeting hall of the Grange where local farmers posted help wanted posters. John posted an ad for a dozen fruit pickers for two weeks work at top wages.

After leaving the Grange, John and Ellis went to the post office where a stack of mail and a telegram waited for them.

The telegram was from Beth's father, informing them that Beth's mother had suffered a stroke.

Emmet was in his office when he was summoned by Judge Thomas. Emmet walked to the courthouse and met Thomas in his chambers.

"Emmet, all those posters and reports you sent out on Joe Pike the past six months may have borne some fruit," Thomas said.

"What do you have?" Emmet said.

Thomas handed Emmet a telegram. It was from a man claiming he knew where Pike was located and was claiming the reward. His name was William Day and he lived in New York City and would be in Sacramento on the two o'clock train tomorrow.

"What do you think, Emmet?" Thomas said.

"We'll talk to him tomorrow," Emmet said. "If it's legitimate, I'll go to New York and arrest Joe Pike for murder and bring him back for trial."

"It's too late," Mr. Olson said. "She's gone."

John, Sarah, Emma and Rip came in one buggy, Ellis, Bettina and their two children in another.

"The doctor is in with her now," Mr. Olson said.

Everybody waited for the doctor in the parlor. Sarah and Bettina made coffee, Finally the doctor entered the parlor and everybody stood.

"She went peacefully in her sleep," the doctor said. "No pain, just sleep."

"We'll bury her here," Mr. Olson said.

"I've written the official death certificate for you, so you can bury her when you want," the doctor said.

After the doctor left, John said, "Ellis, let's go to the barn and build a coffin."

The reward for Joe Pike was ten thousand dollars and offered by the U.S. Marshal's Service. That was for the murder of three Deputy Marshals. There was another five thousand dollars reward offered by the bank.

Emmet sat at his desk and mulled everything over as he drank a cup of coffee. A knock on the door brought a messenger with a telegram.

"Mrs. Olson died?" Anna said. "Oh no."

"They're burying her on the property tomorrow morning after the pastor from the church holds a service," Emmet said. "There's a seven AM train that gets to Stockton at eight-fifteen. Ellis will pick us up in his buggy."

"I only met Mrs. Olson a few times but she seemed like a wonderful person," Rose said.

"She was," Emmet said. "I'll see you at home."

Emmet kissed Rose and then left the hospital and walked to the courthouse to see Judge Thomas.

"I have to go to a funeral tomorrow morning," Emmet said. "A family member back in Stockton."

"I'm sorry to hear that," Thomas said.

"Can you delay William Day until I return around six o'clock?"

"Stay over with your family," Thomas said. "I'll put Day up at a hotel."

"Thanks, Judge," Emmet said. "I'll see you day after tomorrow."

John and Ellis were excellent carpenters. They constructed a fine coffin for Mrs. Olson that Sarah and Bettina decorated with fine linen and lace.

Sarah and Bettina made dinner, which Mr. Olson didn't touch.

After dinner, Mr. Olson, John and Ellis took coffee to the porch.

"John, I'm just about done in," Mr. Olson said. "I'm seventy-one now and my eyesight is failing and so is my memory. I can't run this place anymore. It's too big for me to handle. Somewhere out there is a hundred and fifty horses and a hundred head of cattle. The orange groves and fields of melons and the gold mine, it's all too much for me now."

"Ellis and I can handle the books and hiring farm help and even oversee the paperwork for the mine," John said.

"I appreciate it, John," Mr. Olson said.

"Robert is like a son to me," John said. "As much a part of my family as any of them."

"I'm relieved to hear you say that, John," Mr. Olson said.

"You continue to live here and Ellis and I will take care of the books and your crops," John said.

"I'm obliged to you, John. To all of you," Mr. Olson said. "But what are we to do with all those horses and cattle?"

"Hire a professional cowboy and pay him a top wage to manage things," John said.

"I don't know any cowboys," Mr. Olson said.

"We do," Ellis said.

Ellis met Emmet, Rose, the baby and Anna at the train station and drove them to Beth Olson's ranch. The drive took about an hour and gave them time to talk.

"Did anybody know she was sick?" Emmet said.

"She wasn't sick, not according to the doctor and Mr. Olson," Ellis said. "At least not in any way you could notice."

"I'm reading about strokes in school," Anna said. "It's very complicated and there isn't much in the way of treatment."

Little was said the rest of the way to the Olson ranch.

The reverend from town performed a beautiful service for Mrs. Olson and then Emmet, Ellis and John lowered her coffin into the deep hole they dug beside a large tree. While the women prepared lunch, Emmet and Ellis covered up Mrs. Olson's final resting place.

John and Rip sat in chairs on the porch.

"Your grandmother was a good woman," John said. "I've known her for thirty years or more."

"My mother used to tell me stories about the Big Woods where she is buried," Rip said.

"That's right, the Big Woods," John said. "All this belongs to you now, Rip. Your mother wanted it that way."

"What am I supposed to do with it all?" Rip said.

"Ellis and I will take care of things until you're grown," John said. "But neither of us are cowboys and there are a lot of horses and cattle that need attention. So if it's alright with you, I'd like to ask Josh to take over that end of the business."

"You mean Josh would be the cowboy for

Ma's ranch?" Rip said.

"That's what I mean," John said.

"Ma would like that," Rip said.

"We'll ask him this Saturday," John said.

John stayed behind to keep Mr. Olson company. Emmet drove his buggy home, while Ellis drove the other one.

Anna and Emma made dinner while Emmet, Ellis and Sarah talked on the front porch.

"Emmet, your father is going to ask Josh to take charge of the Olson ranch for the horses and cattle," Sarah said. "We will handle the books and farm until Rip is old enough."

Emmet was about to reply when Sarah held up her right hand. "Now you listen to me, Marshal Boyd. Emma and Josh are very serious about each other and there is nothing you can do about it, so you might as well accept it. Am I understood?"

"Yes, Ma," Emmet said.

Ellis looked away so Emmet wouldn't see him grin.

"I'm going to help the girls with dinner," Sarah said. "Think about what I said."

Sarah went inside. Ellis looked at Emmet.

"What?" Emmet said.

"Not a thing," Ellis said.

■ ■ ■ ■

After dinner, close to sunset, Rip and Emmet walked to the corral and looked at the horses.

"Emmet, why don't you like Josh?" Rip said.

"I never said I didn't like him," Emmet said. "I just want to make sure he respects Emma."

"He's always nice to her, Emmet. Honest," Rip said.

"I believe you," Emmet said. "I guess I can be a bit overprotective when it comes to my sisters."

"What's going to happen, Emmet?" Rip said. "With the ranch and all this stuff my mother left me?"

"We'll take care of it until you're eighteen, then it's up to you," Emmet said.

"That's six more years," Rip said.

"It seems like a lot but it goes by in a blink," Emmet said. "You know, when I was twelve my Pa gave me a special gift and I think you're man enough now for me to pass it along."

Rip looked up at Emmet. "A gift?" he said.

Emmet reached into his right pants pocket

for the pocketknife given to him by John twenty years ago and placed it into Rip's right hand. "It's served me well for twenty years and I hope it does the same for you," Emmet said.

"Gosh, Emmet, I can't take your knife," Rip said.

"It's not a knife, Rip," Emmet said. "It's a passage to manhood."

Rip looked at Emmet and smiled.

"Let's go get some of that apple pie the ladies baked," Emmet said.

In the morning, Ellis drove Emmet, Rose, the baby, Anna and Rip to the train station in Stockton.

After they boarded the train and Ellis and Rip were alone in the buggy, Rip said, "Ellis, Emmet gave me this last night."

Rip showed Ellis the pocketknife. "Emmet gave you this?" Ellis said.

"He said it was a passage to manhood," Rip said. "Do you know what that means?"

Ellis grinned. "I sure do, Rip," he said.

Emmet met William Day in Judge Thomas's chambers shortly after noon. A fresh pot of coffee was on the desk and Emmet poured a cup.

"You're Day?" Emmet said.

"Friends call me Bill," Day said.

Emmet took a sip of coffee. "Tell me what you know and why you know it," Emmet said.

"Knowing is my business," Day said.

"I figured you for a bounty hunter," Emmet said.

"A man's got to earn a living," Day said.

Emmet glared at Day.

"Look, I came out of the war with nothing," Day said. "I had a small farm in Tennessee. No slaves. I never made more than three hundred in a year, but it was mine. I came back in late sixty-five to find it burned to the ground."

"There's other ways to make a living besides hunting bounty," Emmet said.

"Look, Marshal, you do exactly what I do, you just wear a badge doing it," Day said. "The only difference I see is I make considerably more money."

"Suppose you tell me how you came to locate Joe Pike," Emmet said.

"I saw the posters on him in Denver and then again in Saint Louis," Day said. "Fifteen thousand dollars it too much money to pass up."

"That doesn't tell me how you located him," Emmet said.

"Luck more than anything else," Day said.

"A man I sometimes partner with was chasing down a two-bit outlaw hiding out in New York City. He recognized Pike and wired me in Saint Louis. I went to New York and saw Pike for myself. It's him alright."

"Why didn't you go to the New York City police for help?" Emmet said.

"And lose ten thousand dollars," Day said. "Wells Fargo Bank posted five thousand dollars nationally, but the ten thousand is for California only. You're the Marshal for California. I collect the full fifteen thousand if you bring him in."

"He's right, Emmet," Thomas said. "I checked with Washington. The Marshal's Service posted the ten thousand dollars in California only due to an error in the wording."

"Did you ask them to change it?" Emmet said.

"They said we'll be celebrating the Centennial by the time it makes it through all the bureaucratic paperwork," Thomas said.

"I guess I'm going to New York," Emmet said. "And Mr. Day, if Pike isn't where you say he is, you're coming back to Sacramento to answer to Judge Thomas."

"He's there," Pike said. "He's set himself up pretty nice with that Wells Fargo Bank money."

"I'll make arrangements to leave," Emmet said. "Judge, I'll need a written warrant. Day, be at the hotel where I can find you come Monday."

"Oh, Emmet, New York City," Rose said. "And for how long?"

"I don't expect to be there for very long at all," Emmet said. "The train ride is the long part. Five days each way is where the time is spent."

"Do you have to go, Emmet?" Anna said.

"This man killed three deputy marshals and a half dozen other people," Emmet said. "Those deputy marshals worked for me. Yeah, honey, I have to go. I'll ask Ellis to . . ."

"We'll be fine, Emmet," Rose said. "Ellis has his own work to do on the farm. You can't expect him to spend two weeks babysitting us while you're away."

"It's an hour by train from Stockton to Sacramento," Emmet said. "Ellis can take you and pick you up at the station and Ma and Bettina can watch the baby while you're at the hospital. Please, you two, I have enough to worry about without worrying about you while I'm away."

Rose looked at Anna.

"We should pack," Anna said.

"We should," Rose said.

"Josh, we have a business proposal for you," John said.

John, Ellis and Josh were having coffee on the porch.

"Business proposal?" Josh said.

"Rip's grandmother passed away last week," John said.

"I'm sorry to hear that," Josh said.

"His grandfather is too old to manage things so Ellis and I will look after the crops," John said. "But the livestock, the horses and cattle, they need to be managed by someone who knows what they are doing."

"That's you," Ellis said.

"Me?" Josh said.

"You'll live in the house and manage the horses and cattle," John said. "And be paid two hundred and fifty dollars a month."

"A month?" Josh said.

"It's a big job and deserves a big compensation," John said. "Most of the horses go to the Army. You're the only one we know capable of providing them."

"When do you want me to start?" Josh said.

"We'll ride you over on Monday," John said. "Pack your gear tonight."

"I don't know what to say," Josh said.

"Say yes," John said.

"Yes," Josh said.

Emma and Josh walked along the creek after leaving the buggy behind.

They held hands as they walked.

"Do you know what this means?" Emma said. "It means we can get married."

"What do I do?" Josh said.

"Kiss me for starters," Emma said.

"No, I mean, should I ask your father?"

"Silly, you ask me," Emma said.

"I mean for permission to ask you," Josh said.

"Yes. Now what does a girl have to do to get kissed around here," Emma said.

As Emmet unbuttoned his shirt, Rose watched him through the mirror on her dresser as she brushed her hair.

"I can't say I'm too happy about you running around New York City with all those society women on the loose," Rose said.

"Oh for God's sake," Emmet said as he tossed his shirt over a chair.

"Those society women would love to get their hands on a real western Marshal," Rose said.

Emmet tossed his pants on the chair and

got into bed. Rose set her brush down and got into bed beside Emmet. "You behave yourself," she said.

"Want to come with me?" Emmet said.

"New York probably smells worse than Washington and Washington smells like an outhouse in July," Rose said.

Rose curled up beside Emmet. "We need another baby. Interested?" she said.

"This one is only seven months old," Emmet said.

"You and Ellis are only eleven months apart," Rose said. "Do you want Sarah to grow up alone?"

Emmet reached for Rose just as Sarah cried in her crib.

"Hold that thought," Rose said as she got out of bed.

"Sir, with everything that's happened, I would like to ask for your hand," Josh said.

In his chair on the porch, John stared at Josh. Emma stood behind Josh and said, "My hand, Josh? My hand?"

"My hand, sir," Josh said.

"No, Josh . . . my . . . Pa, help us out here," Emma said.

"Josh, are you trying to ask me for permission to marry Emma?" John said.

"Yes sir, I am."

"You messed it up even worse than I did with Emma's mother," John said.

"I'm sorry, Mr. Boyd," Josh said. "I'm just very nervous."

"Don't be, you have my permission," John said.

"Let's go tell Ma," Emma said and yanked Josh into the house.

"Off to a good start," John said.

Ellis picked Emmet, Rose, the baby and Anna up at the train station and drove them to church.

Ellis stopped halfway to the church.

"Emmet, Josh asked Pa for permission to marry Emma and he said yes," Ellis said.

"What? How is he going to support a . . ." Emmet said. "She's not in a family way, is she? Because I'll . . ."

"There's been some new developments," Ellis said. "Pa will fill you in after church."

Rose and Anna grinned at each other in the back seat.

"I can feel you grinning at me, the both of you," Emmet said.

"Let's get to church," Ellis said.

"Emmet, they love each other," John said. "They want to get married and I gave them my blessing."

"And live on what, his pay as a bunkhouse cowboy?" Emmet said.

"We're hiring Josh to be the foreman of the Olson ranch at a considerable salary," John said. "They have contracts with the Army for horses and none of us are qualified for that. There is also the cattle and we know even less about that. It works out all the way around."

"They'll live there, on the ranch?" Emmet said.

"Ironic, isn't it," John said. "Mr. Olson is too old and Rip is too young."

Emmet shook his head.

"Come on, son, dinner is waiting," John said.

After dinner, Emmet and Josh went for a walk through the orange grove.

"Emma is my sister," Emmet said. "To me she will always be my baby sister. If you hurt her, ever hit her, you will wish you were never born."

"As God as my witness, I would never hurt or hit Emma," Josh said. "I love her more than anything."

"I find out otherwise and you'll answer to me," Emmet said.

"I have no doubt you could whip me to a frazzle and I'm useless with a hand gun, but

I'll fight you right now if you ever say I would hit Emma again," Josh said.

"You're willing to take a beating because of what I said?" Emmet said.

"I'll take the beating to prove my point," Josh said.

Emmet extended his right hand. "Welcome to the family, Josh," he said.

Josh shook Emmet's hand.

"Let's go get some pie," Emmet said.

"Emmet, be careful," Rose said as she kissed Emmet goodbye before he boarded the train for New York City. "And watch out for those wicked city women."

"I'll be careful," Emmet said. "I'll wire as soon as I get there."

"Bye, Emmet and do like Rose said, be careful," Anna said.

"Never mind me, you two watch yourselves while I'm away," Emmet said.

After Emmet's train left, Rose and Anna waited in Ellis's buggy for their train to Sacramento.

The ride took just over an hour and they walked to the hospital. Both had a busy day, Anna with scheduled classes, Rose with classes in the morning and assisting a surgeon in the afternoon.

■ ■ ■ ■

Ellis and John met Josh in town and rode with him to the Olson ranch. Mr. Olson welcomed them on the porch with coffee.

"I'm afraid I know nothing about the horses or cattle," Mr. Olson said. "The Army calls for twelve horses a month, but the cowboys we employed have all left to look for gold."

"I'll take a look at the stock as soon as I settle my gear," Josh said.

"Pick which bedroom you prefer," Mr. Olson said.

"I'll be right back," Josh said and entered the house.

"Mr. Olson, Josh and Emma will be getting married," John said.

"I better tell him to take the bigger bedroom," Mr. Olson said.

Of the twelve horses in the corral, just five were fit for Army use. The other seven had small chests and their legs were thin. They would never hold up to the rigors of the hard riding the Army required.

An Army horse needed strength, endurance and speed and most of all, courage. A skittish horse would never stand up to the noise of gunfire.

Josh found Mr. Olson in the kitchen preparing lunch.

"I'm going to check out the horses and pick out the good ones," Josh said.

"Have some lunch first," Mr. Olson said.

Josh rode to the west range where a herd of about thirty horses were gathered. The stallion he saw previously was still there and looked at Josh with recognition.

Josh dismounted and stood beside his horse and looked at the stallion. The stallion looked at Josh. They made eye contact.

"Take a good look, boy," Josh said.

The stallion stomped his right front leg a few times, looked away and then looked back at Josh with defiance.

"You recognize your boss when you see him, don't you, boy," Josh said.

The stallion snorted, shook his head and stomped his right front leg at Josh.

"Say your peace now, boy," Josh said. "You and me will tussle soon enough."

Josh mounted his horse and rode east to a small box canyon where he counted thirty more horses. Then, between the south and north range he counted another sixty horses.

As they rode the train from Sacramento to

Stockton, Rose and Anna sat in the dining car with cups of coffee.

"I could use a hot bath and a good night's sleep," Rose said.

"Rose, do you think I'll ever find a man like Emmet?" Anna said.

"What do you mean like Emmet?" Rose said.

"Emmet is what women call a real man," Anna said. "He's as tough as they come, smart and not afraid to show that he loves you."

"Anna, you fall in love with your heart and not what people call a man," Rose said. "When I met and fell in love with Emmet I knew nothing about him. The learning comes later. What's important is that the man you love, loves you just as much in return."

Anna took a sip of coffee. "It would be nice if he were like Emmet, though," she said.

"You're hopeless," Rose said.

At the dinner table, John said, "I have to see Mr. Olson tomorrow, Emma. I was wondering if you . . . ?"

"Yes," Emma said.

"You didn't let me finish," John said.

"The answer is still yes," Emma said.

"We'll leave right after breakfast," John said.

"You're a fine cook, Mr. Olson," Josh said.

"I always did most of the cooking for the family," Mr. Olson said. "For my wife and my daughter."

"You miss them, don't you?" Josh said.

"To the point I want to join them," Mr. Olson said.

"If you do that, who will cook for me and Emma?" Josh said.

"I've known Emma since the day she opened her eyes," Mr. Olson said. "She is a fine girl."

"Then you better stick around or we'll both go hungry," Josh said.

"When are you getting married?" Mr. Olson said.

"Soon."

"You better move into the master bedroom," Mr. Olson said.

John drove Emma and Rip in the buggy to the Olson ranch right after breakfast. Mr. Olson was having coffee on the porch.

"Good morning," Mr. Olson said as he stood up. "Come have a cup of coffee with me."

John, Emma and Rip went to the porch.

John and Emma had coffee, Rip a glass of milk.

"Where's Josh?" Emma said.

"He said he was going to the west range to stare down a stallion," Mr. Olson said.

"Pa, let's go watch," Emma said.

"Mr. Olson, come with us," John said. "Some fresh air will do you good."

"Maybe you're right," Mr. Olson said.

John drove the buggy to the west field and stopped about a hundred feet behind Josh, who was standing still beside his horse and looking at the stallion.

"What's he doing, Pa?" Emma said.

"Looks to me like he's getting acquainted," John said.

They watched from the buggy for thirty minutes as Josh and the stallion looked at each other. Then Josh removed an apple from his pocket and slowly walked to the stallion.

The stallion backed up several feet.

"It's okay, boy," Josh said. He held up the apple. "I got something good for you."

The stallion took a step forward as Josh approached him.

"You want it," Josh said as he stopped four feet from the stallion. "Come get it."

The stallion looked at the apple in Josh's hand.

"You got to earn it," Josh said.

The stallion took a step forward.

"Couple more and it's yours," Josh said.

The stallion eyed the apple, then stepped forward and took it from Josh's hand. As he ate the apple, the stallion allowed Josh to pat and rub his neck.

"See, nobody is out to hurt you," Josh said.

The stallion turned and ran back to the mob. Josh turned and walked back to his horse and spotted the buggy. He walked his horse to it and said, "How long you been here?"

"Long enough," John said.

"That was amazing," Emma said.

"Josh, I think the ranch side of the business is in good hands," Mr. Olson said.

"He's some horse, isn't he?" Rip said.

Josh looked back at the stallion. "He's the boss," he said. "I get him and I bring in the entire mob."

Josh, Emma and Rip went to the corral while John and Mr. Olson went into the house to do paperwork.

"Only five of these horses are any good for the Army," Josh said.

"How come?" Rip said.

"Small chest, thin legs," Josh said. "Okay

for casual riding, but not for the hard riding soldiers need to do."

"Is that why you want that big stallion?" Emma said.

"He's an officer's horse for sure, but also the others will follow him," Josh said.

"Can you really bring him in?" Emma said.

"He has to trust me first," Josh said. "That could be tomorrow or next month, but I'll bring him in."

John and Mr. Olson came to the corral. "Emma, Rip, time to go," John said.

"Josh, you're coming to dinner Saturday?" Emma said.

"You bet," Josh said.

Mr. Olson pan-fried two steaks for dinner and served them with potatoes, greens and coffee. For dessert, Mr. Olson had fresh apple pie and coffee.

"Mr. Olson, why not come with me on Saturday for supper?" Josh said.

"I don't want to impose," Mr. Olson said.

"Rip is your grandson. You're family. It's not imposing," Josh said.

"Alright, I'll go," Mr. Olson said.

"Tomorrow, I'll work on the stallion in the morning and check the cattle in the afternoon," Josh said.

"Make sure you come back for lunch," Mr. Olson said.

"The way you cook, I wouldn't miss it," Josh said.

"Rose, we have surgery at one o'clock," a surgeon said. "Can you bring a nursing student to assist you?"

"Certainly," Rose said.

Rose went to the cafeteria where Anna was studying. Rose got a cup of coffee and sat at the table.

"Want to assist me?" Rose said.

"With what?" Anna said.

"Surgery."

"Really?"

"Really. Let's go scrub up," Rose said.

Rose and Anna went to the operating ward where they scrubbed up and put on hospital gowns and then met the surgeon.

"Doctor, this is Anna Boyd," Rose said. "She'll be assisting me."

"Actually, she'll be assisting me," the surgeon said. "It's a simple appendectomy. I want you to perform it, and I will assist, and Anna will assist me. Shall we?"

The surgeon showed Anna how to administer the anesthesia while Rose performed the surgery and removed the appendix with little trouble.

"Anna, would you assist me with the stitching?" Rose said.

On Saturday, Mr. Olson and Josh joined everybody for dinner and talk was of Anna's first surgery and the stallion.

"I'm going to try to bring him in tomorrow," Josh said.

"Pa, can we go and watch?" Emma said.

"Josh, would that bother you if we watched?" John said.

"No sir," Josh said. "But I'm afraid I won't make church. I have to ride to the Welding ranch and get some help."

"What time should we arrive?" John said.

"Eleven o'clock should do," Josh said.

After dinner, John took Josh to the porch for a private talk. "Josh, have you and Emma discussed a wedding?" John said.

"Some," Josh said. "We're not sure what to do first."

"First you need to buy her a small engagement ring and a set of wedding bands," John said. "The general store in Stockton has an entire counter just for rings and you don't have to spend too much to get some good ones."

"I don't know anything about rings," Josh said.

"Of course not," John said. "That's why

Bettina and Sarah will go with you."

"I appreciate that, sir, but don't you need to know her finger size?" Josh said.

"The ladies will take care of that," John said. "Now let's go get a slice of pie."

Emmet and Bill Day walked from the train depot to Manhattan's West Side near 34th Street. Each carried a satchel of clothing.

"The last time I saw this many people in one place was in Washington, DC," Emmet said.

"They say a million and a half people live here," Day said.

"It smells like an outhouse," Emmet said. "Where's that hotel located?"

"38th and Broadway. The New Yorker," Day said. "I know the way."

As they walked the streets, Emmet drew stares as the city people rarely saw the likes of Emmet's western clothing and Colt revolver. Carrying firearms inside the city limits was banned since the Civil War, except by police and military personnel.

A block from the hotel, a uniformed police officer approached Emmet and Day. "Fire-arms are not permitted . . . oh, excuse me Marshal, I didn't see your badge," he said.

"U.S. Marshal Emmet Boyd," Emmet said. "I'm here on official business. Can you tell me where I can find whoever is in charge of the police?"

"If you mean who is in charge, you mean the Police Commissioner," the officer said.

"If that's who I need to see," Emmet said.

"The Police Commissioner is James Kelly and he's at Police Headquarters near City Hall," the officer said.

"Obliged," Emmet said.

"You'll need an appointment to see him," the officer said.

"Thanks again," Emmet said.

Emmet and Day walked to the Hotel New Yorker and entered the lobby. It was large, ornate and lavish, with leather sofas and chairs, walled mirrors and decorative rugs.

Emmet signed for two rooms and ordered shaves and baths. "Can you send a telegram for me?" Emmet said.

"Sure can," the desk clerk said.

Emmet wrote out a message to Rose and handed it to the clerk. "Add it to my bill," Emmet said.

"The barber and bath is down that hall to your right," the desk clerk said. "It will be put on your bill, but you can tip for service."

An hour later, Emmet and Day were in a horse-drawn taxi that took them to Police Headquarters near City Hall.

An officer on duty in the lobby looked at

Emmet. "I haven't seen a U.S. Marshal in quite a while," he said.

"Name is Boyd. I'm here to see Commissioner Kelly," Emmet said.

"Do you have an appointment?" the officer said.

"No," Emmet said. "But you tell him that he can wire President Grant to verify who I am and the need to see him."

"I'll send for a runner," the officer said.

Fifteen minutes later, Emmet and Day were inside Commissioner Kelly's office where Kelly had fresh coffee brought in.

"What can I do for you, Marshal?" Kelly said.

"I'm here to arrest a murderer named Joe Pike," Emmet said. "He robbed a Wells Fargo bank, killed three and then killed three deputy marshals in California. This man is Bill Day and he's a bounty hunter who tracked Pike to New York."

Kelly looked at Day. "Bounty hunter?" he said.

"Pike has set himself up as leader of a gang in a section called Five Points," Emmet said. "I aim to take him alive and back to California for trial."

"The Five Points is a miserable, rat-infested place filled with gangs, thugs, murderers and the worst scum on earth,"

Kelly said. "One man alone wouldn't stand a chance. I'll assign thirty men with rifles to go with you."

"I take Pike," Emmet said. "No one else."

"Alright, Marshal," Kelly said. "When do you want to do it?"

"From what I've seen, they never get out of bed before ten," Day said. "Pike is living in this old brewery that's now some kind of complex. He's managed to buy his way into the gang called the Shirt Tails and is now a leader."

"I know that old brewery," Kelly said. "It should be condemned."

"Why isn't it?" Emmet said.

"We don't bother the Points and they don't cause trouble outside of the Points," Kelly said. "It makes life a bit easier for all concerned."

"I'd like to do it say eight o'clock tomorrow morning," Emmet said.

"I'll have thirty men in the lobby at seven," Kelly said. "It's Sunday and lower Manhattan will be quiet."

"Thank you, Commissioner," Emmet said.

"Were you really appointed by President Grant?" Kelly said.

"Send him a wire," Emmet said. "Tell him I said hello."

■ ■ ■ ■

Emmet and Day had steaks at the Hotel New Yorker restaurant.

"If we capture Pike alive, I'll require you to travel back to Sacramento for his trial if you want the ten thousand," Emmet said.

"With fifteen thousand dollars, I can retire and open up a little business," Day said. "Another train ride won't kill me."

"I advise that," Emmet said. "Because sooner or later, every bounty hunter winds up dead before his time."

"You could say the same for U.S. Marshals," Day said.

"I can't argue that point," Emmet said.

"We best get to bed early," Day said. "If we're to meet the police at seven in the morning."

Emmet and Day met Kelly and thirty uniformed officers in front of police headquarters. Thirty-two horses were saddled and ready to go.

"This is Captain Williams of the mounted police squad," Kelly said. "Williams, this is U.S. Marshal Emmet Boyd."

Williams and Emmet shook hands.

"Captain, the objective is the safe capture

of Joe Pike, but any members of the Shirt Tails that interfere are to be arrested," Kelly said.

"Yes sir," Williams said. "Alright men, mount up. Column of two."

Emmet rode beside Williams in the lead and they rode through the streets to the Five Points. Those early risers stared in wonder at the sight of thirty-two mounted police as they rode by.

For more than thirty years, the Five Points was regarded as a slum, a gathering place for murderers, thieves, pickpockets and rapists. The most powerful gang leader was the late Bill 'The Butcher' Cutting, leader of the gang the Nativists.

When they reached the old brewery, Emmet looked up at the rundown, five-story building that was home to several of the gangs.

"Dismount," Williams said. "Winchesters and clubs."

Emmet and Williams led the way as they entered through the unlocked brewery door. Men and women were sleeping in cots and on tables. The stench was a mixture of beer and sweat and stale urine.

"Up. Up. Everybody wake the hell up," Williams screamed. "Men, fan out, find Joe Pike."

Twenty-nine uniformed officers walked from room-to-room and floor-to-floor until a hundred men and women, mostly hungover, staggered out and looked at the police.

"Joe Pike of the Shirt Tails, where is he?" Williams said.

A man on the second floor yelled, "Get stuffed, blue boy."

"Who said that?" Williams said.

Emmet turned and walked to the stairs and up to the second floor and to the man who had shouted.

"Care to stuff me?" Emmet said.

The man pulled a knife and moved toward Emmet. Emmet grabbed his arm and shirt and threw him over the railing to the first floor. The man landed with a loud crash and moaned in pain.

"My name is United States Marshal Emmet Boyd," Emmet said. "Joe Pike is wanted for six murders. I am not leaving here without him, so wrap your minds around that. You can bring him to me, or I will have the fire department set fire to this building and you'll all be living on the street. Either way, I'm not leaving without Joe Pike. You decide. I'll be outside. You have five minutes."

Emmet walked down to the first floor where the man was still moaning, stepped over him and headed to the door. Williams, the officers and Day followed Emmet out to the street.

A hundred or more gang members from other buildings were now on the street, watching.

"What's going on?" a gang member said.

"Not your concern," Williams said. "Don't interfere and you'll have no problems."

"That was quite a stint you pulled in there," Day said to Emmet. "Think it will work?"

"It doesn't, fire will," Emmet said.

The door opened and three men tossed Joe Pike out to the sidewalk.

"One for you, Marshal," Day said.

Emmet walked to Pike.

"Joseph Pike, I have a warrant for your arrest for the murders of . . ." Emmet said.

"Go screw yourself," Pike said.

Emmet punched Pike in the jaw, knocking him to the ground. Then Emmet handcuffed Pike's hands behind his back and yanked him to his feet.

"Let's go," Emmet said.

Josh held eye contact with the stallion without moving for a solid thirty minutes. A hundred feet behind Josh, John, Emma, Rip and a cowboy from the Welding Ranch named Steve watched.

"What's he waiting on?" John said.

"That stallion to tell him it's okay," Steve said.

"How will he know?" Emma said.

"He'll know," Steve said.

With an apple in his right hand and his lasso in his left, Josh slowly walked to the stallion who didn't move.

"Want this?" Josh said and held up the apple.

The stallion took the apple and as he ate it, Josh stroked his neck and slowly slipped the lasso around his neck.

"That wasn't so bad now was it?" Josh said. "Steve."

Steve mounted his horse and rode to Emmet.

Josh handed Steve the rope. "Keep him still until I get my horse," Josh said.

Josh walked to his horse.

"He didn't put up much of a fight," John said.

"That will come later when we try to ride him," Josh said.

Josh mounted his horse and rode to Steve.

"Move him out and I'll follow with the herd," Josh said.

Steve yanked on the rope and the stallion followed Steve's horse. Josh removed his second rope from his saddle and, holding it in his left hand, rode to the herd of twenty horses and used his horse to gather them into a group.

"Let's go, you mob," Josh said.

John, Emma and Rip watched as Josh ran the herd behind Steve and the stallion. "Let's get in the buggy and follow," John said.

Mr. Olson was sitting in a chair on the porch with a cup of coffee. In the distance he spotted a cloud of dust and stood and walked to the corral.

The sight of Josh and Steve herding twenty horses led by the stallion was something Mr. Olson would never forget. As the horses ran into the corral in a cloud of dust, the ground beneath Mr. Olson's feet shook.

"Close 'er up," Josh said when all the horses were in the corral.

"Well, Marshal, you got your man," Kelly said as he served Emmet a cup of coffee.

"Thank you," Emmet said.

"I must say, the New York Police Department could use a man like you in our ranks," Kelly said.

"Thank you, Commissioner, but I'm obligated to Grant for three plus more years," Emmet said. "Plus I have a wife and baby waiting for me in Sacramento."

"We'll hold Pike until you pick him up tomorrow," Kelly said.

"Thanks again, Commissioner. Can I trouble you to send a telegram for me to Judge Thomas in Sacramento and another to my wife?"

"No problem, Marshal," Kelly said.

"Best stew I ever had," Josh said.

"The secret is slow cooking in a Dutch oven," Mr. Olson said. He looked at Emma. "You remember that, young lady."

"I will," Emma said.

"Josh, when is the Army coming to look at the horses?" John said.

"Mr. Olson?" Josh said.

"Next Wednesday," Mr. Olson said.

After lunch, before John, Emma and Rip got into John's buggy, John pulled Josh aside. "Sarah and Bettina will meet you in town at the general store tomorrow to pick out a ring," John said.

John went to the post office for the mail while Sarah and Bettina took Josh into the general store to shop for rings.

The owner of the general store was Mr. Ferguson and he took Sarah, Bettina and

Josh to the counter reserved for rings.

"Emma is a size six," Sarah said.

Josh looked at the rings in the counter.

"Confusing, isn't it?" Sarah said.

"Yes ma'am," Josh said.

"I know my daughters," Sarah said. "Mr. Ferguson, that diamond chip engagement ring and those gold wedding bands next to it."

Ferguson brought out the rings.

"Bettina is a size six, try them on, dear," Sarah said.

Bettina removed her rings and tried on the wedding band and engagement ring.

"Josh?" Sarah said.

"Think she'll like them?" Josh said as he looked at Bettina's finger.

"She will love them," Sarah said.

"Okay," Josh said.

"The engagement ring is seventy-five dollars," Ferguson said. "The wedding bands are fifty for the set."

"I'll go to the bank and be right back," Josh said.

After paying for the rings, John took them to lunch at the café across the street.

"Got a telegram from Emmet," John said and handed it to Sarah.

Sarah ripped open the envelope and read the telegram. "Emmet will be home on

Friday," she said.

After lunch, while Sarah and Bettina did some shopping, John and Josh chatted at the hitching post outside the general store where Josh tied his horse.

"Sir, when should I give the ring to Emma?" Josh said.

"When the time is right," John said. "After church, take her for a walk by the creek."

"How do I . . . ?" Josh said.

"It will come to you," John said.

Josh nodded. He untied the reins from the hitching post and looked at John. "Sir, can I ask you a question?" Josh said.

"Ask."

"Why didn't you open the telegram?"

"You mean why did I give it to Sarah to open?" John said.

Josh nodded.

"There are certain things, Josh, that are reserved for a mother," John said.

"I understand," Josh said.

"Emma, Rip and I will be over on Wednesday to do business with the Army," John said.

"See you then, sir," Josh said.

Captain Tyrell was second in command at the fort and was in charge of buying the horses for the men. As he and Josh looked over the horses in the corral, Josh showed him the stallion.

"The Colonel would love this stallion," Tyrell said.

"He'll take some doing breaking him in," Josh said.

"We have two top busters and some great trainers," Tyrell said. "I'll take all twenty."

Tyrell turned to the squad of men he brought with him. "Sergeant, prepare the horses for transport," he said as he walked to the house.

Josh watched as the Army drovers placed ropes around the necks of each horse. By the time the sergeant had assembled the twenty riders with one roped horse to a man, Captain Tyrell was shaking hands with John on the porch.

Tyrell joined his men and Josh, Emma and Rip watched Tyrell lead his men back to the fort.

"Josh, a moment please," John said.

Josh, Emma and Rip went to the porch.

"Saddle your horse," John said. "We're going to deposit this check for six thousand dollars into Rip's account at the bank."

Emmet brought lunch to Pike in the car reserved for transporting prisoners. The car was divided into two sections. Half was enclosed by iron bars and had a cot, a toilet and a table with water and a glass. The other section was for law enforcement. It had a table and two chairs.

Emmet unlocked the door to the prisoner car with a key and carried a tray of food inside and closed the door. The tray held a steak with potatoes and coffee for Pike and an extra cup of coffee that Emmet removed from the tray and set on the table.

Emmet placed the tray through the slit in the bars and Pike took it to the small table and sat in the chair.

Emmet sat in the chair at his table and took a sip of his coffee.

"Hey, Marshal, my jaw hurts where you punched me," Pike said.

"On behalf of the three deputy marshals you murdered, I can't tell you how little I care," Emmet said.

Pike cut into his steak and grinned at Emmet. "I ain't gonna swing," he said.

"No?" Emmet said.

"Wait and see, Marshal. I ain't gonna swing," Pike said.

"You unrepentant son of a bitch, you don't even care that you killed the deputies and three men robbing that stage," Emmet said.

Pike put a piece of steak into his mouth,

grinned and said, "I care about me. Everyone else can take a flying leap into hell."

"And that's why you'll hang," Emmet said.

"You know, Marshal, if you weren't such a coward, you'd fight me square," Pike said.

"You mean you and me shoot it out?" Emmet said.

"Best man wins," Pike said. "You having any?"

"Unfortunately the law doesn't allow for it, so I guess you'll just have to swing," Emmet said.

"I get the chance I'll kill you," Pike said.

Emmet stood up. "I'll be back for the tray," he said.

John, Emma, Rip and Josh stopped by the bank and met with the bank president.

"Always a pleasure to see you, John. Emma," the bank president said.

"I have a check to deposit into Robert's account," John said and handed the bank president the check.

The bank president looked at the check. "Robert, you are getting to be one wealthy young man," he said. "Give me a minute and I'll get you a receipt."

After Josh rode back to the ranch, John,

Emma and Rip rode to the train station to wait for Rose and Anna.

"Pa, how much is wealthy?" Rip said as they stood on the platform.

"Are you talking strictly money?" John said.

"What other kinds are there?" Rip said.

"Some people consider having a family that they love and that loves them to be the greatest wealth of all," John said.

"Like you and Ma and everybody else?" Rip said.

"Exactly like that," John said. "Then there's the kind of wealth a man gains by living a clean life by not cheating, stealing or lying. That wealth is called respect. Understand?"

"Yes sir," Rip said.

"A man who lies, steals and cheats can't have a clean conscience," John said. "Each time he lies, steals or cheats it's like having a pebble in your shoe you can't remove. It will bother you for all your days."

"And the wealth the man said at the bank?" Rip said.

"That was strictly money and, in that regard, you're worth about four hundred thousand," John said.

"Is that a lot?" Rip said.

"It's more than most people see in their

entire lifetime," John said. "But it's nothing for you to trouble yourself with now."

"Pa, train's coming," Emma said.

"I think I'd rather have my family love me than be wealthy," Rip said.

"That you already have, boy," John said.

As Josh ate a spoonful of beef stew, he looked across the table at Mr. Olson. "How much time do I have before the Army returns wanting more horses?" Josh said.

"One month and they want another twenty horses," Mr. Olson said.

"That gives me time to check on the cattle," Josh said.

"There's something you haven't asked about," Mr. Olson said.

"What's that?" Josh said.

Mr. Olson reached into his suit jacket pocket for an envelope and slid it across the table. "Your wages," he said.

"You know, I almost forgot all about them," Josh said.

"You shouldn't, you earned every penny," Mr. Olson said.

After supper, Mr. Olson and Josh sat in chairs on the front porch and watched the sunset. Mr. Olson brought out two small drinks and gave one to Josh.

"This is brandy," Mr. Olson said. "It's to

be sipped and is excellent for a good night's sleep."

Josh took a sip from his glass. "Reminds me of the cough medicine my mother gave me when I was a little boy and got sick," he said.

"It does, doesn't it," Mr. Olson said.

Emmet opened the cell door and looked at Pike. "Time to go," he said. "Turn around and give me your hands."

"I don't think so," Pike said.

"No?" Emmet said.

"No. Screw you," Pile said.

Emmet drew his Colt and smacked Pike across the face with it and Pike fell to his knees. Emmet flipped Pike around and cuffed his hands behind his back.

"On your feet," Emmet said and yanked Pike to his feet.

Emmet waited for the train to empty, then he walked Pike to the platform where a wagon with two sheriff's deputies waited. "Take him to jail," Emmet said. "I need to see Judge Thomas."

"He give you much trouble?" Thomas said.

"He's mostly talk," Emmet said.

"What about the Wells Fargo money he stole?" Thomas said.

"He didn't have it with him," Emmet said. "And he won't say where he hid it."

"He'll use the return of the money as a bargaining chip at his trial," Thomas said.

"I know," Emmet said. "I'll see you Monday. Right now I'm going to see my wife."

John, Rose and Rip were on the front porch when Ellis arrived with Emmet in his buggy. Before Emmet could dismount from the buggy, Rose was off the porch and running to him. As he stepped down to the ground, Rose grabbed Emmet in a tight hug.

"Is that what you mean by wealth?" Rip said to John.

"You got it, son," John said.

On Sunday, after church, Josh and Emma took a buggy ride to the creek where they walked along the shallow banks.

As they walked, Emma said, "Josh, is something wrong?"

"No. Why?" Josh said.

"You're not holding my hand," Emma said.

"I'm nervous," Josh said.

"Nervous? You've held my hand a hundred times before," Emma said.

"Not that," Josh said. "Well, I think this is

how it's done," he said and dropped to one knee.

"What are you doing?" Emma said.

John removed the ring box from his pocket, held it up and opened it. "Emma, will you be my wife?" he said.

"Oh Josh, put it on my finger," Emma said.

Josh stood up, removed the ring from the box and placed it on Emma's finger.

"Let's go show everybody," Emma said.

"I'll go to town and Bettina and I will make your wedding dress," Sarah said. "Josh, I'm afraid you'll have to buy a suit in town."

"Pa and I will take care of that, Ma," Ellis said.

"We'll need to talk to the preacher about the church," Sarah said.

"If I may suggest an outdoor wedding at the ranch," Mr. Olson said. "Plenty of room for tables and chairs and even a small band for music."

"I can build an archway," Ellis said.

"Bettina, Rose and I can be bride's maids," Anna said.

"I can handle the food," Mr. Olson said.

"Josh, my job is to give the bride away, but you need a best man," John said.

Josh looked at Emmet. Then everybody at

the table looked at Emmet.

"What?" Emmet said.

"Josh is asking you to be his best man," Sarah said.

"And your answer is?" Rose said.

Emmet looked at Rose and he knew what was good for him.

"I'll stand up for you, Josh," Emmet said.

The train from Stockton to Sacramento on Sunday evening was just three cars long, with one hundred passengers on board. It carried no valuable cargo or mail or anything of interest except to the three armed men who saw a hundred wallets, purses and jewelry for the taking.

Emmet, Rose and Anna were seated in the middle car when one of the three men jumped up from his seat and waved his gun in the air. A second man jumped up and pulled the emergency cord. A third man entered the car with a shotgun.

As the train screeched to a violent stop, the man with the shotgun yelled, "This is a Goddam robbery. Do as you're told and you won't get hurt."

Emmet's Colt was out and cocked before he even stood up. "Emmet," Rose yelled as Emmet shot the man with the shotgun in the chest.

The man who pulled the emergency cord reached for his gun and Emmet shot him in the chest, knocking him to the floor.

The man waving his gun in the air looked at Emmet. "No, no," he yelled right before Emmet shot and killed him.

Emmet cocked the Colt and walked to the three fallen men and inspected them, then he de-cocked the Colt and holstered it.

Anna and Rose were hugging each other and finally released their grip.

"Oh my God," Anna said.

Rose stood up. "Emmet?" she said.

"It's okay. Stay there," Emmet said.

The engineer and conductor rushed into the car, both armed with rifles. They looked at Emmet and the three dead men.

"Is anybody hurt?" the conductor said.

"Just these three," Emmet said.

The passengers in the car started to clap and cheer as Emmet returned to Rose and Anna. "You two okay?" he said.

"I'm shaking like a leaf," Anna said.

Rose sat beside Anna and hugged her.

"I best see about those men," Emmet said and returned to the center of the car.

"Rose, Emmet is a real lawman, isn't he?" Anna said.

"As real as they come," Rose said. "As those three found out."

The train was two hours late reaching Sacramento and sheriff's deputies were waiting to take the three dead men away.

"Had some excitement," a deputy said to Emmet.

"Excitement?" Anna said. "My brother shot those men before . . ."

"Anna," Rose said.

"Let's go home," Emmet said as he carried his suitcase and the baby's carrier.

While Rose soaked in a hot tub, Emmet sat on the front porch of the house with a cup of coffee. Anna opened the screen door and came out and sat beside him.

"The baby is asleep," Anna said.

"And how are you?" Emmet said.

"Still a bit shaky, but alright," Anna said. "You know, when you went off to fight in the war, I had no idea what it was like for you. I still don't. But I'm very glad you're a Marshal. People could have been hurt or killed if you weren't on that train tonight."

"I would never let anybody hurt Rose or you or the baby," Emmet said.

Anna put her head on Emmet's shoulder. "You have to buy a real suit for the wedding," she said.

Emmet sighed. "Yeah," he said.

■ ■ ■ ■

Josh studied the twenty or so horses grazing on the north range. He came to check the cattle and about forty were sharing the range with the horses. The cattle were a bit thin and needed some fattening up.

He spotted a painted bay of medium size with a solid chest and sturdy legs. Josh mounted up, removed his lasso from the saddle and rode to the bay.

The bay nervously darted to her right, but Josh snared her with the lasso and tied it to his saddle horn. The bay fought but Josh's big male horse was too powerful for her.

"Nobody is going to hurt you, girl," Josh said. "So get used to the idea and ride along easy."

Thirty minutes later, Josh rode the bay into the empty corral. He put his horse in the barn, went into the house and returned with an apple and a carrot.

At the corral gate, Josh held up the apple. The bay eyed the apple from a distance.

"Well I'm not bringing it to you," Josh said.

The bay and Josh watched each other for several minutes until the bay walked to Josh and took the apple.

Josh rubbed the bay's neck and gave her the carrot. "We have some work to do, you and I," Josh said.

While Rose and Anna had coffee in the hospital cafeteria, several nurses stopped by the table. One had a newspaper and put it on the table.

"Have you seen this?" the nurse said.

Rose and Anna looked at the newspaper. *U.S. Marshal foils train robbery and saves a hundred passengers,* the headline read.

"Oh boy," Rose said.

"You were there?" a nurse said.

"We were there," Rose said.

Anna picked up the newspaper. "They're calling Emmet a hero," she said.

"He won't like that," Rose said.

"Why not?"

"Emmet believes in what he does," Rose said. "He doesn't do what he does for praise."

"Even if it's true?"

"Especially if it's true," Rose said.

"I have to get to the lecture hall," Anna said.

"See you later," Rose said.

After Anna left the table, Rose picked up the newspaper. "Oh dear," she said.

■ ■ ■ ■

"Quite a story," Judge Thomas said as he set the newspaper on his desk.

"I saw it," Emmet said. "From witnesses on the train."

"The railroad said it wants to issue you a citation," Thomas said.

"They can keep it," Emmet said. "About Pike?"

"It's gotten complicated," Thomas said.

"How so?" Emmet said.

"Wells Fargo wants its money back," Thomas said. "They are sending a lawyer to negotiate a deal with Pike for the return of the money, which Pike claims is almost all of it."

"He murdered three deputies," Emmet said.

"So he gets life instead of a rope, is that so bad?" Thomas said.

"Life with parole?" Emmet said.

"I didn't say that," Thomas said.

"But it's possible?"

"It's up to the prosecutor and the Wells Fargo lawyer."

"When?"

"The lawyer will be here Wednesday."

"You have the power to reject any deal,"

Emmet said.

"I do," Thomas said. "I'll hear arguments at two. Please be in my courtroom."

"I'll be there."

"Thank you, Marshal," Thomas said.

With a rope around the bay's neck, Josh guided her in circles around him a few times, then stopped and gave her a carrot. Josh rubbed her neck as she munched.

"She's not a good Army horse," Mr. Olson said as he watched from outside the corral.

"No, but she'll make a fine wedding gift for Emma, don't you think?" Josh said.

"Splendid," Mr. Olson said.

"She's no bronc, but she'll still take some taming," Josh said. "Right now I have to get to town about my suit."

Sarah, Bettina and Emma shopped for fabric in the general store. They chose white for Emma and rose colored for Sarah and Bettina and Anna.

"What kind of lace do you want, honey?" Sarah said.

Emma chose a lace.

"Now for shoes," Sarah said.

John, Ellis, Josh and Rip were in the men's haberdashery one block away.

"It's a fine suit," the tailor said. "Pick it

up in three days when the alterations are complete. Now, about shoes?"

"Shoes?" Josh said.

"You can't get married in your cowboy boots, Josh," John said.

After leaving the haberdashery, John, Ellis and Rip met the women for lunch at the café.

"We have a lot of planning to do," John said. "There are people in town we'd like to invite and Josh, are there any friends from the Welding Ranch?"

"At least a dozen," Josh said.

"We need enough tables and chairs for everybody and of course, the food," John said.

"Bettina, Rose and Anna will help Mr. Olson," Sarah said.

"The preacher, we have to see him," John said.

"Pa, do you remember the Grange party last fall?" Ellis said. "Four members played all the music."

"Let's stop by the hall and contact them," John said.

"About the honeymoon, have you two discussed it?" Sarah said.

"I don't know what a . . ." Josh said.

"We'll talk about it," Emma said.

A member of the Grange having lunch

stopped by the table on the way out. "You must be very proud, John," he said.

"Of what?" John said.

The man set a newspaper on the table. "Good afternoon, folks," he said and left.

John looked at the front page story about Emmet. He handed the newspaper to Sarah. "How many did he kill?" Sarah said.

Rose and Anna walked from the hospital to Emmet's office, which was located on Front Street. Anna held the baby in her arms.

"He's still working," Anna said.

"Of course he is," Rose said.

"Let's drag him out of there," Anna said.

They reached the office, opened the door and stepped inside where Emmet was at his desk. "The women in your life are hungry, Marshal," Rose said.

Emmet stood up from the desk. "Give me a minute to lock up," he said.

A few minutes later, as they walked home, Emmet said, "I'll cook tonight. What would the women in my life like for supper?"

"You're going to cook supper?" Anna said.

"Whatever you like?" Emmet said.

"Rose?" Anna said.

"Baked chicken with potatoes and carrots," Rose said.

"The market is still open," Emmet said.

When they reached the market, Emmet went inside.

"I don't understand," Anna said.

"It's his way of apologizing for us seeing him kill those men on the train," Rose said.

"But he had no choice," Anna said.

"I'm his wife and you're his baby sister, it bothers him," Rose said.

Emmet emerged from the store with a large package. "Alright ladies, let's go home," he said.

As Anna stood behind the bathtub and washed Rose's hair, she giggled. "Besides cooking dinner, Emmet is boiling hot water for my bath."

"I'm afraid it's more about you than me," Rose said.

"I don't understand," Anna said.

"He has a lot of scars," Rose said.

"I've seen them," Anna said. "On his chest and . . ."

"Not physical scars," Rose said. "The scars of all the men he's killed. In the war, as a Marshal, they are worse than any physical scar."

"You said more about me. What do you mean?" Anna said.

"I've seen him in the war and as a Marshal," Rose said. "I accepted it before we were married and I still do. But you're his baby sister. You're not supposed to see men killed, especially if he's the one killing them. The last thing he wants for you is to have the same scars he carries around. Understand?"

"I think so, yes," Anna said.

"So if he wants to cook for you and boil water for your bath, let him," Rose said. "Rinse."

Anna poured a pitcher of water over Rose's hair to rinse away the soap. "And while he's spoiling you, don't feel guilty about it because it's helping him."

The bay did her best to buck Josh off her back, but she was no bronco and tired after about fifteen minutes and settled down.

Josh dismounted and gave her an apple and let her rest.

Watching Josh by the corral gate, Mr. Olson said, "She's coming along just fine, my boy."

Josh grinned. "She'll be rideable by the wedding."

"That reminds me," Mr. Olson said. "We need to get to town to pick up your suit and I need supplies."

"Let me wash the dust off me first and we'll get going," Josh said.

■ ■ ■ ■

"Emmet, this is Mark Andrews, attorney for Wells Fargo Bank," Thomas said. "Mr. Andrews, Marshal Boyd."

"Now then, Marshal, to business," Andrews said.

Thomas handed Emmet a cup of coffee and Emmet took a chair beside Thomas's desk.

"The bank wants its forty thousand dollars returned," Andrews said.

"Pike murdered six people, three of them deputy marshals," Emmet said.

"And he will be punished for his crimes," Andrews said. "I am suggesting twenty years at hard labor to the prosecutor in exchange for the return of the money."

"Twenty years?" Emmet said.

"It's no picnic, Marshal," Andrews said. "He'll be a broken, old man in twenty years."

"Judge?" Emmet said.

"If we hang him or don't offer him a deal, that money is lost," Thomas said. "And like Mr. Andrews said, twenty years at hard labor is no picnic."

"I propose the deal hinge on the recovery of the money," Emmet said. "If the money isn't found first, no deal."

"Mr. Andrews?" Thomas said.

"I'll agree to that," Andrews said.

"Emmet, would you ask a court officer in the hall to have Pike brought to the courtroom while I send for the prosecutor?" Thomas said.

Thirty minutes later, two sheriff's deputies ushered in Pike, who was shackled at the wrists and ankles. He was seated at the table in front of Thomas's bench.

"Do you know why you're here?" Thomas said.

Pike grinned at Thomas. "You tell me," he said.

The prosecutor entered the courtroom. "You sent for me, Judge?" he said.

"Yes," Thomas said. "Let's get started."

Twenty minutes later, the prosecutor said, "Judge, the people can live with twenty years at Yuma Prison in exchange for the stolen money."

"Mr. Andrews?" Thomas said.

"The bank can live with it, Your Honor," Andrews said.

Thomas looked at Pike. "This is your one chance at avoiding the noose, for if this goes to trial you will surely hang," he said.

"I give you the money and I go to Yuma for twenty years. I don't and I swing," Pike said. "Not much of a choice."

"One is life, one is not," Thomas said. "It's up to you."

"I'll take the twenty years," Pike said.

"Open the gate, Mr. Olson," Josh said.

Mr. Olson opened the corral gate and Josh rode the bay outside and paused her. "How does she look?" Josh said.

"She looks fine, Josh," Mr. Olson said.

"I'll be back," Josh said and tugged the reins and the bay moved forward. He kept the pace slow and easy for a half mile, then sped the bay up a bit. After another half mile, he broke her out into a flat run and she ate up the ground without much effort.

When he stopped the bay, she was barely winded. He rubbed her neck. "Emma's going to love you," he said. "Let's go back easy."

At the dinner table, Emmet said, "I have to go to Kansas."

Rose and Anna looked at him.

"To save himself from hanging, Pike has told us where he hid the railroad payroll money, plus money from other robberies," Emmet said. "I'm going to pick it up and return it to Judge Thomas."

"You volunteered to go, didn't you?" Rose said.

"Three of the men he killed were my deputies," Emmet said.

"When are you going?" Rose said.

"Friday," Emmet said. "I should be home by Tuesday."

Rose nodded. "Alright," she said.

John and Ellis went to Stockton for supplies and noticed Mr. Olson's buggy parked in front of the general store. Josh was loading supplies into the back seats.

"Hello, Josh," John said as he and Ellis stepped down from their buggy.

"Hello, sir, Ellis," Josh said.

"Mr. Olson with you?" John said.

"No sir," Josh said. "Sir, I have a small problem."

"What, maybe we can help?" John said.

"Mr. Olson said I'm supposed to dance with Emma at the wedding," Josh said.

"And you can't dance," John said.

"Not a lick," Josh said.

"Ellis," John said.

"Bettina is an excellent dancer," Ellis said. "I'm sure she can give you a few pointers."

"At the ranch?" Josh said.

"I suppose we can come to the ranch," Ellis said. "How is Friday afternoon?"

■ ■ ■ ■

At the Sacramento train station, Emmet kissed Rose and the baby, then turned to Anna and hugged her and kissed her on the cheek.

"I should be back Tuesday night," Emmet said. "If not, I'll send a telegram."

"I feel silly telling you to be careful, but be careful," Rose said.

"I will," Emmet said.

After Emmet boarded the train, Rose and Anna walked to the hospital with the baby in Anna's arms.

"I have a test today," Anna said. "But I'll be done by three o'clock."

"When you're done, join me in the lecture hall," Rose said.

"I feel silly," Josh said.

"Everybody does at first," Bettina said. "It's expected for the new bride and groom to have the first dance, so let's practice."

Seated in a chair on the porch, Mr. Olson suddenly jumped up, said, "Wait, wait," and ran into the house.

Ellis, standing near Bettina and Josh, said, "What was that about?"

Mr. Olson returned to the porch with a

violin and bow.

"I didn't know you played the fiddle," Ellis said.

"Violin, dear boy and I only played for my wife," Mr. Olson said. He took his chair and said, "Try this."

Mr. Olson played a soft waltz and Bettina took Josh by the hands and led him through a dance. "Whatever you do, do not step on her feet," Bettina said and a moment later, Josh stepped on her feet.

After five or six dances, Josh relaxed and managed to get through an entire dance without stepping on Bettina's feet.

"You'll do fine, Josh," Bettina said.

"Well done, young man," Mr. Olson said. "Josh, why don't you show them your wedding gift for Emma?"

"Wait by the corral," Josh said.

Ellis and Bettina went to the corral while Josh went into the barn. A few moments later, Josh walked the bay to the corral.

"She's beautiful," Bettina said.

"Emma's wedding gift," Josh said. "Do you think she'll like her?"

"You caught and broke her yourself?" Ellis said.

"The boy sure did," Mr. Olson said as he came to the corral.

Josh looked at Bettina. "Would you ride

191

her?" he said.

"Me?" Bettina said.

"Up until now I'm the only one on her back," Josh said.

"Go ahead, hon," Ellis said. "You know how to ride."

"Alright, but just for a bit," Bettina said.

Josh grabbed the saddle off the corral railing and saddled the bay. Ellis helped Bettina into the saddle.

"Now take it easy, honey," Ellis said. "I don't want you falling off and . . ."

Bettina yanked the reins and the bay trotted away from the corral, then Bettina yanked the reins again and the bay broke out into a full run.

Ellis, Josh and Mr. Olson watched as the bay vanished in a cloud of dust.

"Yeah, she knows how to ride," Josh said.

Bettina returned ten minutes later, stopped the bay at the corral and dismounted. "Emma will love her," she said.

"You won't tell her," Josh said.

"Not a word," Ellis said.

"We better get going," Bettina said. "We have to pick Rose and Anna up at the station."

"Emmet is pretty upset with himself for having to kill those men on the train in front

192

of Anna," Rose said to Sarah as the two women shared a cup of coffee on the porch.

"How does Anna feel?" Sarah said.

"We talked," Rose said. "She understands it's his job and is okay with it."

"And now he's off again," Sarah said.

"That Pike made a deal for his life," Rose said. "Emmet is going to pick up the money he stole from the bank."

"I read the story in the newspaper," Sarah said. "About the men on the train. Emmet is about the most respected man in California."

"And he doesn't realize it," Rose said.

"It's not his way," Sarah said.

Anna came out with the baby wrapped in a blanket. "She's had her bath," she said.

"Thank you, hon," Rose said.

"Let's see about dinner," Sarah said.

Emmet stepped off the train in Topeka, the capital city of Kansas. A sprawling town of ten thousand residents, Emmet walked through busy streets, drawing stares along the way. His first stop was the sheriff's office on Front Street.

Sheriff Paul Wilkinson was at his desk when Emmet entered the office.

"I'm U.S. Marshal Emmet Boyd," Emmet said as he set down his satchel.

Wilkinson stood up from his desk. "I know the name," he said and shook hands with Emmet. "What brings you to Topeka?"

"Joe Pike," Emmet said.

"I read in the newspapers you captured him and brought him to California for trial," Wilkinson said.

"Sheriff, I've had a long train ride. Maybe you'll join me for breakfast and I'll tell you why I'm here," Emmet said.

"The Mexican Café across the street serves a mean breakfast," Wilkinson said.

They went across the street to Juan's Café. Breakfast was rice, beans, three fried eggs, toasted bread and strong, Mexican coffee.

"The Wells Fargo Bank made a deal with the prosecutor for the return of the money," Emmet said. "Twenty years at Yuma instead of the noose. Pike told me where the money is hidden."

"He robbed a Wells Fargo bank in Arizona of railroad payroll, that money?" Wilkinson said.

"That money," Emmet said. "Pike claims that he has fifty-four thousand dollars hidden at his sister's place north of Topeka."

"I heard he had brothers, but not a sister," Wilkinson said.

"She's married," Emmet said. "First name

is Elizabeth. Married name is Jordan. Know them?"

"No. How far north?" Wilkinson said.

"He said about twelve miles north of the Kansas River," Emmet said.

"My guess is if they do any business, they do it in Kansas City," Wilkinson said.

"I need to rent a horse and a hotel room," Emmet said.

"You can rent one at the livery and I suggest the Topeka House up the street," Wilkinson said. "Get settled and I'll go with you."

Emmet and Wilkinson crossed the Kansas River on raft pulled by four men. The cost was two dollars a man and horse.

Along the way, they stopped at several farmhouses to ask about Elizabeth Jordan. One family knew them and gave directions.

They arrived at the Jordan farm, one hundred and sixty acres of corn, a house, barn and corral. A shirtless man was out front chopping wood when they dismounted.

He looked at Emmet.

"We don't know where he is," the man said.

"But he was here?" Emmet said.

"Maybe three months back," the man said.

"Are you Jordan?" Emmet said.

"I'm Jordan."

A woman came out of the house and walked down the steps. "I'm Elizabeth, Joe's sister," she said. "My husband told you he isn't here."

"I know he isn't here because I got him locked up in a Sacramento prison," Emmet said.

"Then what you want?" Elizabeth said.

"Your brother made a deal to escape hanging," Emmet said. "In exchange for twenty years he gave me the location of where he hid the money he stole."

"Here?" Elizabeth said. "You think I have his money?"

"According to your brother," Emmet said.

"The lying, murderous son of a bitch hid his money on our farm?" Elizabeth said.

"Where?" Jordan said.

"Before I say anything else, I need you to read this warrant," Emmet said. He produced the warrant and handed it to Elizabeth.

"What's it say?" Jordan said.

"Says they have the right to search the property for the stolen money," Elizabeth said.

"Please don't interfere and allow me to do my job," Emmet said.

Elizabeth nodded and stepped out of the way. Emmet and Wilkinson walked to and entered the barn. Elizabeth followed them.

The barn had six stalls, which were occupied by four horses and two mules. The loft was full of hay. Tools lined the walls. Three covered barrels were centered inside the barn's interior.

"Which barrel has flour?" Emmet said.

"Middle one," Elizabeth said. "He hid the money in the flour?"

"Under it," Emmet said.

Emmet grabbed the flour barrel and rolled it out of the way. "Sheriff, find a shovel," he said.

"Against the wall," Elizabeth said.

Wilkinson grabbed the shovel and gave it to Emmet. Wilkinson and Elizabeth watched as Emmet dug down about three feet and stopped when the shovel struck metal.

Emmet pulled up a burlap sack that was tied closed with twine. He cut open the sack with his field knife and removed a strongbox locked with a padlock. He set the box on top of the flour barrel, removed his Colt and smashed open the lock with the butt, then holstered the Colt.

"That snake, son of a bitch brother of

mine," Elizabeth said.

Emmet opened the box and it was filled with money.

"Mrs. Jordan, we won't bother you anymore," Emmet said.

"Hold it," Jordan said.

Emmet, Wilkinson and Elizabeth turned and Jordan had entered the barn armed with a Winchester rifle.

"That money is on our property," Jordan said. "That money is ourin."

"Don't be a fool, Jordan," Emmet said.

"You leave right now and I won't shoot you," Jordan said.

"Dan, stop it," Elizabeth said. "That money isn't ours and you know it."

"Look at it, Liz," Jordan said. "More money than we could ever earn growing corn in our whole life."

"Jordan, put down that rifle right now," Emmet said. "I've killed too many men in my life to add you to the total."

"Dan, listen to him. Please," Elizabeth said.

"Look at it, Liz," Jordan said. "All that money in our barn and we never even knew it."

"Last warning, Jordan," Emmet said.

"Dan, please," Elizabeth said.

"That money is ours," Jordan said and

cocked the lever of his Winchester.

Emmet drew his Colt, cocked it and shot Jordan in the left shoulder. At the force of the blow, Jordan dropped the Winchester and fell to the ground.

Elizabeth ran to Jordan. "Dan," she said.

"Sheriff, hitch their wagon," Emmet said. "We'll take him to a doctor in Kansas City."

Emmet, Wilkinson and Elizabeth sat in chairs in the doctor's waiting room.

"I appreciate you not killing my husband, Marshal," Elizabeth said. "I know you could have if you wanted. We had a bad year last year and won't break even this year. The sight of all that money made him go a bit crazy."

The doctor entered the waiting room. "Mrs. Jordan, you can see your husband now," he said.

Elizabeth and the doctor left the waiting room.

"We have three hours of daylight left, I suggest we get moving," Emmet said.

"What about Jordan?" Wilkinson said.

"You mean am I charging him?" Emmet said. "No, I'm not."

Sarah, Rose and Anna sat in chairs in the parlor and watched Rose's baby crawl around on the floor.

"I've never seen a baby who wanted to walk as badly as your little girl, Rose," Sarah said.

"That's the Emmet in her," Rose said.

"He walked at eleven months," Sarah said. "Ellis at a year."

"What about me and Emma?" Anna said.

"Somewhere between twelve and thirteen months," Sarah said.

Rip entered the parlor. "Ma, Bettina said to get Rose right away," he said.

They rushed to the kitchen where Bettina was holding her youngest child, John, who was two years old. "He has a fever," Bettina said.

"Since?" Rose said.

"I put him down to take a nap before dinner about an hour ago," Bettina said. "I just went to get him and he's burning up."

"Anna, get my bag," Rose said.

Anna rushed out of the kitchen and returned a few seconds later with Rose's bag. "Let's get him to a bed," Rose said.

Bettina carried John to a bedroom and set him on the bed. Emma and Rip entered the bedroom and Anna said, "Go get Ellis and Pa. Hurry."

Rose used her stethoscope.to listen to John's lungs. "Anna, my thermometer,"

Rose said.

John and Ellis came in as Rose was taking the baby's temperature. "We have to get him to the hospital in Stockton right away," Rose said.

"What's wrong with him?" Ellis said.

"Pneumonia," Rose said.

It was after nine o'clock at night by the time Emmet and Wilkinson returned to Topeka, so Emmet put the strongbox into the hotel safe.

Then they went to the hotel dining room for steaks.

"A very interesting day, Marshal," Wilkinson said.

"And long," Emmet said.

"Mind a question?" Wilkinson said.

"Why did I not arrest Jordan?" Emmet said.

"Yes."

"He lost his head and almost his arm," Emmet said. "He's been punished enough."

The entire family waited in the cramped waiting area at the Stockton hospital. It was a small hospital compared to the one in Sacramento, but it was clean and the medical staff was excellent.

Rose and Anna went into a room with a

doctor and another nurse.

After an hour, Anna came to the waiting area. "It's pneumonia, but the doctor said it was mild and John should recover quickly."

"Oh thank God," Bettina said. "Can I see him?"

"I'll ask the doctor," Anna said and went to check.

"Our daughter has become quite the little nurse," John said.

"What's pneumonia?" Rip said.

"An infection in the lungs," John said.

Anna returned. "Bettina, Ellis, it's okay," she said.

Bettina and Ellis followed Anna to the room where the doctor was checking the baby's fever.

"Rose and Anna will stay the night, so you might as well go home and come back in the morning," the doctor said. "Expect the baby to be with us a week or so."

Bettina looked at Rose.

"Go home and get some rest," Rose said. "We'll be here all night."

Bettina hugged Rose and Anna. "Thank you," she said.

After everybody left, Rose looked at Anna. "Well, let's see about getting some cots in here."

On Monday morning, Emmet stepped off the train in Sacramento and walked straight to the courthouse to see Judge Thomas.

"Fifty-four thousand and six hundred dollars," Emmet said.

"Have any trouble?" Thomas said.

"Just the long train ride," Emmet said.

"Tomorrow we'll do the official sentencing," Thomas said. "I imagine you want to see your wife and baby."

"And I'm going to do exactly that," Emmet said.

He left the judge and walked to the hospital. Rose and Emma weren't there and a doctor said they sent a telegram that they had a family emergency they had to take care of.

Emmet went to the livery where he stabled. "Did he get ridden?" Emmet asked the manager.

"Every day like you asked," the manager said.

"Saddle him for me," Emmet said.

In Stockton, Emmet walked Bull off the platform, mounted the saddle and rode to the farmhouse. The ride took about an hour and when he arrived, John and Sarah were on the front porch.

"This doesn't look like much of a family emergency to me," Emmet said as he dismounted.

Emma and Rip came out to the porch and Emma handed Emmet a cup of coffee. Emmet kissed Sarah on the cheek and took a chair.

"Baby John took down with pneumonia on Saturday," John said. "Rose and Anna have been with him at the hospital since. Bettina and Ellis went there after breakfast."

"Emmet, we made lunch if you're hungry," Emma said.

"After lunch, we're all going to take a ride to the hospital," John said.

Bettina and Ellis were in the waiting room when the family entered.

"How is he?" Sarah said.

"Rose said he's coming along fine," Bettina said.

"Where is Rose?" Emmet said.

"Down the hall, first room," Bettina said.

Emmet went down the hall and entered the room. Anna was reading a book beside the bed where baby John was asleep. Next to the bed, Rose was sleeping in a cot.

Anna stood up, put a finger to her lips

and ushered Emmet to the hall.

"Rose sat up with him all night," Anna said. "She's finally getting some rest."

"But . . ." Emmet said.

"No buts," Anna said. "Rose needs to sleep. In here you're not the Marshal. In here Rose is the boss."

Emmet grinned. "And apparently so are you," he said.

Anna kissed Emmet on the cheek. "Tell everybody to come back later," she said.

As they had done hundreds of times, as brothers growing up, Emmet and Ellis chopped wood on the block behind the house.

"Still know how to swing an ax, huh," Ellis said.

"I can beat you any day," Emmet said.

"We're just about done," Ellis said. "Let's go fishing, just the two of us."

Emmet looked at his brother.

"Come on," Ellis said.

After washing up, Emmet and Ellis walked to the creek at the edge of the property and dug for worms on the banks.

They baited their hooks and cast out their lines.

"This reminds me of . . ." Emmet said.

"Johnson's Creek back in The Big Woods,"

Ellis said.

"When I took Beth back to bury her, the place had changed," Emmet said. "Grown. I'm sure it's even bigger now."

"Emmet, Rose saved my son's life," Ellis said. "If she wasn't here, we might not have gotten him to the hospital in time. I just wanted you to know how grateful I am. To Anna, too. Our little sisters have become quite the women now."

"I noticed," Emmet said.

"Emma's getting married and Anna's almost a nurse," Ellis said. "I remember changing their diapers."

"Rip, come out from behind that tree if you want to fish," Emmet said.

Rip poked his head out. "How did you know I was there?" he said.

"I'm the Marshal," Emmet said. "I know everything."

Holding his fishing pole, Rip walked to Emmet and Ellis. "It's not polite to snoop around and spy on people," Emmet said.

"I wasn't spying, I just wanted to fish," Rip said.

"Well, grab a worm," Emmet said.

"It will be dark in an hour, son, why not stay the night and head out come morning?" John said.

"I need to get back to Sacramento," Emmet said. "I'll stop and see Rose and Anna before taking the late train."

Emmet mounted the saddle and rode away from the house to the road. The ride took about an hour and he reached the hospital a few minutes before dark.

Rose and Anna were in the room with baby John when Emmet walked in. Rose greeted him with a warm hug and kiss.

"Had supper yet?" Emmet said.

"No, we've been . . ." Rose said.

"How about I take my two best ladies for some dinner?" Emmet said.

"I'll get a nurse to sit with John," Rose said.

After getting a nurse from the ward, Emmet took Rose and Anna to the hospital cafeteria.

"So how is he?" Emmet said.

"Fever is gone and his lungs are about eighty percent clear," Rose said. "He'll be home by Friday."

"And when are you two coming home?" Emmet said.

"We should be home Wednesday on the five o'clock train," Rose said.

"I'll be there with the buggy," Emmet said. "So listen, you know I'm not a man of words, but I want to tell you both how

207

proud of you I am."

Rose took Emmet's hands and smiled at him. "The kid here is no slouch with a sick patient," she said.

Emmet looked at Anna. "You've come a long way since I used to change your diapers and powder your little bottom," he said.

"Emmet, please," Rose said as she watched Anna blush.

Emmet stepped off the train at one o'clock in the morning. He retrieved Bull from the boxcar and rode straight home.

Behind the house was a large lean-to Emmet built for times when he needed Bull in the morning. He bedded him down, then entered the house. It was dark and quiet. He struck a match and lit the lantern on the table.

He locked the door, took his satchel with the cashbox in it to the bedroom and fell asleep on top of the covers.

He was in Judge Thomas's chambers at nine the following morning. Thomas, Andrews and the prosecutor counted the money and Thomas issued a receipt to Andrews.

"This closes the case on Joseph Pike," Thomas said.

After Andrews and the prosecutor left

chambers, Thomas said, "Marshal, when was the last time you took a vacation?"

"The next time will be the first," Emmet said.

"Then it's long overdue," Thomas said. "Think about it."

After leaving Thomas, Emmet went to the small café across the street from his office and had breakfast. He picked up a newspaper at the counter and read while he ate.

A man approached Emmet's table. "Excuse me, but aren't you Marshal Emmet Boyd?"

"I am. You are?" Emmet said.

"William Titus. May I sit for a moment?"

Emmet took a sip of his coffee and looked at Titus, who was wearing a suit from back east. "Sit," Emmet said.

Titus took a chair and removed his wallet and produced a business card. "I write for the Beadle and Adams Publishing Company in New York City," he said. "I wrote the expose of Wild Bill Hickock's first ever gunfight in Springfield in sixty-five. It made him famous. I would like to do the same for you, Marshal."

"Do what?" Emmet said.

"Write what they call a dime store novel about your adventures," Titus said.

"From New York City?" Emmet said.

"The people back east eat them up like candy," Titus said. "We sell millions of copies a year and most of the stories are, well, bullshit to be honest. The real thing such as yourself will sell like wildfire."

"And you think people will want to read about me back east? Why?" Emmet said.

"You're the genuine article from all accounts," Titus said. "Fought in the war, helped build the railroad, tamed Cheyenne, appointed by Grant, why you'll be bigger than Hickock even."

"Mr. . . . Titus, is it?" Emmet said. "I'm not in the least bit interested in being bigger than Hickock."

"You could make twenty, maybe even thirty-thousand dollars in royalties," Titus said.

"Still not interested," Emmet said. "Now, if you'll excuse me I have work to do."

Emmet left a dollar and fifty cents on the table and walked out to the street. Titus turned and followed him.

"Marshal, I don't think you understand," Titus said.

"Mr. Titus, is it, I understand perfectly," Emmet said. "And the answer is still no."

With Titus walking with him, Emmet walked to his office, unlocked the door and entered, followed by Titus.

"Mr. Titus, I have a lot of work to do," Emmet said.

"You're a married man, aren't you, Marshal?" Titus said.

"Mr. Titus, walk out or be thrown out," Emmet said.

Titus nodded. "We'll talk again," he said.

After Titus left, Emmet built a fire in the woodstove and put on a pot of coffee. While the coffee boiled, he went to the post office and returned with a stack of mail. The coffee was ready and Emmet filled a cup, sat at his desk and opened the mail.

"So how good are you?" Titus said.

"Good enough," Dick Teasel said.

"Good enough to take Marshal Boyd?" Titus said.

"I think so," Teasel said.

In the Three Aces Saloon, Titus poured another drink for Teasel. "Two hundred and fifty now, the rest when the job is done. But it has to be a fair fight on a main street. Agreed?"

Teasel tossed back his drink and held the glass. Teasel filled it from the bottle. "Agreed," Teasel said.

"Tomorrow. I'll tell you when. Be across the street from the Marshal's office at noon," Titus said.

"You said half in advance," Teasel said.

"So I did," Titus said.

Mr. Olson stood at the corral gate and watched as Josh worked with the bay. He had taught her to prance, trot and bow. Today he was teaching her to ride in circles.

"She's a fine student, Josh," Mr. Olson said. "Any woman would be proud to receive such a wedding gift."

"I hope so," Josh said as he dismounted and walked to the gate.

"Josh, would you like to hear the song I've been practicing for your wedding dance?" Mr. Olson said.

"I'd be pleased," Josh said.

"Come to the porch," Mr. Olson said.

Bettina sat in a chair and held baby John. Ellis stood beside her.

"The doctor is making his rounds," Rose said. "He should be here shortly, but it appears he'll be going home on Friday."

"We don't know how to thank you," Bettina said.

"There is one thing you can do," Rose said. "You can take me and the sidekick to the train. I have a neglected husband waiting at home."

"Be right back," Ellis said to Bettina.

In Sacramento, Rose and Anna stepped off the train and walked to Emmet, who was waiting beside their buggy.

They greeted him with a kiss and a hug.

Emmet helped them into the buggy, which had room for three up front. Before taking the reins, Emmet reached under the seat and produced two perfect roses and gave one to Rose and the other to Anna.

"For my two best girls," Emmet said.

"Well, this will get you a lot of points," Rose said.

As he snapped the reins, Rose and Anna looked at each other and grinned.

The ride home took just ten minutes. While Emmet put his horse in the lean-to, Rose and Anna entered the house.

The house was neat as a pin. The aroma of dinner cooking filled the air.

"What . . . ?" Rose said.

Rose and Anna went to the kitchen where the chef from the café in town was at the oven.

"Mr. Brady, what on earth are you doing?" Rose said.

"The Marshal hired me to prepare a special dinner for you both tonight," Brady said.

"Emmet did that?" Anna said.

"If you care to go to the bathing room

you will find Mrs. Orr from the boarding house waiting with plenty of hot water for baths," Brady said.

"I don't understand," Rose said.

Emmet entered the kitchen.

"Emmet, what is going on here?" Rose said.

"A small thank you for saving my brother's son's life," Emmet said.

From the bathroom, Mrs. Orr said, "Mrs. Boyd, your bath is ready."

Rose took Anna by the arm. "Shall we?" she said.

An hour later, Brady served Cornish hens with roasted potatoes and carrots, greens, fresh bread and left a warm blueberry pie on the counter.

"Goodnight, Marshal, ladies," Brady said and left the kitchen.

"How long is Ma keeping our little Sarah?" Emmet said.

"We'll pick her up on the weekend," Rose said. "Enjoy the two nights of peace and quiet."

Emmet whittled down the stack of mail on his desk as he drank a cup of coffee. Thirty new wanted posters came in the mail, along with several detailed reports on wanted outlaws that may be seeking refuge in

California.

Around noon, he left the office and was crossing the street when Dick Teasel stepped off the wood sidewalk.

"Marshal," Teasel shouted.

Emmet paused and looked at Teasel. "Yes?" Emmet said.

"I'm calling you out, Marshal," Teasel said.

Immediately, people on the street got the hell out of the way.

"Do I know you?" Emmet said.

"Not yet. You will," Teasel said.

"Gunfighting is illegal," Emmet said. "I'm afraid I'm going to have to ask you for your gun."

"Come and get it, Marshal," Teasel said.

"What's your beef with me?" Emmet said.

"I don't like lawmen, especially marshals," Teasel said.

"I'm coming over there and I'm taking your gun," Emmet said.

"No you ain't, Marshal," Teasel said. "Take one step and I draw."

"I'm taking your gun," Emmet said.

Emmet took a step and Teasel reached for his gun. Emmet drew his Colt and shot Teasel in the upper right chest. Teasel dropped his gun as he fell to the street.

Emmet walked to Teasel, who was seriously wounded but alive.

"You're good, Marshal," Teasel said. "Real good."

A crowd had gathered around Emmet. "Some of you men get him in a wagon and get him to the hospital," Emmet said.

As several men lifted Teasel and put him in a wagon, Emmet scanned the buildings and spotted Titus peeking out a second-floor window of the Hotel Sacramento.

The crowd on the street watched as Emmet crossed the street and entered the hotel. A dozen people in the lobby parted as Emmet walked past them to the stairs. He went up to the second floor to the room where he saw Titus at the window.

"Titus, open up," Emmet said. "It's Marshal Boyd."

The door opened and Titus stepped back. "Marshal, I saw that from the window," he said. "He was a gunfighter, wasn't he?"

"You should know," Emmet said.

"What do you . . . I don't understand, Marshal," Titus said.

"Gun fighting is illegal," Emmet said. "And so is hiring a gunfighter. Teasel is alive and if he talks, I'll be back to arrest you," Emmet said.

Emmet walked out of the room and down to the lobby where the town sheriff and two deputies waited.

"Sheriff, keep Titus in room 212 under house arrest until I return," Emmet said.

"How is he?" Emmet said to the doctor tending Teasel.

"He'll pull through as soon as I remove the bullet," the doctor said.

Emmet looked at Teasel, who was on an operating table. "Who hired you?" Emmet said.

"Some book writer from back east named Titus," Teasel said. "Promised me five hundred dollars."

"If you swear to that in court, it will go easier on you," Emmet said.

Teasel nodded. "I'll swear to it," he said.

Emmet left the room and stopped when Rose and Anna ran to him.

"We heard," Rose said. "Are you alright?"

"Fine," Emmet said. "I have to arrest somebody. I'll see you both at home."

Emmet entered the lobby of the hotel where the sheriff and two deputies were monitoring Titus's room.

"Sheriff, go to the street and arrest Mr. Titus," Emmet said. "Charge of hiring a gunfighter to kill me."

"The street?" the sheriff said.

"He'll be right down," Emmet said.

The sheriff and two deputies went outside to the street while Emmet went up to the second floor.

"How are we going to arrest him from here?" a deputy said.

Titus came flying out the window, landed on the hotel awning and rolled off it and fell to the street in front of the sheriff.

"Well," the sheriff said to his deputies. "Pick him up."

Emmet waited by the archway and looked at the seated crowd of forty plus people. The pastor stood behind a podium. To Emmet's left, Josh, in his new suit looked as if he might pass out at any moment.

On the porch, the band plus Mr. Olson got the nod and they started playing the wedding song. Slowly, the bridesmaids, Rose, Bettina and Emma, walked from the side of the house to the podium and stood to the left.

Then, escorted by John, Emma walked from the side of the house to the podium where John released her arm.

In the front row, Sarah started to cry. Ellis and Rip looked at each other and Rip rolled his eyes.

"Who gives the bride away?" the pastor said.

"I do," John said.

"Will the bride and groom face each other, hold hands and repeat after me," the pastor said.

Josh and Emma turned and held hands.

"Who keeps the rings?" the pastor said.

Emmet handed the rings to the pastor.

After the short speech on marriage by the pastor, he handed Josh and Emma the rings and asked them to say their vows. Then they placed the rings on each other's finger and the pastor pronounced them husband and wife.

John turned to the seated crowd. "Everybody to the tables for lunch," he said.

During lunch, the mood was festive as the band played softly in the background. Then Emmet made a short speech and it was time for Josh and Emma's first dance. To Emma's delight, Josh gave a good account of himself.

"We need to change clothes," Josh said.

"Why?" Emma said.

"It's a surprise," Josh said.

"What's going on," Sarah said when she spotted Josh and Emma going into the house.

"A surprise," John said.

"What kind of . . ."

"You'll find out in a few minutes," John said.

When Josh and Emma reappeared, Josh was in cowboy garb and Emma in work pants and shirt.

"What in the world?" Sarah said.

Josh took Emma's hand and led her to the head table. "Wait here with your parents, I'll be right back," Josh said.

He walked quickly to the barn.

Emma looked at Sarah. "Ma?"

"No idea, honey," Sarah said.

A few minutes later, Josh walked the saddled bay from the barn to Emma, a gesture that brought everybody to their feet and loud applause.

Josh placed the reins in Emma's hands. "My wedding present, honey," he said.

Emma hugged Josh and started to cry.

"Well done, Josh," John said.

"Can I ride her?" Emma said.

"That's why she's saddled," Josh said.

Josh helped Emma mount the saddle. "Now don't bust her out until you get a feel for her," Josh said. "She's very fast for a . . ."

Emma yanked the reins and the bay took off running down the road in a cloud of dust.

Ellis turned to Emmet. "Aren't you glad you didn't shoot him now?" Ellis said.

■ ■ ■ ■

"What do you think, Rip? Who's boss of this mob?" Josh said.

Josh, Emma and Rip were studying the mob of horses near the hills of a box canyon. Emma rode her bay that she named Dolly.

"That big stallion there in front," Rip said.

"That's right, he's boss," Josh said. "And he's going to fight."

"Do we get to help Steve?" Rip said.

"Both of you," Josh said. "Just follow what he does and we'll have a corral full of horses by suppertime."

Josh looked up on the hill where Steve waited. "Emma, Rip, get ready," he said.

Josh ran his horse down to the mob, lasso at the ready. He cornered the big stallion and roped him around the neck. The big stallion wasn't pleased. He fought hard for about twenty minutes until he tired and resigned himself to his fate.

"Now big fellow, let's go," Josh said.

Josh led the stallion and Steve, Emma, and Rip herded the mob into a close-knit group and followed the stallion.

"You put in a full day's work, son, eat hearty," Mr. Olson said.

Rip cut into his steak. "Today was fun," he said.

"It was fun," Emma said.

"And just in time," Josh said. "The Army will be here tomorrow."

"That reminds me," Emma said. "The day after that is Christmas Eve. Mr. Olson, you'll be going with us, right."

"Please, grandpa," Rip said.

"I wouldn't miss it," Mr. Olson said.

Anna, Emma, Josh, and Rip decorated the eight-foot-tall tree Ellis had cut down, while Christmas Eve supper was being prepared by Sarah, Rose and Bettina.

John, Ellis, Emmet, and Mr. Olson drank coffee in the parlor and talked of the winter days in the Big Woods.

"Those were good days but I don't miss the freezing cold and the snow," John said.

Rose came into the parlor. "Alright, you men, dinner in fifteen minutes," she said.

Josh came in behind Rose. "Miss Rose, Emma isn't feeling well. Could you take a look?" he said.

Rose followed Josh to Anna's bedroom where Emma was on the bed and Anna was sitting next to her. "Honey?" Rose said.

"I'm alright," Emma said.

"What happened?" Rose said.

"She's feverish and was nauseous," Anna said.

"Josh, would you excuse us please," Rose said.

After Josh left the room, Rose said, "How long have you had these spells?"

"It started about a week ago," Emma said.

Rose looked at Anna. "I'll get your bag," she said.

The entire family waited in the parlor while Rose examined Emma. Finally, Rose walked into the parlor with Anna.

"Josh, Emma is waiting for you," Rose said.

Josh nodded and left the parlor.

"Well, is she sick?" John said.

"Nothing nine months won't cure," Rose said.

Chapter Three:
1876

"I want to go with you," Emma said.

"You heard Rose," Josh said. "No riding after six months."

"But I feel fine," Emma said.

"She explained about all the bouncing on a horse could hurt the baby," Josh said. "Remember?"

"What if I took the wagon?" Emma said.

"Ask Mr. Olson to go with you," Josh said. "I'll hitch the buggy."

After hitching the buggy, Emma and Mr. Olson followed Josh as he rode to the north range to check the herd of cattle.

They needed a tally. Each took a separate count. "I got a hundred and three," Josh said.

"Same," Emma said.

"One hundred and three it is," Mr. Olson said.

"Not counting strays," Josh said.

"When will you drive them to market?"

Mr. Olson said.

"I'll need to hire a few hands," Josh said. "Steve and maybe two more. A week should do."

"Offer them ten dollars a day plus a bonus of ten when the cattle reach the market," Mr. Olson said.

"I'll see the boys tomorrow," Josh said.

"We should get back and see how John and Ellis are doing in the groves," Mr. Olson said.

John, Ellis and Rip walked through the groves and watched as pickers worked filling their sacks with oranges.

"It's going to come in at fifty thousand oranges," John said.

"That should bring twenty-thousand-dollars or more," Ellis said.

"Here comes Mr. Olson with Emma and Josh," John said.

"I expect we're in for lunch," John said.

Mr. Olson had prepared fried chicken and they ate at the backyard patio table.

"Pa, I want to be a cowboy like Josh," Rip said.

"Son, you're off to a good start," John said. "You're fourteen now and in a few years, the place is yours to run."

"Josh, can I have cattle and horses?" Rip said.

"You own the place, Rip," Josh said. "You can have whatever you want."

"That's what I want," Rip said. "Cattle and horses."

"You need to finish school, though," John said. "The business end of it is very complicated and without an education you might not be able to manage things properly."

"I'm afraid he's right, Josh," Mr. Olson said. "The bookwork is quite complicated."

"Josh doesn't do bookwork," Rip said.

"I don't own this place, Rip," Josh said. "If I did, I imagine I'd spend half my time doing bookwork like Mr. Olson does."

"You're a lucky boy, Rip," John said. "You're learning in school and from Josh and from Mr. Olson, so by the time you're eighteen, you'll be totally prepared to take charge."

"I guess so," Rip said. "But I still like working with Josh the best."

"The baby kicked," Emma said as she settled into bed on her back. "I remember Bettina and Rose saying that same thing."

"I wonder if it's a boy or a girl?" Josh said.

"I don't know, but we need to think of names," Emma said.

"That's not all we need to think about," Josh said. "We need a place of our own."

"We don't have nearly enough money yet," Emma said. "For a place of our own."

"I know. The two thousand we have in the bank won't get us much," Josh said. "Not if we're to buy our own land, cattle and horses."

"Josh, we have a lot of family," Emma said.

"No, we're not taking their money," Josh said. "We'll make our own way."

"Oh, the baby is kicking again," Emma said.

"Let me feel," Josh said.

The graduating class of seventy-six was small, with just six doctors and twelve nurses, of which one doctor was Rose and one nurse was Anna.

The entire family was on hand to witness Rose and Anna graduate. Afterward, as the graduation took place on a Friday, the entire family took the train to Stockton for a weekend-long celebration.

In the bedroom they shared for many years, Anna and Emma talked as they had so many times before.

"The baby is due in about a month," Anna said.

"And the way it's kicking, it can't wait to pop out," Emma said.

"It could take a while, you know," Anna said. "I saw some deliveries at the hospital that took twenty-four hours or longer."

Emma rubbed her swollen belly. "Hear that?" she said. "You better make it quick."

On the front porch, John, Ellis, Emmet, Josh and Mr. Olson sat in chairs and drank coffee.

"A proud day," John said. "A doctor and a nurse in the family."

"So what's next, Emmet?" Ellis said. "Are they going to work at the hospital?"

"For now," Emmet said. "Rose has always had the idea that she wants to be where she can make the most difference. Like when she worked in Fort Laramie Hospital."

"She's married with a baby and you're committed to President Grant for another two years," John said.

"I didn't say Rose wasn't a patient woman," Emmet said. "She'll work it out in her mind what she wants to do."

"What about you, Josh?" John said. "You're about to become a father, what are your plans?"

"Me and Emma want to get our own ranch," Josh said. "Raise our own cattle and horses."

"That's a big undertaking, son," John said. "It requires a lot of money to start a ranch. Cattle require a lot of land. You'll need a home, horses and a lot of luck."

"California is not really ranch country," Ellis said. "It's farming country. The land is too valuable for farming for ranches to take a big hold."

"Wyoming is good cattle country," Emmet said. "I saw it firsthand. The valley is full of open ranges and it's better than Montana because of the railroad. In Montana you'd have to drive a herd a thousand miles to get it to the railroad. Wyoming is the place for a young rancher."

"First things first, Josh," John said. "You have a baby on the way."

In the parlor, Sarah, Bettina and Rose sat on the sofa with cups of tea.

"You'll work at the hospital in Sacramento?" Sarah said.

"For now," Rose said.

"You're restless to be a real doctor, aren't you?" Sarah said.

"There are some places in this country where there isn't a doctor for a hundred miles," Rose said.

Sarah and Bettina grinned.

"What?" Rose said.

"I hear a baby crying," Bettina said.

"I best go see," Rose said.

"And I need to check on dinner," Sarah said.

"I feel so big, I think I'm going to explode," Emma said.

Josh was rubbing the lotion Rose gave him on Emma's stomach as they lay in bed.

"Just a few more weeks," Josh said.

"I feel like a big, old hog," Emma said.

"Don't be silly," Josh said.

"Josh, you're still going to want me after, right?"

"What are you talking about?" Josh said.

"Look how fat I am," Emma said. "If I was a man, I wouldn't want me."

"Honey, you're talking nonsense," Josh said.

"My stomach is upset. Can you get me some milk?" Emma said.

"Be right back," Josh said.

He left the bedroom and went down to the kitchen for a glass of cold milk. Mr. Olson was at the table, drinking a cup of coffee and reading a newspaper.

"Emma's tummy is upset?" Mr. Olson said.

"A little."

"When you have some time, I'd like to talk to you for a minute," Mr. Olson said.

"Be right back," Josh said.

He took the milk up to the bedroom and then returned to the kitchen. Mr. Olson filled a cup with coffee for Josh and refilled his own.

"I've been thinking about Wyoming, about what Emmet said," Mr. Olson said.

"Me, too," Josh said.

"I've been doing some figuring based upon what I've learned the past ten years," Mr. Olson said. "At twenty dollars an acre, you'll need twenty thousand dollars to buy a thousand acres of land to get started. And at least five thousand to build a house, corral and barn."

"I've got a little more than two thousand in the bank," Josh said. "Even saving all my wages it would take ten years before I saw that."

"Maybe," Mr. Olson said. "Maybe not."

"Ellis, the elections at the Grange are coming up in a month," John said. "I'll be stepping down and I'm nominating you."

"Aw, Pa, all that paperwork," Ellis said.

"You're thirty-two now, son," John said. "It's time to leave your mark on things. The Grange has grown considerably and needs young, smart men like you to keep it moving."

"We'll talk about it at the meeting," Ellis said.

In the hospital cafeteria, Rose and Anna grabbed some lunch and a table.

"I have the operating room at one-thirty," Rose said. "You'll assist me."

"Rose, does Emmet know you sent a telegram to that hospital in Wyoming?" Anna said.

"Not yet," Rose said.

"It's not like you to hide something from Emmet," Anna said.

"I'm not hiding it, I just don't have a response yet," Rose said.

Anna stared at Rose.

"Alright, I should have told him I sent the telegram," Rose said. "I'll tell him tonight."

"Let's go scrub up," Anna said.

Emmet took a cup of coffee to the front porch to enjoy the cool, night air. October was a much cooler, comfortable month than the summer months where the heat can stifle a man.

The front door opened and Rose, holding a coffee cup, came out and sat beside Emmet.

"Emmet, I have to tell you something,"

Rose said. "And I feel sort of guilty about it."

"You sent a telegram to Fort Laramie Hospital," Emmet said.

Rose, surprise on her face, said, "Yes. How did you know that?"

"I'm the Marshal," Emmet said. "Sooner or later, I know everything."

"That little weasel Charlie at the telegraph office told you," Rose said.

"In passing," Emmet said. "I was picking up my mail and telegrams and Charlie said he didn't get a response yet. I asked him to what and he told me."

"How long have you known?"

"Three days."

"And you let me stew in a pot of guilt all this time?" Rose said.

"I figured you're entitled to privacy like anybody else," Emmet said. "Besides, I've always known how much you want to be a doctor."

Rose set her cup on the porch floor and stood and then sat on Emmet's lap. "If you weren't already my husband, I'd marry you," she said.

A few minutes later, Emma came out to the porch to find Emmet and Rose kissing. "Oh brother," she said.

■ ■ ■ ■

After church on Sunday, the family gathered in the dining room for the customary early supper. Drinking a glass of milk, Emma put the glass down and looked across the table at Rose.

Rose stood up. "Josh, get Emma to her bedroom right now," she said.

"What is . . . ?" Josh said.

"Now, Josh," Rose said. "Anna, get my bag. Sarah, you and Bettina boil water. A lot of water. And we need a lot of clean linen."

"What's happening?" Josh said.

"Her water broke, Josh," Rose said.

"What water? What are you talking about?" Josh said.

"She's going to have a baby, Josh," Anna said.

"But . . ." Josh said.

"Get her up to the room," Rose said.

"Come on, Ellis, we best get some extra wood," Emmet said.

Several hours later, Sarah and Bettina did needlepoint in the parlor. Emmet and Ellis chopped wood on the side of the house. Mr. Olson taught Rip how to play chess in the kitchen. Josh wore out the rugs between rooms as he nervously paced the floors. John tinkered in the barn.

In the parlor, Sarah said, "Josh, come in here, please."

Josh entered the parlor. "No sense pacing like a nervous cat," Sarah said. "These things take time. Go find something to do."

"Yes ma'am," Josh said.

Josh went to the kitchen and looked at the chess board. "What's this?" Josh said.

"It's a game called chess," Mr. Olson said. "I was hoping to teach you one day."

"It's been four hours," Josh said and walked out to the porch and around to the side of the house where Emmet and Ellis were chopping wood.

"Hi, Josh," Ellis said.

"Grab an ax," Emmet said. "Work off some steam."

"It's been four hours," Josh said.

"Josh, come over here," John said from the barn.

Josh turned and walked to the barn.

"Yes sir?" Josh said.

"Could you give me a hand with something?" John said.

Josh followed John into the barn. "I'm repairing this old dresser and need some help," John said. "Maybe you could give me a hand."

In the parlor, Anna walked in and said, "I'm going to make some coffee for Rose and me."

"How's it going up there?" Sarah said.

"Emma's starting to push, but it will be a while," Anna said.

"I'll make the coffee and bring it up to you," Sarah said.

"Okay, Ma," Emma said.

"Maybe we should heat up the food?" Bettina said. "Nobody ate much."

"Good idea," Sarah said. "I'll round up the men."

Thirty minutes later, everybody sat at the table to eat. From the bedroom upstairs, Emma started to scream.

"They're killing her," Josh said.

Sarah and Bettina grinned at Josh. "No, Josh, she's giving birth," Sarah said.

"Ellis, could you pass the rolls?" John said.

"Josh, if you ever come near me again, I'll kill you, so help me God," Emma screamed from the bedroom.

"That's nothing, Josh," Ellis said. "Bettina called me a son of a . . ."

"Ellis, not at the table," Sarah said.

By nine o'clock, Sarah and John were dozing on the sofa. Emmet and Rip were playing checkers in the kitchen. Ellis and Bettina and their two children, plus Rose and

Emmet's daughter were sleeping in John and Sarah's large bed. Mr. Olson was on the front porch with Josh and Mr. Olson was teaching Josh the game of chess by lantern light.

Everything stopped, everybody woke up when they heard a loud slap and a baby cry. The entire family gathered in the living room.

Anna came down the steps to the living room.

"Josh, come meet your son," Anna said.

Emmet sat at his desk and opened the mail. Besides the usual, there was a telegram from Sheriff Jack Clark in the small, ocean town of Santa Barbara. Clark was holding a wanted criminal named Jake Benchman on charges of robbery and murder.

Emmet went to see Judge Thomas.

"Go get him, bring him before me," Thomas said.

"Okay, Judge," Emmet said.

At the dinner table, Emmet said, "I have to go to Santa Barbara to pick up a prisoner in the morning. I'll be gone overnight."

"No longer than that," Rose said. "I want to check on Emma and the baby."

"I'll be back in plenty of time," Emmet said.

Anna looked at Rose and nodded.

Rose said, "Emmet, I received a response from Fort Laramie Hospital. They have no openings at this time."

"There are other places, honey," Emmet said. "Send out telegrams everywhere. There's a lot of wilderness where doctors and nurses are needed."

Rose stood up and then sat on Emmet's lap and kissed him.

"Here we go," Anna said.

In the morning, Emmet and his deputy Max Cody took the train to Santa Barbara. If there were no delays, the ride would take seven hours.

Around one in the afternoon, Emmet and Cody ate lunch in the dining car.

"I read the report on this Benchman," Cody said. "Murder, bank robbery, horse theft, cattle rustling. Thomas will give him life if not the noose."

"Most likely the noose," Emmet said. "He shot three people in the bank in Nevada before killing several members of a posse."

"The report doesn't say how he wound up in Santa Barbara," Cody said.

"No it doesn't," Emmet said. "But we'll

get all the facts from Sheriff Clark when we get there."

"That's not what I'm thinking about," Cody said.

"You're wondering how one man could rob a bank, steal cattle and horses and escape a posse," Emmet said.

"He's got friends, Emmet," Cody said.

"And you're wondering if those friends will show up and try to break him loose," Emmet said.

"Aren't you?"

"Of course," Emmet said.

"What are we going to do about it?" Cody said.

"Nothing," Emmet said.

"Nothing ain't a strategy, Emmet," Cody said.

"Let's try the apple pie for dessert," Emmet said.

Emmet and Cody stepped off the train in Santa Barbara at five in the afternoon and walked the streets to the sheriff's office.

A coastal town of three thousand residents, mountains loomed in the background, the ocean at its front door.

They reached the sheriff's office and entered. Sheriff Clark was behind his desk and stood up. "Marshal Boyd," he said.

"And Deputy Cody," Emmet said.

"Everything is arranged," Clark said.

"Good," Emmet said. "Did you get us a room at the hotel?"

"Second floor with a view of the street," Clark said.

"Bring him over around nine o'clock," Emmet said.

"It beats the hell out of me how you can sit in that bathtub as if you don't have a care in the world," Cody said. "Benchman's gang could be in a saloon, plotting his escape this very minute."

"Clark has six deputies on the streets," Emmet said. "He'll let us know. We haven't eaten since one, let's get a steak in the hotel restaurant."

"Jesus Christ, Emmet, if you don't beat all," Cody said.

At nine o'clock, Sheriff Clark and two deputies brought Benchman to Emmet and Cody's hotel room.

Benchman was shackled around the wrists and angles.

"He's all yours, Marshal," Clark said.

"Keep watching the streets," Emmet said. "Let me know if you see any sign of them."

After Clark and his deputies left, Bench-

240

man flopped onto a bed and grinned. "You may get me on that train, but you ain't getting me off," he said.

"Got your men camped outside of town just waiting to hold up the train, don't you?" Emmet said.

"Now Marshal, I ain't a man to kiss and tell," Benchman said. "I'm gonna take a nap. Wake me when it's time to leave."

At eleven-thirty, Emmet shook Benchman awake. "Time to go," Emmet said.

Emmet and Cody led Benchman down the rear staircase to the back alleyway of the hotel where a wagon and horse waited.

"Benchman, get in the back," Emmet said. "Cody, keep him quiet."

"What is this?" Benchman said.

"Cody, gag him," Emmet said.

After Cody and Benchman were prone in back of the wagon, Emmet drove it to the freight lines at the railroad depot where a two-car train awaited.

"Let's go," Emmet said.

"What is this?" Benchmark said.

"This," Emmet said. "This is a private prisoner car reserved for Federal Marshals, of which I am one of, and by the time your buddies try to stop the train north to Sacramento, they'll find themselves surrounded by thirty sharpshooters from the Army. Cody, get him on the train."

The prisoner train went northwest to Bakersfield and then turned north to Sacramento. The long car was divided into two rooms, one side for the prisoner and one side for passengers.

Besides the engineer, a conductor was on board, and he fixed a pot of coffee and hot roast beef sandwiches for the trip.

"This is brilliant, Emmet," Cody said. "Why didn't you tell me your plan?"

"I didn't get confirmation from the railroad the prisoner train was available until eight o'clock tonight," Emmet said. "Otherwise we'd have to use plan b."

"What was plan b?" Cody said.

"Rent horses and ride to Bakersfield and take a regular train," Emmet said.

"I like plan A better," Cody said.

At nine o'clock the following morning, Emmet and two sheriff's deputies escorted Benchmark before Judge Thomas.

"Your arraignment will be tomorrow morning at ten," Thomas said. "Deputies, please take him to the city jail."

After the deputies took Benchmark out of Thomas's chambers, Thomas said, "Emmet, go home and get some sleep. I want to see you at five this afternoon."

"Alright, Judge," Emmet said.

He went straight home where Rose and Anna were having breakfast in the kitchen. He kissed Rose on the lips and Anna on the cheek, then filled a cup with coffee and sat beside Rose.

"You look tired, honey," Rose said.

"Long trip," Emmet said.

"Want some breakfast?" Anna said.

"I just want to grab some sleep," Emmet said. "I need to see Judge Thomas at five o'clock."

"Okay then, we need to get to work," Rose said.

"I'll stop by the hospital after I see the Judge," Emmet said.

"You're looking some better, Emmet," Thomas said.

"A little sleep helps," Emmet said.

"I didn't go into this earlier because I was still in communication with Carson City," Thomas said.

"Nevada?" Emmet said.

"They want Benchmark," Thomas said. "He killed three people in the bank and they're entitled to him."

"Want me to deliver him?" Emmet said.

"I hate to ask," Thomas said.

"It's my job," Emmet said. "That prisoner train is still in the yard. I'll make arrangements for day after tomorrow."

"Thanks, Emmet," Thomas said.

After leaving Thomas, Emmet stopped by the railroad depot and made arrangements for the trip to Carson City, then walked over to the hospital.

Rose and Anna were just finishing up their shift.

"Mind if I take my two best girls to dinner?" Emmet said.

"Better not let Ma hear you say that," Anna said.

"I know my husband, Anna," Rose said. "He has a guilty conscience. Let him feed us and clear his chest."

Rose and Anna each took an arm and Emmet took them to the restaurant at the Sacramento Hotel.

"Don't let him off without dessert," Rose said.

After they were seated, Emmet said, "Thursday, I have to take a prisoner to Carson City, but I'll be taking a private train and will be back in time for dinner."

"Well that isn't much," Anna said.

"I didn't say it was," Emmet said.

"Do we still get dessert?" Anna said.

■ ■ ■ ■

John called the two hundred members of The Grange to order. "The first order of business is to nominate my replacement as Chairman of the Grange of California," he said. "And I can think of no one better suited than my son Ellis."

The nomination was unanimous.

Seated next to Ellis, Bettina said, "Better brush up on your bookwork."

"Ellis, come up here and accept," John said.

Ellis stood and went up to the podium.

As they gave the baby a bath, Josh said, "At least he doesn't look like a grape left in the sun too long anymore."

"Josh, our son is beautiful," Emma said. "He has your hair."

"When can you ride again?" Josh said. "We haven't ridden together in so long the bay won't know you anymore."

"Don't be silly," Emma said. "I'll ask Rose when she comes to see us this weekend."

"Maybe we can . . . ?" Josh said.

"Not until she checks me," Emma said.

"I swear, I'm about to bust."

"You busting is how we got him," Emma

said and picked up the baby.

"They'll hang me in Carson City," Benchmark said.

Emmet placed Benchmark in the iron cell in the prisoner car and locked it. "Hanging is no less than you deserve," Emmet said.

"How about some coffee?" Benchmark said.

"I'll have my deputy bring you a cup," Emmet said and closed the door that connected the cell to the riding car.

The conductor was at the woodstove, boiling a pot of coffee. "Got some fresh biscuits to go with the coffee," the conductor said.

"Cody, bring him some coffee and a few biscuits," Emmet said.

Cody filled a cup with coffee, grabbed a few biscuits and opened the door to the cell. "Brought you some coffee and biscuits," Cody said.

"Thank you kindly, Deputy," Benchmark said.

Cody passed the coffee and biscuits through the bars.

"Stay a minute, Deputy," Benchmark said as he bit into a biscuit. "Good biscuit."

"What do you want?" Cody said.

"Talk," Benchmark said. "This is a really good biscuit for sure."

"Enjoy," Cody said.

"Now hold on, Deputy. Just hold on," Benchmark said. "I admit dumb luck got me caught and your Marshal there out-smarted my boys, but — and this is a big but, you never recovered the twenty-seven thousand dollars I stole from the bank."

Cody stared at Benchmark.

"That's right, boy. Twenty-seven thousand dollars," Benchmark said. "And only I know where it's hid."

"Tell it to the judge," Cody said.

"Oh no, boy, I want to tell it to you," Benchmark said. "You see, I'll split it with you right down the middle. All you got to do is get me out of here."

"I get you out and I get half?" Cody said.

"Right down the middle," Benchmark said. "More money than you could earn wearing that badge the next ten years."

"And all I got to do is let you escape?"

"That's it, just let me escape."

"How?"

"Hit the Marshal over the head, open the door and let me out," Benchmark said.

"No horses, no food, no water, then what?" Cody said.

"You say I jumped you, made you open the door," Benchmark said. "With the Marshal dead, who is to say otherwise.

Think of all that money in your hands, boy."

"You want me to kill the Marshal?" Cody said.

"You let me out, give me a gun and I'll do it," Benchmark said.

"Okay," Cody said.

Benchmark grinned. "Open the door, boy," he said.

"You hear that, Emmet?" Cody said.

Emmet walked up behind Cody. "I heard," Emmet said.

"You son of a bitch, you," Benchmark said. "You knew the Marshal was there all along."

"Open the door, Deputy," Emmet said. "Give him your gun."

"Oh, Marshal, you do like to stir the pot," Benchmark said.

"We'll be in Carson City in thirty minutes," Emmet said. "Now is the only chance you're going to get. Cody, open the door."

Benchmark stepped back and placed his back against the wall.

"Looks like he isn't having any, Deputy Cody," Emmet said.

Carson City, Nevada was a boom town and the capital of Nevada. After the train arrived at ten-thirty, Emmet and Cody delivered Benchmark to Sheriff Don Blocker.

Blocker locked Benchmark up in his jail, then said, "Marshal, how about a cup of coffee before you leave."

"We missed breakfast," Emmet said. "Just a few biscuits on the train."

They went across the street to Rosie's Restaurant and ordered breakfast. "First time in Carson City for me, Sheriff," Emmet said. "It's a right prosperous town."

"Cattle is a prosperous business, Marshal," Blocker said. "Oh, people came to Nevada fifteen years ago for the silver mines, but they stayed for the cattle country in the Valley, especially along the Carson River."

"What are you building at the end of the street?" Emmet said.

"A hospital," Blocker said. "Or was. Funds ran short and our only doctor died last winter."

"Sorry to hear that," Emmet said.

"We're trying to raise money now," Blocker said. "Last year we spent a goodly sum building a school. We'll get there."

"Let's take a walk around before we leave," Emmet said.

Emmet and Cody shook hands with Blocker before boarding the private train.

"The Army in California is holding three

of the seven members of Benchmark's gang," Emmet said. "They killed four. I'll bring you the three as soon as we pick them up."

"Thanks, Marshal," Blocker said.

"See you soon," Emmet said.

"Okay, Emma, you can get dressed now," Rose said.

"Am I alright?" Emma said.

"You're fine. Perfectly healthy," Rose said. "Now let me take a look at the little one."

Emma opened the bedroom door. "Anna, you can bring him in now."

Anna carried the baby into the room and set him on the bed. Rose examined him carefully, then said, "He's in very good condition. Where is Josh?"

"On the porch with the men," Anna said.

"Could you tell him I'd like to see him for a moment," Rose said. "Alone."

"Is something wrong?" Emma said.

"No, dear, everything is fine," Rose said.

Emma took the baby and then she and Anna left the bedroom. A few minutes later, John knocked on the door.

Rose opened the door and Josh entered.

"Emma said you wanted to see me?" Josh said.

"I just wanted to tell you that Emma and

the baby are doing just fine," Rose said. "As her doctor, I can tell you she is fit for her regular activities."

"That's great to hear," Josh said. "Thank you."

"And as her doctor, let me caution you on one thing," Rose said. "By regular activities, that includes sex. Emma is a little bit of a girl and if you rush in like you're breaking a Mustang, well, you could do some damage. Understand?"

"Yes. No, not really," Josh said.

"How sore would your nose be if you pushed an apple through one nostril?" Rose said.

Josh looked at Rose. "Oh," he said. "Oh."

"Exactly," Rose said. "So be gentle. She'll thank you for it."

"I will. Thank you," Josh said and left the room.

Rose sat on the bed. "Oy," she said aloud.

"I don't understand why Anna and I are going with you to deliver prisoners to Carson City," Rose said.

The conductor brought a tray with a pot of coffee and cups to the table where Rose, Anna, Emmet and Cody sat. "Would anyone care for biscuits?" the conductor said.

"Bring us a plate, thank you," Emmet said.

The conductor brought a plate of biscuits.

"So, Marshal Boyd, why are Anna and I on this trip?" Rose said.

"This biscuit is really good," Anna said.

"I know, right," Cody said.

"Emmet?" Rose said.

"Mr. Conductor, do you have a recipe for these biscuits?" Anna said.

"I'll write it down for you, miss," the conductor said.

"Emmet?" Rose said.

"Have a biscuit, hon," Emmet said. "They're really good."

"They really are," Anna said.

Rose picked up a biscuit and took a bite. "Mmm," she said.

"See," Anna said.

"See that place called Rosie's across the street there? Wait for me there," Emmet said. "Alright you three. Move."

Emmet shoved the three prisoners.

Rose and Anna went to Rosie's and ordered coffee. They watched through the window as Emmet and Cody brought the three prisoners to the sheriff's office.

"I don't understand this, do you?" Anna said.

"I don't understand half what that man does," Rose said. "Come to think of it, I don't understand the other half much either."

"He's a mystery, my brother," Anna said. "Tough as nails with outlaws and such and like a kitten with you and even me."

"He loves us," Rose said. "Me as his wife and you as his baby sister. There is no mystery to it."

"Here he comes," Anna said.

Emmet entered Rosie's and sat opposite Anna and next to Rose. He waved the waitress over and asked for coffee. She smiled and said, "Right away, Marshal."

"Emmet, why are we here?" Rose said.

The waitress returned, set a cup in front of Emmet, leaned over and smiled. "If you want anything else, just ask," she said, turned and walked away.

"Wow," Anna said. "She's pretty bold."

"Why that little . . ." Rose said.

"You want to be a real doctor and make a difference," Emmet said. He looked at Anna. "And you want to be a real nurse and make a difference. That's why you're here."

"Somewhere in that brain of yours that makes sense to you," Rose said. "But not to us."

Emmet left a dollar on the table and stood

up. "Come on," he said.

On the way out, the waitress said, "Come again, Marshal. Anytime."

"Why that little . . ." Rose said.

"Let's go," Emmet said.

"Where?" Rose said.

Emmet linked arms with Rose and Anna and walked two blocks and stopped in front of a partially constructed, two-story building.

"Carson City, the capital of Nevada doesn't have a doctor at the present time," Emmet said. "This was to be a hospital, but they ran out of funds. For twenty thousand, we can build a hospital for you and Anna."

"What?" Rose said.

"Here comes the mayor right on time," Emmet said.

"Marshal Boyd, Mayor Glenn Cosby," Cosby said.

"My wife, Doctor Rose Boyd and her nurse Anna Boyd," Emmet said. "We'd like to see the building."

"Right this way, Doctor," Cosby said.

On the return trip to Sacramento, Rose, Anna and Emmet sat at the table, drank coffee and munched on biscuits. Cody sat in a seat beside the window and read a newspaper.

"It can be a beautiful medical facility, but twenty thousand dollars, Emmet," Rose said.

"We have thirty-five thousand in the bank," Emmet said. "We can use that to secure a loan, or just pay for it outright."

"And you?" Rose said. "You still owe Grant two years."

Emmet removed a folded telegram from his pocket and handed it to Rose. "Grant approved my relocation to Carson City as the Marshal recently retired," he said.

Rose read the telegram. "Anna?" she said.

"Rose, let's do it," Anna said.

"But your parents," Rose said.

"The ride from Carson City is just fifteen minutes longer," Emmet said.

"Rose?" Anna said.

Rose picked up a biscuit and took a bite. "Boy these are good," she said.

"That's damn fine news, Emmet," John said. "Ellis and I are fair carpenters, maybe we can help."

"In that case, Bettina and I can help, too," Sarah said.'

"When can we see the place?" John said.

"We're going on Tuesday to see the mayor about a deposit," Emmet said. "We'll meet you at the station in Sacramento for the ten-

255

fifteen train."

"Now that we settled that, let's eat," John said.

At the dinner table, Emmet said, "Josh, Emma, maybe you'd like to go to Carson City with us. Nevada is fine cattle country."

Josh looked at Emma. "Want to take a ride, hon?" he said.

Emmet, Rose, Anna and the baby waited on the platform for the ten-fifteen train to arrive. It arrived a few minutes early.

The entire family took the ten-thirty train to Carson City, which arrived at noon.

The first stop was to the hospital. They inspected the interior. John and Ellis made pages of notes on carpentry and what rooms would be best suited for what. Then, while Rose, Emmet and Anna went to meet Mayor Cosby at the bank, the rest of the family toured Carson City. They agreed to meet back at the hospital building in one hour.

In the bank, Mayor Cosby said, "The town holds the note on the building. It's valued at ten thousand, but as we need a hospital and a doctor, we'd be willing to let it go for eight,"

Emmet looked at Rose and she nodded.

"Mr. Cosby, I can give you a deposit right now of one thousand dollars and return in two days with the remaining seven," Emmet said.

Cosby looked at the bank president. "Draw up the papers," he said.

As they walked to the hospital building, Rose said, "Emmet, we're using our own money?"

"No mortgage to hold," Emmet said. "Let's figure out what it will take to turn it into a real hospital."

They met the family at the hospital building and John and Ellis made notes and drafted prints on what materials were needed. Rose and Anna toured the rooms, deciding what room would be what and then they made lists of the necessary medical equipment.

Mayor Cosby stopped by and Emmet pulled him aside. "Where did the previous Marshal live?" Emmet said.

"Oh, a fine house off Front Street," Cosby said.

"And his office?" Emmet said.

"Across the street from the Town hall," Cosby said.

Emmet showed the telegram from President Grant to Cosby. "Well, welcome to Carson City, Marshal. Would you like to see your house and office?"

"Let me grab my wife and sister," Emmet said.

Cosby led Emmet, Rose and Anna to the house on Front Street, just six blocks from the hospital building. It was a two-story home, with four bedrooms, a kitchen with a pump, parlor, den and living room and an attic and garden in the backyard.

"What do you think, girls, can we live here?" Emmet said.

On the train ride home, John, Ellis and Rose went over design plans, while Sarah and Bettina discussed decorating. Emmet and Anna and Rip were content to sit back and watch.

Emma and Josh looked out a window at the Nevada scenery.

"Your brother was right, hon," Josh said. "Nevada is some of the best looking cattle country I've ever seen."

With the baby asleep over her shoulder, Emma said, "What are you thinking, Josh?"

"I'm thinking we could really build a life there," Josh said.

"What's the matter, Josh?" Mr. Olson said. "You haven't had an appetite in days."

"We saw some of the best cattle country I've ever seen in Nevada and there is nothing I can do about it," Josh said. "It would take ten times what we got in the bank to get started."

"I'm seventy-two years old," Mr. Olson said. "After my wife died, I felt old and useless and ready to die. Today I feel like I want to live forever and it's because of you two."

"Us?" Emma said.

"Your youth and vitality have revitalized me and made me want to continue," Mr. Olson said. "With that thought in mind, I would like to suggest a fifty-fifty partnership between you two and myself."

"A partnership?" Josh said.

"For the past fourteen years or so, all I have done is save and invest my money, although I don't know why," Mr. Olson said. "My wife and daughter are gone and my grandson doesn't need me, not really. And now I see why I saved and invested all those years. In my twilight, I would like the three of us to go to Nevada and build a ranch of our own."

"Wait. What?" Josh said. "Mr. Olson, it takes a lot of money to . . ."

"Money I have, time I do not," Mr. Olson said. "I would like to see this done before my time on this earth expires."

"You said an equal partnership," Josh said.

"I supply the money and you supply the

labor," Mr. Olson said.

"But what about this place and Rip?" Emma said.

"Details we will work out this weekend when we go to dinner," Mr. Olson said.

Emma looked at Josh. "Josh?"

"Mr. Olson, you got yourself partners," Josh said.

After a week of construction, the building was beginning to resemble a real hospital. A dozen rooms with beds, two examination rooms, a room for emergencies, two operating rooms, a check-in room and two offices.

Carson City buzzed with excitement at having its own hospital and, although women doctors were scarce, the general population didn't seem to mind as the nearest hospital was an hour-long train ride into California.

John and Ellis put their carpentry skills to use and assisted the local carpenters Rose hired. Sarah and Bettina sewed drapes and curtains for all the windows.

Emmet acclimated himself to his new state and met the twelve deputies assigned to Nevada by holding a meeting at the town hall. As they came from across Nevada, the meeting took place on Friday afternoon.

Lewis R. Bradly, Governor of Nevada attended the meeting and introduced Emmet to his deputies. "Men, I have just returned from a governor's meeting in Washington and spoke to President Grant and if his recommendation means anything, we have the finest Marshal in the country," Lewis said when he introduced Emmet.

Emmet took the podium, thanked the governor, then said, "There are more than one hundred outstanding warrants on my desk. Murderers, cattle thieves, claim jumpers and more. Starting today, we are going to bring these outlaws to trial and make Nevada a safe place for families to raise their children."

On Saturday morning, Emmet, Rose and Anna took the train to Stockton where Ellis waited with a buggy.

The family ate a light, early lunch together as dinner would be a heavy meal.

"I've contacted the medical journals for a second doctor and nurse," Rose said. "And we hired a receptionist for the lobby."

"When do you think you might open?" John said.

"If all our equipment is delivered on time, two weeks," Rose said.

"We need balloons," Rip said. "Like at the state fair."

Everybody looked at Rip.

"Now here's a boy who can think," John said.

"Did anybody notice I got a haircut?" Emmet said.

Everybody looked at Emmet.

"Now that you mention it," Rose said.

"Looks very nice, son," Sarah said.

"The reason I brought it up is because the barber, without any training at all, acts as the town dentist," Emmet said.

"Oh for God's sake," Rose said. "Anna, we can bring in a dentist."

"We can reconfigure one of the rooms for a dentist office," John said. "Ellis, where are those plans?"

After looking at the plans and deciding on a dentist office, Mr. Olson said, "Everybody, Josh, Emma, and myself have a little announcement of our own."

"Well, don't keep it to yourself," John said.

"Josh, Emma, and myself are going to partner up on building our own ranch in Nevada," Mr. Olson said.

"It takes a great deal of money to start a ranch," John said.

"That's where the partnership comes in," Mr. Olson said. "I supply the necessary money and Josh supplies the labor. We're going to the land office in Carson City on

Monday to search for land in what they call the Valley."

"You'll need a house, barn and corral just for basics," John said.

"I'm handy with a hammer," Josh said.

"We'll be through with the hospital in a week, Pa," Ellis said.

"Josh, Emma, if you'd allow us to help, we'd be happy to," John said.

"Pa, no need to ask," Emma said.

"Mr. Olson, why not come with us Sunday night?" Emmet said. "We have plenty of room and you can get to the land office early on Monday."

"I need to consult with my partners," Mr. Olson said.

"You heard my brother, they have plenty of room," Emma said.

Emmet walked Rose and Emma to the hospital, then turned and went to his office. Sheriff Blocker was waiting for him on the wood sidewalk.

"Morning, Sheriff," Emmet said.

"Marshal," Blocker said.

Emmet opened the office door and stepped inside, followed by Blocker. Emmet filled a coffee pot with water and coffee and placed it on the woodstove, then made a fire.

"The sheriff in Virginia City sent me this," Blocker said and handed Emmet a telegram. "He doesn't know we got us a new Marshal."

"He's holding a man for bank robbery," Emmet said. "He'll need to be tried here in Carson City as bank robbery is a federal offense."

"The railroad go to Virginia City?" Emmet said.

"Not yet," Blocker said. "The Overland does."

"How long a ride?"

"Four hours each way."

"Send the sheriff a telegram," Emmet said. "Tell him I'll be there tomorrow."

"That coffee smells pretty good," Blocker said.

Emmet filled two cups and he and Blocker went outside and sat in chairs in front of the office. "Who presides on federal cases at the courthouse?" Emmet said.

"Judge Bear Briscoe," Blocker said.

"Bear?"

"It's a name they hung on him one year when he went hunting and tagged himself a bear," Blocker said.

"I'll go see him and get a warrant to bring him in," Emmet said.

"You make good coffee, Marshal," Blocker said.

Mr. Olson, Josh and Emma entered the land office that was located in City Hall at nine o'clock sharp.

The city clerk showed them maps of available land for sale in the plush valley south of Carson City.

"Right here," the city clerk said and traced a plot of land with his finger. "Is one thousand acres of prime cattle country. Excellent grazing land with several natural streams running throughout the land."

"Asking price?" Mr. Olson said.

"Fifteen thousand dollars," the city clerk said. said.

"When can we see this land?" Mr. Olson said.

"I have appointments the rest of today," the city clerk said. "How about ten o'clock tomorrow morning?"

"We'll meet you here at ten tomorrow," Mr. Olson said.

Judge Roy 'Bear' Briscoe stood five-feet-two-inches tall and was sixty years old. His grey hair was to his shoulders and he wore a long, greying moustache.

"So you're the new Marshal I've heard so

much about," Briscoe said.

"How are you, Judge?" Emmet said.

"Overworked and underpaid, same as you," Briscoe said.

"I need a warrant for this man," Emmet said and showed the telegram from Virginia City to Briscoe.

Briscoe wrote out a warrant and handed it to Emmet. "I have about a hundred more for you when you get back," he said.

"I'll see you sometime late tomorrow afternoon," Emmet said.

Teamsters were unloading medical equipment and supplies when Emmet arrived at the hospital. John, Ellis and six carpenters were hammering away as Rose and Anna directed where equipment and supplies were to be designated.

"One more week and we'll be ready to open," Rose said.

"Can I take you ladies to lunch?" Emmet said.

"Little Miss Waitress?" Rose said.

Anna grinned.

"Who?" Emmet said.

"John, Ellis, come to lunch," Rose said.

On the way to Rosie's, they met up with Mr. Olson, Josh and Emma. The restaurant didn't have a table for eight but pushed two tables together against a wall.

Once everybody was seated, the waitress came to the table. "Hello, Marshal," she said.

Rose looked at the waitress.

"Can we get some menus?" Emmet said.

"You can have whatever you like, Marshal," the waitress said.

Anna and Emma looked at the waitress.

"Be right back," the waitress said and winked.

"Wow," Emma said.

"I know, right," Anna said.

"What?" John said.

"I thought she was going to drool over Emmet," Emma said.

"I thought she was nice," Josh said.

"Oh you did, did you?" Emma said.

"What?" Josh said.

"I'll give you what," Emma said.

"How did you make out at the land office?" Emmet said.

"Fifteen thousand for one thousand acres," Mr. Olson said. "If we may impose on you for another night, we will see the land tomorrow morning."

"Of course," Rose said.

The waitress returned with menus. She looked at Emmet. "If you want something special, just ask," she said and walked away.

"That's enough," Anna said and stood up only to be promptly yanked down by Rose.

"So, what's good here?" John said.

Rip watched Sarah and Bettina feed Emma's baby and Rose's baby, while Bettina's three-year-old and six-year-old played on the floor.

"What happens to me if they move to Nevada?" Rip said.

"Nothing, honey," Sarah said. "You stay with us until you're eighteen and old enough to take over your mother's business."

"But who will take care of things until then?" Rip said.

"Josh's friend Steve will handle the ranch and we hired a very capable gardener to oversee the groves," Sarah said. "And several times a week you and John and Ellis will go over and see how things are progressing. In the meantime, can you fetch us some wood so we can start dinner?"

"I'm going to punch that waitress right in the eye," Anna said.

"That table goes against the wall," Rose said to two men carrying an examination table. "And you'll do no such thing, Anna."

"She's trying to steal Emmet away from you," Anna said.

"She's looking for bigger tips," Rose said.

"No, she's not, Rose," Anna said. "She's looking for a husband. Your husband."

"Okay, fellows, that's it for today," Rose said. "See you all in the morning."

Anna stormed outside and stood in front of the hospital. She spotted Emmet walking to the hospital and waited for him to arrive.

"Hey, little sis . . ." Emmet said and Anna punched him in the left arm. "Ow. What was that . . . ?"

"You stay away from that waitress," Anna said.

"Anna, that's enough," Rose said as she came up behind her.

"You pack a pretty good punch for such a tiny thing," Emmet said.

"Keep that in mind," Anna said.

After dinner, Emmet, Josh, Mr. Olson and Emma took coffee in the parlor. Mr. Olson had a copy of the 1876 edition of the *Farmer's Almanac*.

"Average temperatures in December and January are fifty degrees in the daytime," Mr. Olson said. "And it rarely snows. That means we can work through the winter on building a house."

"Where would we live?" Emma said.

"Have you ever seen an Army officer's

tent?" Emmet said. "Some of them have three rooms and a wood floor and a potbelly stove for heat. I knew Grant to live in his for an entire winter."

"Where can we get some of these tents?" Josh said.

"I'll get them," Emmet said. "I could have them in a week."

"We're grateful to you, Marshal," Josh said.

"After you get the land, you need blueprints for the house," Emmet said. "A barn is a barn, a corral is a corral, but the house needs to be perfect. You decide what you want and we'll get an architect to draw up the prints. Pa and Ellis, plus local help will put it together in no time."

"Sound good, Josh?" Mr. Olson said. "Emma?"

"It sounds like a dream come true," Josh said.

Anna entered the parlor. "Rose said to come get some apple pie," she said.

Everybody stood and left the parlor except Emmet because Anna blocked his way.

"You stay out of that little coffee shop," Anna said.

"Oh for God's sake, Anna," Emmet said.

"That waitress is looking to give you more than a slice of pie, Emmet," Anna said.

270

"Now promise me."

"Alright and don't worry," Emmet said.

Sound asleep, Emmet woke up when Rose sighed and tossed in bed.

"What?" Emmet said.

"I'm thinking," Rose said.

"At this hour?" Emmet said. "What about?"

"Little Miss Waitress," Rose said.

"Not you too?" Emmet said.

"I think Anna may be right," Rose said.

"Has everybody in this house gone crazy?" Emmet said.

"She's younger than me," Rose said. "And quite pretty."

"I'm going back to sleep," Emmet said. "I have to catch the stage at eight o'clock in the morning."

"I don't want to sleep," Rose said.

"No?"

"I have a better idea," Rose said.

Emmet stepped off the stagecoach in Virginia City, along with seven other passengers. The driver had promised them they would arrive on time and he got them there ten minutes early.

As he walked to the sheriff's office, Emmet was surprised at how large a town Virginia

City was compared to Carson City. A silver strike fifteen years earlier created the boom town that grew overnight to seven thousand residents.

The sheriff's office was a one-story, red brick building with three modern jail cells. Only one cell was occupied when Emmet entered and introduced himself to Sheriff Brooker.

Brooker read the warrant from Judge Briscoe and said, "The return stage is in one hour, want to get some coffee."

Emmet and Brooker went to a café across the street for coffee.

"So what's the details of the robbery?" Emmet said.

"This damn fool walks into the bank at high noon and demands at gunpoint the amount of two hundred dollars," Brooker said.

"Two hundred dollars? That's it," Emmet said.

"That's all he wanted," Brooker said.

"How was he captured?" Emmet said.

"One of my deputies entering the bank drew down on him," Brooker said. "Turns out he was packing an 1860 Navy Colt, cap and ball that wasn't even loaded."

"Is there something wrong with this man?" Emmet said.

"Nothing that seven years at hard labor won't fix," Brooker said.

"Did he make a statement, say anything?" Emmet said.

"He said just one thing," Brooker said. "He said he failed his wife."

"Failed his wife?"

"That's what he said," Brooker said.

"Let's get him ready to transport," Emmet said.

Henry Howe was twenty-nine years old, a farmer from southern Oregon. He was a stout man and could use a shave and a bath and a change of clothes.

"Sheriff, this is how you prepare a man to go before a federal judge?" Emmet said.

"He robbed our bank," Brooker said. "What do you want me to do, give him flowers and a box of chocolate?"

"Mr. Howe, come with me," Emmet said.

Emmet took Howe across the street to a barber shop. The stunned barber looked at Emmet as he said, "A shave and a haircut for this man."

"But he robbed our bank," the barber said.

Emmet glared at the barber.

"In the chair," the barber said.

Howe took the chair and the barber went

to work. Emmet stood out front and Brooker joined him.

"What do you think you're doing?" Brooker said.

"Getting my prisoner presentable to stand before a federal judge," Emmet said.

"This is not how we do things here," Brooker said. "He robbed our bank and . . ."

"Does he have a horse?" Emmet said.

"At the livery."

"Get his saddlebags," Emmet said.

"What?"

"Sheriff Brooker, I don't care how you do things, I'm a U.S. Marshal and I will shut this entire town down. Now go get his damn saddlebags."

The barber was finishing with Howe when Brooker returned with the saddle bags.

"Mr. Howe, do you have a clean shirt and pants in your bags?" Emmet said.

"Yes," Howe said.

"Go in the back room and change," Emmet said. He looked at the barber. "Give him some body powder."

"Who is paying for this?" the barber said.

Emmet gave the barber two dollars.

After Howe changed, Emmet said, "Mr. Howe, when did you eat last?"

"Yesterday morning."

"Grab your saddle bags and come with

me," Emmet said.

Howe followed Emmet to the street where Brooker waited. "Sheriff, tell the stage driver that the U.S. Marshal is taking charge of the stage. He is not to release it until I get there."

Brooker looked at Emmet.

"Do it or I'll take your badge," Emmet said. "Howe, come on."

Emmet led Howe to the café he visited earlier with Brooker. "Order whatever you like," Emmet said.

"I have no money," Howe said.

"If the sheriff was doing his job, you would have had a full breakfast," Emmet said.

Howe ordered eggs with bacon and potatoes and coffee. Emmet asked for a coffee and a slice of pie.

"You're no bank robber, Howe," Emmet said. "Why don't you tell me what this is all about."

"In my saddlebags you'll find a letter," Howe said.

Emmet fished out the letter. If was from a hospital in Bend, Oregon. His eight-year-old daughter would go blind if she didn't have an operation. The procedure cost two hundred dollars.

"That's why you only wanted two hundred

from the bank?" Emmet said.

"My wife and me got a small farm just across the border," Howe said. "It don't amount to much. We had a bad year. I know it was stupid. Hell, that Navy Colt belonged to my father from the war. I don't even have powder or bullets. I guess I lost my head."

Emmet replaced the letter into Howe's saddlebags.

"As soon as you're ready," Emmet said.

Judge Briscoe read the letter and then looked at Emmet. "Send a telegram to this hospital and wait for a reply," he said. "Then bring it to me immediately."

Emmet left Briscoe's chambers and walked to the telegraph office and sent the telegram, requesting an immediate reply. Ten minutes later, the reply came. On the way to the courthouse, Emmet stopped by the hospital.

Rose and Anna were setting up equipment.

"I'm afraid we'll be a while," Rose said.

"Me too," Emmet said.

"Mr. Olson is making dinner," Rose said.

"I'll see you at home," Emmet said.

Emmet returned to Briscoe's chambers and handed him the reply. "Have Howe brought to my courtroom," he said.

Fifteen minutes later, Howe stood before Briscoe's bench. Emmet was the only other person in the courtroom.

"Mr. Howe, I've given the circumstances of your case a lot of thought," Briscoe said. "I'm foregoing a trial and getting straight to sentencing."

"Yes sir," Howe said.

"I sentence you to one year in prison, minus eleven months," Briscoe said. "You will serve the remaining thirty days performing labor for the town of Carson City. For your labor, a sum of two hundred dollars will be wired to your wife. Case dismissed."

Howe burst into tears. "Judge, I don't . . ." he said.

"Case dismissed, Mr. Howe," Briscoe said. "Marshal, you know what to do."

"It's beautiful land, Emmet," Emma said. "Wait until you see it."

"It's a lot like California, only the grass is richer and better suited for cattle," Josh said.

"When can we see it?" Emmet said.

"We'll be back in two days to pay off the balance," Mr. Olson said. "It's only an hour's ride southeast of here."

Rose and Anna entered the dining room with the turkey Mr. Olson cooked and set it on the table.

"Emmet, would you do the honors?" Rose said.

After dinner, Emmet, Mr. Olson, Josh and Emma took coffee in the parlor.

"The architect who designed the hospital is right here in Carson City," Emmet said. "I stopped off to see him and he's done a lot of fine homes in the area."

"Josh, Emma, let's see him tomorrow before we take the train home," Mr. Olson said.

"Ma must be going crazy with all those babies to take care of," Emma said.

"It won't take long," Mr. Olson said. "We'll catch the noon train."

Anna entered the parlor. "If you want a slice of the pumpkin pie Mr. Olson baked, come and get it," she said.

Before turning in, Anna and Emma sat in chairs on the front porch and talked the way they had all their lives.

"Are you happy?" Anna said.

"Of course," Emma said. "I have a wonderful husband and a beautiful baby and we're building our own ranch. What about you?"

"I love what I'm doing," Anna said.

"But what about a husband?" Emma said.

"Any man I marry would have to be the equal of Emmet," Anna said.

"That is not going to happen," Emma said. "We both know that."

"I know," Anna said.

"You don't want to wind up an old maid, do you?" Emma said.

"I'd rather that than marry a man I don't love," Anna said.

"We're not even twenty," Emma said. "There is somebody out there for you. Just wait and see."

Emmet walked with Howe to the town square. Howe pushed a maintenance cart. The park in the Town Square was a quarter acre, with several benches and a statue.

"After you rake the leaves and pick up trash, come find me," Emmet said.

"I will," Howe said. "Marshal, I need to thank you for what you've done for me and my family."

"You want to thank me, don't rob banks," Emmet said.

"Yes sir," Howe said.

Mr. Olson, Josh and Emma met with the architect, Mitchel Curry, in his office on Main Street. Curry, from Boston, moved west twenty years earlier to design bridges for the Army and developed a reputation for home design.

"What design did you have in mind?" Curry said.

"A ranch house with the porch facing the sun," Mr. Olson said. "Four bedrooms, a den, parlor, dining room and kitchen with pantry and a front and back deck for the sunrise and sunset."

"Rustic or modern?" Curry said.

"Rustic," Emma said. She looked at Josh and he nodded.

"Square footage in mind?" Curry said.

"I don't . . . what does that mean?" Josh said.

"How much room do you want?" Curry said.

"Two thousand square feet," Mr. Olson said.

"Pump in the kitchen?" Curry said.

"Essential," Mr. Olson said.

"Ice box in the kitchen?" Curry said.

"Also essential," Mr. Olson said.

"I'll draw up several variations for you to choose from or mix and match," Curry said. "I'll have them ready in a week."

"Do you need a deposit?" Mr. Olson said.

Emmet saw Mr. Olson, Josh, and Emma to

the train station.

"We'll be back in two days," Mr. Olson said.

"Don't forget my daughter," Emmet said.

After the train left, Emmet went to the park where Howe was loading his cart with trash.

"Mr. Howe," Emmet said. "As the court must provide you with lunch, let's go get some."

About to suggest Rosie's, Emmet remembered Emma's warning and took Howe to a small restaurant near the courthouse.

The special of the day was beef stew with bread and Emmet ordered two bowls.

"Where do you need me after lunch?" Howe said.

"The park near the railroad station," Emmet said. "Until five o'clock."

"Marshal, can you check on my horse?" Howe said.

"I can," Emmet said. "And I'll check on your wife and daughter, too."

"I'm obliged to you, Marshal," Howe said.

"What's the name of that hospital your wife took your daughter to?" Emmet said.

"Sounds like a fine plan," John said. "When do you figure to break ground on the house?"

"They have mild winters, so right after the new year," Mr. Olson said. "If we decide on the blueprints."

"Me and Ellis will be able to help with construction," John said. "Now that we're done with the hospital."

"Mr. Boyd, you've done so much already," Josh said.

"Josh, family helps family," John said. "Never forget that."

Holding her son, Emma entered the parlor. "Pa, Ma wants you in the kitchen," she said.

"Best go see," John said.

Emma took John's chair. "Josh, we best name our son or he'll be the only kid in school without a name," she said.

"I have an idea, but I'll tell you about it later," Josh said.

Emmet was at his desk, writing a report on his deputies' activities for the previous month. Eleven wanted outlaws had been apprehended and brought to trial in various courts throughout the state.

He crossed off each apprehended outlaw in a logbook and wrote trial status pending next to the name.

As he was getting a cup of coffee from the woodstove, a telegram clerk entered the office. "Got two replies for you, Marshal," he said.

Emmet took the coffee to his desk and read the telegrams. The first one was from Howe's wife. The surgery went well and the doctors gave her daughter a very good chance at keeping her eyesight, although she would probably require eyeglasses. She was grateful for the kindness showed to her family and hoped her husband was behaving himself.

The second telegram was from Sheriff Brooker. Anticipating Howe wouldn't need his horse for seven years, the horse was sold at auction.

It was close to five o'clock and Emmet walked over to the park by the railroad and escorted Howe back to the courthouse jail.

"Got something for you to read," Emmet said and handed Howe the telegram from his wife. Howe read it, teared up and said, "Thank God."

"Let's get you back in time for supper," Emmet said.

After dropping Howe off at the courthouse holding jail, Emmet went to see Judge Briscoe, who was in his chambers.

"Judge, have a look at this," Emmet said and handed Briscoe the telegram from Brooker.

Biscoe read it, then looked at Emmet. "What do you plan to do about this?" he said.

"Take the stage to Virginia City in the morning," Emmet said.

Emmet stopped by the hospital where Rose and Anna were talking to a small group of people in the lobby.

"Emmet, come in," Rose said. "Everybody, this is my husband, the U.S. Marshal for Nevada."

Three of the women were fulltime nurses. One woman was an admitting nurse. Two men were janitors. One woman was a dentist assistant.

Lacking was a second doctor and a dentist.

"I'm afraid we'll be late," Rose said.

"If you're not home by six-thirty, I'll come looking for you," Emmet said.

On the way home, Emmet stopped by the general store and butcher and had a pot of beef stew with potatoes and carrots with fresh bread cooking by the time Rose and Anna arrived home.

"The tub is full of hot water, you got thirty minutes before supper is ready," Emmet said.

"Food and a hot bath is the way to a woman's heart," Rose said.

■ ■ ■ ■

Emmet caught the eight o'clock stage to Virginia City that arrived at ten minutes before noon. He rode with seven other passengers and spent most of the trip reading a novel by Jules Vern titled *Michael Strogoff*.

The stagecoach docked in front of the Hotel Virginia City, four blocks from Brooker's office. As he walked the four blocks, people on the streets sensed something was brewing and followed Emmet from a safe distance.

Brooker was at his desk with his feet up, drinking coffee and smoking a rolled cigarette. A deputy was with him, sitting on the edge of the desk and cleaning a rifle. The deputy stood when Emmet entered the office.

Brooker swung his feet off the desk. "Marshal, what are you doing here?" he said.

"Relieving you," Emmet said.

"What? Are you crazy?" Brooker said.

"Stand up when I'm talking to you," Emmet said.

Brooker got to his feet.

"You're a disgrace as a lawman, Brooker," Emmet said.

"Now see here, Marshal," Brooker said.

"I'll have your badge," Emmet said. "You're done as sheriff in Virginia City. Deputy, who is senior deputy?"

"Charlie Stroud," the deputy said.

"Go get him," Emmet said.

The deputy rushed out to the street.

"I'll have your badge," Emmet said.

Brooker glared at Emmet. "Because I sold his horse?"

"Because you're too damn stupid or lazy or both to occupy that desk and wear that badge," Emmet said. "Now give it to me or I take it."

Brooker removed his badge and set it on the desk.

"What did you do with the money you got for selling his horse?" Emmet said.

Brooker stared at Emmet but didn't answer.

"Now get out," Emmet said.

Brooker left the office.

Emmet grabbed a cup from the table beside the woodstove and filled it with coffee. He was sipping when the deputy returned with Charlie Stroud.

"You're the senior deputy?" Emmet said.

"Yes sir," Stroud said.

"You're acting sheriff until an election can be organized," Emmet said.

The door opened and the mayor of Virginia City rushed in. "What in blazes is going on here?" he said. "There's a crowd outside like a carnival is in town."

"I relieved your sheriff and appointed Stroud here as acting sheriff until you can hold an election," Emmet said.

"Can you do that?" the mayor said.

Emmet looked at the mayor.

"I guess you can," the mayor said.

"You have thirty days to hold an election," Emmet said. "If you fail to elect a new sheriff within thirty days, I will return with six deputy marshals and I will put your town under federal authority. Any questions?"

The mayor shook his head. "No," he said.

"Let me know when the election is," Emmet said. "I'll come back and verify the results. In the meantime, Deputy Stroud, do your best to be the sheriff Virginia City deserves."

When Emmet entered his house, he was greeted by Rose, Anna, Emma, Josh and Mr. Olson. "Where are the babies?" he said.

"The rest of the family will be here tomorrow," Rose said.

"Is it somebody's birthday?" Emmet said.

"Uh oh," Anna said.

Rose glared at Emmet.

"Our anniversary?" Emmet said.

"Oops," Emma said.

Rose's mouth formed a hard, thin line as her eyes formed slits.

"Oh, wait," Emmet said. "I think I know this."

Emmet left the living room.

"That man is going to give me an ulcer," Rose said.

"What's an ulcer?" Josh said.

Emmet returned with two small, gift-wrapped boxes. "One for you," he said and handed a box to Rose. "And one for you," he said and gave the second box to Anna.

"What is it?" Anna said.

"I guess you'll just have to open them to find out," Emmet said.

Rose and Anna ripped off the wrap and opened the boxes. Each box contained a silver chain with a small medallion with the image of Saint Raphael the Archangel.

"It's beautiful, Emmet," Anna said. "Who is it?"

"Saint Raphael, the Patron Saint of doctors and nurses," Rose said.

"Allow me," Emmet said.

Emmet placed one chain around Rose's neck and the other around Anna's.

Emma looked at Josh, who was wiping his

right eye. "Oh, brother," she said.

"Dinner is ready," Mr. Olson said.

At the dinner table, Mr. Olson, Josh and Emma talked about buying the land at the land office. "Tomorrow we will see Mr. Curry after the opening ceremony at the hospital," Mr. Olson said.

"With some luck, we'll start building right after Christmas," Josh said.

After dinner, Emmet took coffee on the porch with Josh. "I need to ask a favor," Emmet said.

"Of me?" Josh said, surprised.

"I need a horse," Emmet said. "A good one, ready to ride. Sturdy. Can you get one for me?"

"Is something wrong with your horse Bull?" Josh said.

"No. It's a gift for a friend," Emmet said.

"I can have him in a week," Josh said.

"Thank you," Emmet said.

Mayor Cosby, Governor Bradley, Rose, and Anna stood at the red ribbon that was stretched across the main doors to the hospital and smiled for the reporter from the *Nevada Appeal Newspaper* as he took their photograph.

The mayor made a short speech, followed by a short speech by the governor, then

Cosby, Bradley, Rose, and Anna cut the ribbon.

Then it was time to get to work. A line of about a hundred entered the hospital the moment the doors were opened.

Mr. Olson, Josh and Emma went to see Mr. Curry.

Emmet took John, Sarah, Bettina, Ellis, Rip and the children to Rosie's while they waited for Mr. Olson, Josh and Emma.

"Hello, Marshal, where you been hiding?" the waitress said as she came to the table.

"I've been busy," Emmet said.

"No need to hide from me, Marshal," the waitress said.

"We'll all have coffee and pie," Emmet said.

"Coming right up, sweetie," the waitress said.

After the waitress left, Sarah said, "Honestly, Emmet."

"Son, I'd steer clear of this place if I was you," John said.

The waitress returned with a large tray full of pie and coffee and milk for Rip. "Anything else you want, Marshal, just ask," she said, winked and walked away.

"I'm going to give that woman a piece of my mind," Sarah said.

John put his hand on Sarah's arm. "Eat

your pie," he said.

After renting three buggies, everybody except Emmet took a ride to see the land purchased by Mr. Olson for the ranch.

Southeast of Carson City, the thousand acres were rich, grazing land with three streams running through the property.

"Here," Mr. Olson said after they parked the buggies close to a stream. "What do you think?"

Josh and Emma walked to the stream. "What do you think, hon?" Josh said.

"I think it's perfect," Emma said.

John, Ellis and Mr. Olson spread out the blueprints on the ground. "Emma, Josh," John said.

Emma and Josh walked to John.

"Front porch facing east, corral out front, barn to the west," John said. "What do you think?"

"I think we need to get started," Josh said.

"The blueprints call for forty by twenty-five," John said. "Ellis, get the stakes and measuring tape."

Ellis and John measured out forty feet and Ellis hammered a stake into the ground with a wood mallet. Once all the stakes were in the ground, John tied twine from stake to stake, creating an outline of the house.

"Josh, Emma, let's go to the lumber yard," Mr. Olson said.

After a week of being open, the hospital settled into a regular routine. Office hours were between ten AM to six PM. If any patients needed a hospital bed, one nurse stayed overnight. If there was an emergency during the night the nurse couldn't handle, she would send for Rose and Anna.

Business hours would be extended once a second doctor came on board.

During the second week, a dentist from Chicago was hired to work at the hospital during regular business hours. His name was Homer Whitlow and he was thirty-seven and had never been west of Illinois until arriving in Carson City.

Rose and Anna put in ten-hour days during the week and four hours every Saturday. Many of their patients came from as far away as thirty miles. Their days were full and satisfying, but they would welcome a second doctor to lighten the load.

A young doctor from Kansas City wrote that he was interested in the position and would arrive right after Christmas.

Rose decided that keeping the books of expenditures and income was too much work in addition to her duties as a doctor and she hired an accountant from town. He did a weekly count and deposit at the bank and the hospital was in the black by a large amount.

Rose and Anna decided that because of the surplus they could afford to do charity work for those who couldn't afford to pay.

A week before Christmas, Virginia City held an election to elect a new sheriff to a four-year term.

Emmet made the trip to Virginia City to oversee the election results. Deputy Stroud was elected the new sheriff by a wide margin.

For the first time in a decade, Christmas wasn't celebrated at the family farm and was instead celebrated in Carson City.

The house had four bedrooms, enough for Ellis and Bettina and their two children and John and Sarah. Rip slept on the large sofa. Emma and Josh and Mr. Olson got rooms at the Hotel Carson City.

After church, the women prepared Christmas dinner while the men took advantage of the fifty-degree day by taking coffee on the porch.

"Supplies will be delivered before the new year," Mr. Olson said. "If the weather stays mild, we could be living in our new home by early spring."

"I have the tents and cots at the livery in storage," Emmet said.

"Ellis and I will give you three days a week to go with the crew you hired," John said.

"At my age, such an adventure," Mr. Olson said.

On December 30th, Emmet and Judge Briscoe met Howe at the release gate of the courthouse jail.

Howe was wearing clean pants and shirt, was freshly shaved and had a haircut.

"What do I do now, catch the stage to Virginia City to get my horse?" Howe said.

"No, Mr. Howe," Emmet said. "Do you see that young stallion tied to the post over there?"

Howe looked at the stallion. He was young and strong and had a fine saddle on him. Attached to the saddle was a good Winchester rifle in a saddle sleeve.

Emmet, Briscoe, and Howe walked to the stallion.

"You'll find a hundred dollars in your wallet in the saddlebags. Have a safe trip home, Mr. Howe," Emmet said.

Howe looked at Emmet and Briscoe. "But . . . I don't . . ."

"Court's adjourned, Mr. Howe," Briscoe said. "Have a safe trip home."

With tears in his eyes, Howe mounted the saddle.

"And Mr. Howe," Emmet said. "Don't rob any more banks."

Howe grinned. "Yes sir," he said.

CHAPTER FOUR:
1877

Doctor James Glass walked into the hospital, carrying a briefcase, and stopped at the desk where one of the nurses sat.

Glass was young, with dark hair and eyes and chiseled features and a warm smile.

"Hello," he said to the nurse. "I'm here to see Doctor Boyd."

"Do you have an appointment?" the nurse said.

"In a way," Glass said. "I'm Doctor James Glass and I wrote to Doctor Boyd about a position that was advertised in the medical journals."

The nurse stood up. "Wait here," she said.

She went down a hallway to Rose's office and knocked on the door. "Doctor?" she said.

"I'm with a patient," Rose said. "I'll be a few minutes."

"Where is Miss Anna?" the nurse said.

"Making rounds," Rose said.

The nurse found Anna in room 7, where she was changing a bandage. "Anna, there's a Doctor Glass waiting out front."

"I'm done here," Anna said. "I'll have Rose stop in and see you," she said to the man in bed.

"Thank you, nurse," the man said.

Anna and the nurse walked back to the reception desk where Glass waited.

"I'm Anna Boyd," Anna said.

"I was expecting you to be a bit older," Glass said.

"Why?" Anna said.

"It takes years to become a doctor," Glass said. "You would have had to start college at the age of twelve."

"I'm not a doctor, I'm a nurse," Anna said. "And you look about twelve yourself."

"I'm twenty-seven, twenty-eight in March," Glass said. "And if you're not the doctor, who is?"

"Rose Boyd is the doctor," Anna said.

"Your sister?"

"She is married to my brother Emmet, who is the U.S. Marshal for Nevada," Anna said.

"I see," Glass said. "How did you and Rose come to work together at this hospital?"

"We built it," Anna said. "From the

297

ground up."

"Well, Doctor Glass, it's nice to meet you," Rose said as she entered the reception area.

"Rose, Rip looks older than he does," Anna said. "Nobody is going to take him seriously."

"Anna, don't be rude," Rose said.

"I'm not," Anna said. "I'm just being honest."

"Miss Boyd, I graduated first in my class at Boston medical school and interned two years in Kansas City. My youthful appearance aside, I consider myself an excellent doctor and I have the references to back that up."

"I don't even think you shave yet," Anna said.

Rose looked at Anna. "I thought you were making rounds," she said. "Doctor Glass, let's go to my office."

Anna and the admitting nurse watched them walk down the hall to Rose's office.

"He's a handsome lad, isn't he?" the nurse said.

"If you like twelve-year-old boys," Anna said and walked away.

Emma came out of the two-room Army tent and stirred the large pot of stew that was hanging over a fire. John and Ellis, Josh and the hired crew from town were framing the house. The floors were complete and at the rate they were working, the house would be finished by March.

She checked the large pot where a dozen biscuits were baking and then set it aside. She picked up the bell and rang it several times.

"Lunch," Emma said.

The six-man crew, John, Ellis, and Josh came to the long table where bowls were already in place. Emma brought the hot biscuits to the table, put the gallon coffee pot next to it and then filled each bowl with stew.

"Excellent biscuits, hon," John said.

"Pa, Mr. Olson is coming with Mr. Curry," Emma said.

"Set them up a bowl," John said.

Mr. Olson stopped his buggy near the table and he and Curry walked to the table.

"Hello, everyone," Curry said.

"Mr. Curry, take a chair and join us for lunch," John said. "My daughter is an excellent cook."

"Don't mind if I do," Curry said.

As they ate, Curry said, "I make it a policy to check the work as it progresses to ensure quality control and make adjustments if needed."

"I think you'll be pleased at the progress we've made, Mr. Curry," John said. "I expect they'll be moving in come March if the weather holds."

"Have a biscuit, Mr. Curry," Emma said.

Anna watched as Rose walked Glass to the front door where she shook his hand. After Glass walked out, Anna said, "Don't tell me you hired that kid."

"Anna, that kid is an excellent doctor and surgeon and we need him if we're to ever get any sleep around here," Rose said. "And he's very nice if you give him a chance."

"When does he start?" Anna said.

"Tomorrow at four o'clock," Rose said. "Maybe we can get home in time to cook dinner for Emmet."

"I think he enjoys cooking for us," Anna said.

"Maybe, but he still has the entire state of Nevada to worry about," Rose said. "And he can't do that washing dishes and changing diapers."

"I forget that sometimes," Anna said.

"Alright, we have patients to see," Rose said.

Curry inspected the work and compared

the framing to his blueprints.

"Excellent work," Curry said. "My compliments to you and the crew."

"When will you have the plans ready for the barn?" John said.

"Next week, I'll bring them out," Curry said.

"Mr. Curry, I'll take you back to town now," Mr. Olson said.

"I'll see you all next week," Curry said.

"Alright everybody, let's get back to work," John said.

Emma washed the dirty dishes by dipping them into a pot of boiling water and rinsing them in a pot of cool water. Once that was done, she tended to her son. He was eleven months old now and refused to stay where she put him. He would grab onto anything and fight his way to his tiny feet and try to walk.

After feeding him, Emma wrapped him in a warm blanket and walked to the house and watched for a while. Josh, Ellis and John were framing the roof. The rest of the crew were putting up walls inside.

Emma took her son's tiny arm and pointed it at Josh. "That's your daddy up there," she said.

Emmet left his office and was walking to

the courthouse to see Judge Briscoe about signing a warrant. I was a nice day for February, with the temperature around fifty degrees and lots of sunshine. He wore a vest and didn't bother with a jacket.

"Well hello, Marshal," the waitress from Rosie's said as she came up behind him.

"Hello," Emmet said.

"Mind if I walk with you a bit?" the waitress said.

"Look, Miss . . . ?" Emmet said.

"Julie."

"Look, Julie, I'm married," Emmet said.

"I know," Julie said. "To the doctor. I don't care. I want you anyway."

"Look, Julie, I'm afraid I'm going to have to ask you to leave me alone," Emmet said.

"Afraid, Marshal?" Julie said. "Of me? Or yourself?"

"I love my wife," Emmet said. "And that's the end of it."

Emmet crossed the street and walked toward the courthouse.

Julie watched him go. "It's not the end of it, Marshal. You'll see," she said.

Emma, Josh and Mr. Olson ate dinner at the table facing the sunset.

"It's going to be a beautiful ranch," Mr. Olson said. "I wish my wife could be here to see it with me."

Inside the tent, the baby started to cry and Emma went inside to tend to him.

"Josh, you really need to name him," Mr. Olson said.

"We tried every name we can think of, but nothing sticks," Josh said.

"It will come to you," Mr. Olson said.

"Well, I best bed down the horses," Josh said.

Josh walked to the field where the bay, his horse and Mr. Olson's horse were feeding on grass and he took the reins of his horse and walked him to the large tent set up where they sleep. The other two horses followed.

After bedding down the horses, Josh closed the tent flap and looked at the last bit of sun as it touched the horizon. The grass glowed orange. He looked back at the tent where Emma sat at the table with Mr. Olson and they were laughing about something.

"Yeah, it's going to be a beautiful ranch," Josh said.

"Anna, I have to remove an appendix," Glass said. "Would you assist me?"

"Somebody has to make sure you don't screw it up," Anna said.

They went to the scrub-up room to wash, then put on gowns and went to the operating room where the patient, a man of about thirty was already out on a table.

"Keep him under while I begin," Glass said.

"Try not to kill him," Anna said.

"I've done thirty of these types of procedures alone," Glass said.

"How many survived?" Anna said.

"Are you ready, nurse?" Glass said.

"If you are," Anna said. "Doctor."

In another room, Rose and a nurse named Gail were setting an eleven-year-old boy's broken left leg. The boy's mother watched as Rose and Gail set the leg and applied a plaster cast.

"Will it be alright?" the boy's mother said.

"Right as rain in six weeks," Rose said. "I'll keep him overnight and you can get him in the morning." Rose looked at the boy. "And no more trying to do tricks on a horse for at least five more years," she said.

Rose and Gail went to the wash-up room and passed the operating room where Glass and Anna were performing surgery. They paused to listen at the door.

"Well at least you didn't butcher him," Anna said.

"You know perfectly well the operation

was successful," Glass said.

"I guess we'll see when he wakes up," Anna said. "If he wakes up."

Rose and Gail went to the wash-up room to scrub plaster off their hands.

"Do you think those two know they're in love?" Gail said.

Rose reached for a bar of soap. "Not yet," she said.

At the dinner table, Rose said, "I think we should have Doctor Glass over for dinner sometime. What do you think, Anna?"

"Why?" Anna said.

Emmet looked at Rose and then at Anna.

"Just to be nice," Rose said.

"To that . . . that . . . boy," Anna said.

Emmet looked at Rose.

"Anna, you've been working with him now for two weeks," Rose said. "Isn't it time you were a bit nice to him?"

"Him?" Anna said. "When is he going to be nice?"

"I'm inviting him to dinner," Rose said.

"Fine. I'll eat out that night," Anna said.

After dinner, Emmet and Rose took coffee on the porch.

"Do they know they're in love?" Emmet said.

"Not yet," Rose said.

■ ■ ■ ■

Emma held the baby as she and Mr. Olson watched John, Ellis, Josh and the crew install the windows.

"It really looks like a home now, doesn't it?" Emma said.

"A fine one," Mr. Olson said. "A home to be proud of. Of course the real work will come later raising cattle."

"How long before we move in do you think?" Emma said.

"After the windows, they'll do the doors and build the porch," Mr. Olson said. "In the meantime, we need to order furniture and things for the kitchen and bedding. I'd say the second week of March should do."

"It will be nice to sleep in a real bed again, won't it?" Emma said.

"It sure will," Mr. Olson said. "On Saturday. I'll take a ride to town for supplies as we're running low."

"Josh and I will go," Emma said. "You deserve a rest for once."

"I shall take you up on that provided you pick up a nice bottle of wine for supper," Mr. Olson said.

"Anything you want," Emma said. "Here hold him, I'm going to help put in windows."

Emma handed Mr. Olson her son and ran to Josh.

John, Ellis, and Rip inspected the orange groves at the Olson farm. Five hundred trees were starting to bud with the promise of seventy-five thousand oranges to come.

"By the time this grove is in full bloom, you'll be fifteen, Rip," John said.

"Can I get a cowboy hat like Josh and Steve?" Rip said. "A real one."

"I think that can be arranged," John said.

"We need to check the books, Rip," John said.

"Can I wait with Steve at the corral?" Rip said.

"Sure," John said.

Rip left the groves and walked to the corral where Steve and two other cowboys were breaking in a large bay for the Army.

"Hi, Steve," Rip said.

"Hey, Rip," Steve said. He and the two cowboys were sitting on the fence, watching the large bay.

"She's beautiful," Rip said.

"And a handful," Steve said.

"Steve, with Josh gone, will you be staying here when I turn eighteen?" Rip said.

"This is the best job I ever had," Steve said. "I'll stay as long as you want me to."

"Good, because I need someone to teach me how to be a real cowboy," Rip said.

"The first thing you need is a good hat," Steve said. "And a rope and you need to learn how to use it."

"Josh taught me a little, then he got married and ruined it all," Rip said.

Steve grinned. "A man has to follow his heart, Rip," he said. "And if your heart tells you to be a cowboy, then be a cowboy."

"Yeah, but what am I going to do with all these oranges?" Rip said.

"Is this your first time west of the Mississippi?" Emmet said.

"Prior to this, Kansas City, Missouri was the furthest west I've ever been," Glass said. "And coming from the east, it was quite an adjustment."

"I'll bet," Anna said. "Out here we don't have overpainted women in high shoes that don't fit."

Emmet looked at Anna.

"I don't see what that has to do with anything," Glass said. "A doctor goes where he feels he is needed most."

"Maybe so, but I didn't hear you deny you like overpainted women in high shoes," Anna said.

Rose looked at Anna. Emmet looked at Glass.

"Rose, I'm sorry but I think my coming to dinner was a mistake," Glass said.

"I'll say," Anna said.

Glass stood up. "I'll say goodnight and see myself out."

As he walked to the front door, Rose looked at Anna. "Are you going to let him walk out like that," Rose said.

"Yes," Anna said.

The door closed.

"No," Anna said, stood and rushed to the front door.

"What just happened?" Emmet said.

"Love," Rose said.

Anna caught up with Glass on the front steps. "Wait," she said.

Glass paused and turned around. "What for?" he said.

"If you don't kiss me right now, I'll punch you, right in the nose," Anna said.

"We'll be back from town with supplies by lunch," Josh said as he helped Emma into the buggy. She held the baby wrapped in a blanket in her arms.

"You can leave the boy, I'll look after him," Mr. Olson said.

"He's due for a checkup with Rose,"

Emma said.

Josh climbed aboard the buggy. "I won't forget that bottle of wine, Mr. Olson," he said.

While they were gone, Mr. Olson did some chores. He got fresh water from the stream, swept out his tent and peeled carrots and potatoes to make stew for lunch. There was just enough fresh meat in the cooler box, a large metal box with a block of ice on the bottom, to make the stew.

He gathered up enough wood from the wood box to start a fire in the Dutch oven and made fresh coffee.

Then he sat in his chair outside his tent and looked at the fine ranch house that was nearly complete and for a very old man, he felt so very young.

After Rose and Anna examined the baby and pronounced him very fit, Anna and Emma went to the small lunchroom for coffee.

"I have a beau," Anna said.

"About time. Who?" Emma said.

"Doctor Glass, the doctor Rose hired," Anna said.

"Doctor? Is he old?" Emma said.

"No, silly, he's only twenty-seven," Anna said. "And he's very cute."

"Where is he?" Emma said.

"He won't be here until four," Anna said. "But you'll meet him tomorrow for Sunday dinner."

"Okay. I better go find Josh now," Emma said.

Mr. Olson added a bit of flour to the stew to thicken it and when he looked up he spotted two riders headed his way. They were too far to make out faces, so he poured a cup of coffee and sat in his chair by the fire to wait.

Presently, the two riders arrived. One rode a paint, the other a brown bay with white stockings and a white star on her nose.

"Hello to camp," one of them said.

"Spare a cup of coffee?" the second man said.

"I can spare you some stew if you have a mind for some," Mr. Olson said.

The two men dismounted. "Right neighborly of you," the first man said.

Mr. Olson filled two plates with stew and the men sat in chairs.

"That's a fine big house you're building," the first man said.

"It will be soon enough," Mr. Olson said. "You men looking for work?"

"We're just passing through, headed

south," the second man said.

"This is going to be a cattle ranch if you're looking for work," Mr. Olson said.

"Like he said," the first man said. "We're just passing through."

The second man tossed his empty plate on the ground. "I thank you kindly for the stew and anything else you have around here," he said.

"I'm afraid I don't understand," Mr. Olson said.

The first man drew his Colt and cocked it. "Understand now?" he said and shot Mr. Olson in the chest.

"Get his money, watch, whatever," the first man said. "I'm gonna check those tents."

The second man went through Mr. Olson's pockets and took his gold watch and some coins. The first man went through the tents and found Mr. Olson's cash box that contained his papers and one thousand dollars.

"Let's go," the first man said.

"He's still alive," the second man said.

"He'll bleed out," the first man said. "We need to put some distance between us and him."

The two men mounted up and rode on.

Twenty minutes later, Josh and Emma arrived in the buggy. "Mr. Olson," Emma cried, handed the baby and jumped down. She ran to Mr. Olson and knelt beside him.

"Josh, he's been shot," Emma said.

"Is he alive?" Josh said as he climbed down with the baby.

"Yes," Emma said. "Put the baby in the crib and go get Rose. Hurry, Josh. Please."

Josh put the baby in the crib, returned to the buggy and raced back to town.

Emma cradled Mr. Olson's head and he opened his eyes. "Emma," he said.

"I'm here," Emma said.

"Not much time," Mr. Olson said. "Tell Emmet . . . two men. One rode a paint, the other a brown bay with white stockings and a white star on her nose. The horses wore the Double Deuce brand. I saw it."

"I'll tell him," Emma said as she started to cry.

"In my tent, my will. Read it," Mr. Olson said. He turned his head and looked at the ranch house. "Be happy," he said.

Then he closed his eyes and went limp.

"No, no," Emma cried. She held him tight and wept.

Emma was seated in a chair with the baby on her lap when Emmet arrived first on Blue. She had covered Mr. Olson with a blanket and stared at it as Emmet dismounted.

"Emma, what happened?" Emmet said.

Emma looked up at him. "I don't know," she said. "Somebody passed by and shot him."

Emmet pulled back the blanked, knelt and examined the wound. It was from a Colt .45 revolver. He replaced the blanket, stood and looked at the two empty plates on the ground. Then he looked for and found the tracks of two riders heading south.

A few minutes later, Rose, Anna and Josh arrived in the buggy.

"He's gone," Emmet said as Rose, Josh and Anna left the buggy.

"Oh no," Rose said.

After loading Mr. Olson into the back of the buggy, Rose and Anna rode back to town. Emmet, Josh and Emma rode their horses. Anna held the baby. Emma took the papers from Mr. Olson's box and put them into her saddlebags.

At the hospital, Emmet carried Mr. Olson in through the back door to an operating room.

"Rose, I want that bullet," Emmet said.

While Rose and Anna removed the bullet,

Emmet took Emma and Josh to Rose's office.

"Sit down you two," Emmet said.

Emma and Josh took chairs. Emmet leaned against the desk. "Tell me what happened," Emmet said.

"We went to get supplies," Josh said. "Mr. Olson wanted to go, but we told him to rest."

"When we got back, he was on the ground bleeding," Emma said. "Josh went to get Rose and he died in my arms."

"Was he conscious?" Emmet said.

"Yes," Emma said. "He said, two men, one rode a paint, the other a brown bay with white stockings and a white star on her nose."

"Anything else?" Emmet said.

"He said the Double Deuce brand and then told me to read his will," Emma said. "And then he died."

"Okay," Emmet said. "Let's get you to my house."

Emma sat in a chair beside the bed and watched her son sleep. She was trying to make sense of it all, but it made no sense.

Mr. Olson was the kindest, gentlest man she had ever known and whoever shot him deserved to hang.

Josh entered the room with a cup of tea. "Rose and Anna are making supper," he said.

"I'm not hungry," Emma said.

"Me neither, but we have to eat," Josh said.

"I'll be down soon," Emma said.

"Okay," Josh said and left the room.

After Josh was gone, Emma picked up her saddlebags from the floor and removed Mr. Olson's papers. She found his will and opened it.

I, Jorn Frederickson Olson, being of sound mind and body, make this following statement. After the death of my wife, I felt my life no longer had meaning and I was just waiting to die. Two young people came to me full of life and love and I felt once again I had a purpose. To those young people, Emma and Josh Paden, I leave the bulk of my estate that is in the First Bank of Carson City, a total of forty-seven-thousand-dollars. I hope I live long enough to see the ranch, but if I don't, Josh and Emma, make it a grand one. If possible, I wish to be buried beside my beloved wife. Sincerely, Jorn Olson.

Emma lowered the will and wept.

■ ■ ■ ■

Emmet, Rose and Josh were at the dinner, picking at their food. No one was hungry, but they made a show of eating the meal.

Emma finally came to the table, holding the will. "Emmet, will you read this out loud, please," she said and handed him the will.

Emmet read the will and Rose teared up, as did Josh. Crying out loud, Emma just sat there. Finally Rose stood up. "I'll make some coffee," she said.

A little while later, as Rose, Emma and Josh sat in the parlor with cups of coffee, Anna and Glass came from the hospital.

Anna sat beside Emma and put her arm around her. "I don't know what to say," she said.

"Doctor Glass, are you returning to the hospital?" Rose said.

"Yes. I just wanted to take Anna home," Glass said.

"Could you prepare Mr. Olson's body for transport?" Rose said. "He will be buried in Stockton next to his wife."

"Of course," Glass said.

"Have a cup of coffee before you leave," Rose said.

■ ■ ■ ■

In the morning, Emmet sent a telegram to the railroad depot in care of his parents, telling them to stay put and he would meet them on the platform at ten-fifteen.

"I'll be back tonight," Emmet said.

"I'm going with you," Emma said.

"Your place is here with Josh and your son," Emmet said.

"I'm going with you," Emma said.

Emmet looked at Rose and she nodded.

"Alright," Emmet said.

After the coffin was loaded into the cargo car, Emmet and Emma got into a riding car for the ninety-minute ride to Stockton.

Emma looked out the window. Emmet read a newspaper.

John, Sarah, Ellis, Bettina, their children and Rip waited on the platform.

"Emmet, what in blazes is going on?" John said.

"Mr. Olson was killed," Emmet said.

"What?" John said.

"My Grandpa?" Rip said.

"Let's go get some coffee and I'll explain," Emmet said. "Ellis, we'll need the wagon."

Emmet, Ellis and Emma took the wagon to

318

the Olson ranch. The air was filled with the scent of oranges as the groves were coming into bloom.

"I'll break ground," Emmet said as he removed his holster.

Using a pickax, Emmet went to work breaking ground to dig the grave beside Mrs. Olson. The ground was hard, with thick roots, but after an hour, Emmet was ready for the shovel. Ellis removed two shovels from the wagon and he and Emmet got to work.

Emma went to the barn and returned with a shovel, got in the hole beside Ellis and started digging.

Emmet and Ellis looked at her. "For God's sake, Emma, will you get out of here," Emmet said.

"No," Emma said. "I will not."

Emmet sighed. "Ellis, give her your extra work gloves before she rips up her hands," he said.

After several hours, Ellis and Emma went to the wagon for water, while Emmet continued digging.

"He never gets tired, does he?" Ellis said.

"No," Emma said.

Finally, Emmet climbed out of the deep hole. "Ellis, let's get his coffin beside the hole," he said. "We'll stop at the church on the way to town for the preacher."

On the ride back to Carson City, Emma placed her head against Emmet's shoulder.

"Tired?" Emmet said.

"I feel like I could sleep for a week," Emma said.

Emmet took her right hand. "You tore them up," he said.

"I'm okay," Emma said. She closed her eyes and fell asleep with her head on Emmet's shoulder and didn't awake until the train reached Carson City.

The minister gave a beautiful service for Mr. Olson. Sarah, Bettina, Rose, Anna, and Rip cried the entire time, but Emma stared at the coffin and didn't shed a tear.

Then John said a few words and then it was time to lower the coffin. Once it was in the ground, Emmet said, "You all go in the house, I'll take care of this."

Emmet got a shovel and covered up the grave. It took him about an hour and by that time lunch was ready.

Steve and several other hands came to pay their respects and room was made for them at the table.

When Emmet entered the house, Emma stood from the table and walked to him.

"You get them," she said. "Don't send anybody, just you. I don't care if it takes the rest of your life, you get those bastards so I can watch them hang. You promise me that."

The entire family watched in shock as Emma began slapping Emmet in the chest. "Promise me," she cried, slapping Emmet so many times she fell to her knees exhausted.

Emmet picked her up and she hugged him around his neck. "Promise me," she said.

"I promise," Emmet said and carried her to her old bedroom and set her on the bed.

Emmet returned to the dining room. Everyone was silent as he took a chair beside Rose.

"This is one promise you better keep," Rose said. "Marshal."

After lunch, John, Ellis, and Emmet took coffee on the porch.

"Pa, I'm thinking you and Ma should stay with Emma and Josh for a while," Emmet said. "She's taking this pretty hard."

"I was thinking that very thing," John said. "Sarah?"

"Of course," Sarah said.

"Rose, Anna and I are catching the five o'clock train home," Emmet said. "You can bring Emma and Josh with you in a few days."

"Alright, son," John said. "Son, about that promise you made."

"Don't worry, Pa," Emmet said. "I've never broken a promise yet."

While Rose and Anna had breakfast before leaving for the hospital. Emmet came to the table. "Want breakfast?" Rose said.

"Just coffee," Emmet said.

Rose filled a cup and set it in front of Emmet.

Rose and Anna stared at him.

"What?" Emmet said.

"How are you going to keep that promise to Emma," Rose said. "You have no idea who they are or where they went."

Emmet finished his coffee and stood. "I'll see you tonight," he said. He reached for his holster that was hanging from his chair and strapped it on, then left the dining room.

"How is he going to find them?" Anna said.

"Don't ever sell your brother short," Rose said. "Many have and regretted it. Come on, let's get to the hospital."

Emmet entered the building at the end of

Front Street where the Stock Grower's Association for Nevada was located.

A small man at the front desk said, "Marshal Boyd, what can I do for you?"

"I'm interested in the Double Deuce brand," Emmet said. "What do you have registered under that brand?"

"Let's go take a look," the man said.

He and Emmet went to a large desk where a number of register books were stacked. The man opened the book for the letter D.

"Double Deuce, you say?" the man said.

"What do you have?" Emmet said.

"That brand is registered to the Garth Ranch in Wyoming," the man said.

"Wyoming? Where in Wyoming?" Emmet said.

"Northwest of Fort Laramie," the man said.

"Okay, thanks," Emmet said.

Emmet left the Stock Grower's building and walked to his office. Deputy Marshal Cody was on duty.

"Morning, Marshal," Cody said.

"I'm going to Wyoming for a few days," Emmet said. "I'll need you to handle things while I'm gone."

"Is this about Olson's murder?" Cody said.

"It is," Emmet said. "I'll fill you in when I

get back."

"How long will you be gone?" Rose said at the dinner table.

"Three days, no more than that," Emmet said.

"Your parents and Emma and Josh are coming tomorrow," Rose said.

"Tell them I'll stop by when I get back," Emmet said. "You can tell Emma I'm keeping my promise."

"She knows," Anna said.

As was his usual custom, Emmet watched Rose brush her hair while in bed. She generally brushed for one hundred strokes.

"Our son is eighteen months old now," Rose said.

"I know," Emmet said.

"My temperature is over one hundred," Rose said.

"Are you sick?" Emmet said.

"No."

"You don't have a fever for no reason," Emmet said.

"I have a reason," Rose said as she set the brush aside and stood up. She removed her nightgown and slid into bed beside Emmet. "It's time we had another baby," she said.

"That's why you have a fever?" Emmet said.

"I'm a doctor," Rose said. "Remember?"

John, Sarah, Emma, baby in arms and Josh stepped off the train and met Rose and Anna on the platform.

"Where's Emmet?" John said.

"He went to Wyoming," Rose said. "Josh, I have the buggy for you."

"I'll get our luggage," John said.

After the buggy was loaded, Rose said, "We'll be out to see you as soon as Emmet returns."

John drove the buggy to the ranch where the crew was installing doors and building deck railing for the porch.

"Let's get settled in the tent and I'll give them a hand," John said.

"Josh, can you drive me back to town for supplies?" Sarah said.

"Sure," Josh said.

After Josh and Sarah left, John said, "Emma, let's go check your house."

Emma carried the baby as she and John walked to the house.

"Hello Mr. Boyd, Emma," the crew chief said. "It won't be long now. Why not go in for a look."

John and Emma went up the stairs and

opened the door and entered the house. The massive living room was the showpiece, with a large stone fireplace and windows that faced the morning sun.

"Mr. Olson will never see this," Emma said. "Why, Pa?"

"I can't answer why, honey," John said. "But I can tell you that Mr. Olson sees this and he approves. Now you and Josh have to do your part. You have to make this the best ranch as you can to honor his memory."

Emma looked at the stone fireplace. "We will, Pa," she said.

Anna and Glass took a break and went for coffee in the small break room.

"Are we officially courting?" Anna said.

"You know we are," Glass said.

"Then you have to ask my father," Anna said.

"I know and I will as soon as I can," Glass said.

"Then let's talk about my brother," Anna said.

"The Marshal?" Glass said. "He seems like a real decent man."

"He is," Anna said. "Unless he thinks I've been dishonored. In that case, run. As far and as fast as you can."

"Dishonored? But I haven't . . ." Glass said.

"I know," Anna said. "He needs to know it. He's a bit fanatical when it comes to his sisters and you don't want to be on the wrong end of his temper."

"How do I do that?"

"Tell him your intentions," Anna said. "He went to Wyoming, but he'll be back in a few days. Come to dinner and have a talk with him."

"I will," Glass said. "Right now I have to make rounds."

"I'll see you later," Anna said.

After Glass left, Rose entered the break room, grabbed a cup of coffee and sat with Anna.

"Did you give him the Emmet talk?" Rose said.

"I did," Anna said.

"Well, if that doesn't scare him off, you got yourself a husband," Rose said.

Emmet walked Blue from the train station through the streets of Cheyenne. Much had changed since he was Marshal here in seventy. At least half the buildings were made of red brick instead of wood and there was a large school and a new church.

Saloons were more upscale and some

featured live entertainment. He drew looks from people on the street, some because he wore a Marshal's badge, others because they remembered him.

In front of the governor's office, Emmet tied Blue to a post, then opened the door and entered. A woman sat at a reception desk in the lobby.

"Hello . . . Marshal can I help you?" she said.

"Marshal Emmet Boyd to see Governor Thayer," Emmet said.

"Let me check," she said, stood and entered Thayer's office. She returned a few moments later. "Marshal," she said.

Governor John Thayer stood from behind his desk and extended his right hand to Emmet after Emmet entered the office.

"Marshal Boyd," Thayer said. "You're something of a legend around here. Are you here on business or just passing through?"

"Business," Emmet said.

"Please, sit," Thayer said. He reached for a coffee pot on the desk and poured a cup for Emmet.

"Thanks," Emmet said. "Governor, I'm after two men. Stone cold killers. I believe they have ties to the Double Deuce ranch."

"That's Garth's spread about ten miles north of Laramie," Thayer said.

"Who is marshal now?" Emmet said.

"Waite. Jon Waite," Thayer said. "A good man."

"I'll see Waite and head out in the morning," Emmet said.

"This doesn't have anything to do with Garth, does it?"

"No."

After leaving Thayer, Emmet walked Blue to the marshal's office that he built in sixty-nine. It had been redone and was now constructed entirely of red brick. He tied Blue to the post and entered the office.

Marshal Jon Waite was behind a large desk, drinking a cup of coffee. He was around forty, tall and thin. He wore a Smith & Wesson, Schofield .45 in his holster. He looked at Emmet's badge.

"Marshal Emmet Boyd," Emmet said.

Waite extended his right hand and they shook. "You're something of a legend around here," Waite said.

"That's mostly talk," Emmet said. "I just spent sixteen hours on a train and I could use a hot bath and a steak. I'm going to check in at the hotel and I'll buy you dinner around seven and tell you why I'm here."

"The Double Deuce is Garth's place," Waite said. "He came up from New Mexico in seventy-five and purchased two thousand acres northwest of Laramie. He runs two thousand head and employs a dozen hands."

"I'm sure he has nothing to do with it, but he might know the two men riding those horses," Emmet said. "I'm catching the eight o'clock train to Laramie, you're welcome to come."

"Sure," Waite said.

"Good," Emmet said.

The waiter brought two steaks to their table. "Enjoy," the waiter said.

John roasted two chickens on a spit, while Sarah roasted vegetables in a pan and also baked biscuits.

"Pa, it seems so empty here without Mr. Olson," Emma said. "And without him, what are we going to do with all that house?"

"I have a suggestion," Sarah said.

Emma looked at Sarah.

"Fill it with children," Sarah said.

"There is no denying that when it comes to his sisters, Emmet can be a bit overprotective, but he isn't that bad, not really," Rose said.

Rose, Anna, and Glass were having dinner at the house after work.

"Not that bad?" Anna said. "He told Josh that if he disrespected Emma his body would never be found."

Glass looked at Emma. "I was on the boxing team in medical school," he said.

Rose and Anna broke out laughing.

"James, honey, as a doctor I prescribe that the last thing you ever want to do is raise a fist to my husband," Rose said. "It would be much better for your health if you simply talked to him man-to-man and stated your intentions."

"Okay, I can do that," Glass said.

Anna grinned.

Rose grinned.

"Would you like some apple pie?" Rose said.

The train ride to Laramie took just one hour. Emmet and Waite retrieved their horses and rode northwest for ten miles and reached rich grazing land.

"I expect we're on Garth's land right now," Waite said.

They rode a mile or so more and encountered a range with close to a thousand head of cattle on it. Six cowboys were sitting around a campfire, drinking coffee. Emmet and Waite stopped by the campfire.

"Morning, boys," Emmet said.

They looked at Emmet's badge. "Morning, Marshal," one of the men said.

"Where can I find Mr. Garth this time of day?" Emmet said.

"The house," the cowboy said. "Keep going a half mile and turn right on the road. It takes you right to it. Is something wrong, Marshal?"

"Thanks," Emmet said.

Emmet and Waite rode until they reached the road and turned right. A half mile later, they arrived at a large ranch house. Some cowboys were working with a bronco in the corral. A large barn and bunkhouse were several hundred feet from the house.

Emmet and Waite dismounted at the corral. "Morning, boys," Emmet said. "We're looking for Mr. Garth."

"He's in the house," a cowboy said.

"Thanks," Emmet said.

Emmet and Waite walked to the house and took the steps to the porch. A man wearing an apron opened the screen door and stepped out. "May I help you?" he said.

"United States Marshal Emmet Boyd and Jon Waite to see Mr. Garth," Emmet said.

A few minutes later, Emmet and Waite were being served coffee by the man in the apron in Garth's den. Garth was sixty years old, average height and stocky.

"I know the two men you're talking about," Garth said. "The Henderson brothers. Mitch and Jonas. They were here for about six months. They were okay hands, but nothing special. I believe Mitch rode the paint, Jonas the other."

"How did they come by your horses and why did they leave?" Emmet said.

"A man hires on without a horse, he uses one of mine," Garth said.

"And they didn't have their own?" Emmet said.

"No," Garth said. "Then, about a month ago, they just took off."

"With your horses?" Emmet said.

"Those are three-hundred-dollar horses," Garth said. "I'd like to get them back."

"Do you know where they're from?" Emmet said.

"No. My foreman might," Garth said. "He's in the corral."

Emmet, Waite, and Garth went to the porch. Garth called for his foreman and he came to the porch.

"Yes sir, Mr. Garth," the foreman said.

"The Marshal has some questions about the Henderson boys," Garth said.

"Those two," the foreman said.

"Men in bunkhouses talk," Emmet said. "Did they ever say where they were from?"

"They said Texas, but I never believed that," the foreman said. "A couple of nights before they took off, I heard them talking outside. They said they wanted to stop off and see their sister in Santa Fe."

"And then they took off with Mr. Garth's horses," Emmet said.

"Rode out when they were supposed to be working," the foreman said. "They were gone ten hours before anyone knew it."

"Santa Fe is a piece from Nevada," Emmet said. "Any idea why they would be in Nevada?"

"Nevada? It never came up," the foreman said.

"Thanks for the information," Emmet said.

"Marshal, I sure would like to have those horses back," Garth said.

Emmet and Waite shook hands on the platform before Emmet boarded the train.

"Hope to see you again," Waite said.

"You bet," Emmet said.

Emmet boarded the train for the sixteen-hour ride home.

"Emmet's train arrived at ten o'clock," Rose said. "What do you say we take a walk over and meet him?"

"I'll tell James we'll be gone for a bit," Anna said.

Rose and Anna left the hospital and walked toward the railroad station. A few blocks from the station, Julie, the waitress walked directly at them, less than a block away.

"Look who it is," Anna said.

"Anna, don't start anything, please," Rose said.

"I won't start a thing," Anna said.

They kept walking until Julie stopped in front of them.

"Would you excuse us, please," Rose said.

"I figured you for thirty-five, but up close I'd say you were past forty," Julie said. "No wonder he keeps coming around for coffee."

"Stay away from my brother, you whore," Anna said.

"What did you call me?" Julie said.

"You heard me, you bitch," Anna said. "Now get the hell out of our way."

"That's enough, Anna," Rose said.

"Yeah, Anna, that's enough," Julie said.

"Last time, get out of our way," Anna said.

"Or what?" Julie said.

Anna punched Julie in the face, knocking her down.

"That," Anna said.

As Anna took a step, Julie grabbed her skirt and Anna fell forward. The two women rolled around, punching, kicking and biting each other.

A small crowd gathered around and cheered Anna and Julie on.

"Oh for God's sake," Rose said.

Somehow, Anna managed to get on top and was punching Julie in the face when Anna was lifted from behind and set on the wood sidewalk.

"Who . . ." Anna said and looked up at Emmet. "Oh, Emmet. Hi."

"And this is about?" Emmet said.

"Her," Anna said and pointed to Julie.

Emmet reached down and lifted Julie to her feet. "I want her arrested, Marshal. She attacked me," Julie said.

"Emmet, it wasn't like that at . . ." Rose said.

"I'll speak to you later," Emmet said. He looked at Julie. "I told you once before to leave me and my family alone. If I have to tell you again, I'll have a restraining order slapped on you. Anna, home."

"Yes, sir," Anna said.

Emmet, Blue in tow and Anna started walking home.

"She started it," Anna said.

"Don't say a word until we get home,"

Emmet said.

"Yes, sir," Anna said.

They reached the house. Emmet tied Blue to the hitching post and they went inside.

"I'll boil some water for you to take a bath," Emmet said.

"I have to get back to work," Anna said.

"Look at yourself," Emmet said.

Anna looked in the mirror in the hallway. Her skirt and blouse were ripped. Her hair was down and covered with dirt. A red welt was under her right eye. Her lips were bloody.

"Oh boy," she said.

An hour later, Anna, dressed in a clean skirt and blouse and sporting a red welt under her right eye and a swollen lower lip, had coffee at the kitchen table.

"Can I speak now?" Anna said.

Emmet nodded as he sipped coffee.

"She wouldn't let us pass," Anna said. "And insulted Rose. She had it coming."

"Do you really think I would ever do anything to hurt Rose, or you?" Emmet said.

"No."

"Then the subject is closed," Emmet said. "Permanently. I'll walk you back to the hospital."

■ ■ ■ ■

"You look like you need a doctor," Rose said when Anna entered the hospital.

"I guess I was wrong," Anna said.

"Emmet give you a scolding?" Rose said.

"He did."

"I guess I'll get one later," Rose said.

"You will," Anna said.

"Well, come on, we have patients to see," Rose said.

"Mitchel and Jonas Henderson?" Judge Briscoe said.

"They're the two men who murdered Mr. Olson," Emmet said. "I'd like a warrant for their arrest and a warrant to speak with their sister in Santa Fe."

"They were murdered in my county," Briscoe said. "I'll post a ten-thousand-dollar reward for their capture."

"Write a separate document explaining the reward," Emmet said.

"When are you going to Santa Fe?" Briscoe said.

"Tomorrow," Emmet said.

Ellis and Rip sat in the shade of a large tree and tossed fishing line into the stream that ran through the farm.

"Ellis, now that Grandpa is gone I have no real family," Rip said.

"We're your family, Rip," Ellis said. "All of us."

"Not by blood," Rip said.

"Bettina was his daughter," Ellis said. "That makes you blood. But blood or not, you are as much a part of the family as any of us."

"Can we go to the ranch tomorrow?" Rip said. "I want to see Steve and the horses."

"Not tomorrow," Ellis said. "But you can go to Carson City with me and help with the work now that you're older."

"I'd rather go fishing," Rip said.

"Me too," Ellis said.

Rose and Anna sat at the kitchen table while Emmet stood.

"Am I clear about this waitress nonsense now?" Emmet said.

"Yes, Emmet," Rose said.

Emmet looked at Anna.

"Clear," Anna said.

"Alright, let's have dinner," Emmet said.

As they ate, Emmet said, "Tomorrow, I'm going to Santa Fe, for at least three days."

"About Mr. Olson?" Anna said.

"Yes," Emmet said. "I know who the two

men are who murdered him, now I have to track them down."

Emmet stood up from the table. "I need to pack," he said.

After Emmet left the table, Anna said, "He'll find them won't he?"

"Oh yes," Rose said. "You can count on that."

The crew was building a brick chimney and John and Josh were planning windows and doors when Ellis, Bettina, their children and Rip arrived.

Sarah and Emma were at the fire, getting ready to prepare lunch.

"Come on, Rip, let's go lend a hand," Ellis said.

An hour later, Rose and Anna arrived in their buggy.

"What happened to you?" Emma said when she saw Anna's face.

"Remember that waitress?" Anna said. "We had a discussion."

"Must have been some discussion," Emma said.

"Where is Emmet?" Sarah said.

"He went to Santa Fe," Rose said. "He knows who the men are that murdered Mr. Olson."

"Good," Emma said. "Good."

■ ■ ■ ■

The ride to Santa Fe would take sixteen hours and Emmet was prepared with a book and two newspapers to occupy his time.

He read the newspapers first, then had lunch in the dining car and started to read the novel *The American* by Henry Jones. It was a large novel and took the rest of the day, through dinner and right up to the train docking in Santa Fe before he reached the midpoint.

The capital of New Mexico Territory, Santa Fe was a bustling town of five thousand residents. As he walked Blue from the train station to the center of town, music played from every saloon and cantina along the way. With a heavy Mexican population, most of the music was Spanish as were most of the people on the street.

Emmet had wired ahead to the Hotel Santa Fe for a room and after tying Blue to the hitching post, he entered the hotel, carrying his saddle bags, satchel and Winchester.

"Marshal Emmet Boyd," Emmet said to the desk clerk.

"Got your room all ready for you, Marshal," the clerk said.

"Reserve me a shave and a bath in the morning and stable my horse," Emmet said. "Add any extras to my bill."

Emmet's room was on the second floor and it had a balcony. He set his things on the bed, removed his boots and opened the balcony doors. The music from below reached his room.

There was a knock on the door and a voice in the hall said, "Marshal Boyd, this is Marshal Wilford Byrd."

Emmet drew his Colt, went to the door, cracked it and looked at the badge on Byrd's vest. He holstered the Colt and opened the door.

"Come in," he said.

Byrd was several inches shorter than Emmet, stout and wore a handlebar moustache. "I asked the desk clerk to let me know when you arrived," Byrd said.

"I would have stopped by your office in the morning," Emmet said.

"I know," Byrd said. "I never go to bed early anyway. So let me ask what your business is in Santa Fe?"

Emmet dug out the warrants and showed them to Byrd. "I know the Henderson woman," he said. "Has a small spread maybe two hour's ride to the west. Used to be married but he died. She doesn't get to town maybe three times a year."

"What about her brothers?" Emmet said.

"I don't know them," Byrd said. "I've been here eighteen months and this is the first I've heard of them."

"Who's sheriff here?" Emmet said.

"I handle both duties," Byrd said.

"How long has the Henderson woman lived here?" Emmet said.

"From what little I know, she came here in sixty-nine with her husband," Byrd said. "He died a few years later."

"So if she's been here eight years, some long standing residents might know her brothers?" Emmet said.

"We can ask around in the morning," Byrd said. "If anybody knows, it's the shopkeepers."

"I'll see you for breakfast around eight," Emmet said.

"Yeah, I know the Henderson woman," the clerk at the general store said. "Chloe, and if ask me, she's plum loco in the head."

"Why do you say that?" Emmet said.

"I don't see her but three, four times a year," the clerk said. "Never says a word. Just hands me a list long enough to last for months, pays and goes."

"How much does she buy and how does

she pay?" Emmet said.

"About a hundred dollars' worth of supplies and pays in gold eagles," the clerk said.

"She ever bring crops to town to sell?" Emmet said.

"Not that I know of," the clerk said.

"So where does she get gold eagles?" Emmet said.

"No idea. All I know is they're good," the clerk said.

"Ever meet her brothers?" Emmet said.

"Just the one, but he's gone two years or more," the clerk said. "Why, does she have others?"

"Thanks for your time," Emmet said.

Back in the street, Emmet said, "I'm going to ride out and see Chloe Henderson."

"I'll get my horse and go with you," Byrd said.

Emmet and Byrd took the west freight road out of town and stayed on it for about an hour until it forked, then they took the fork west.

The countryside was bleak and dry as dust, with cactus as the main vegetation.

"Get much rain in these parts?" Emmet said.

"Maybe six or seven snowfalls in winter and two months of heavy rain in July and

August," Byrd said. "Just enough to keep the wells full."

Chloe Henderson's place was around a bend in the road. There was a rundown house, a barn in dire condition, a small shed and a corral with two horses. Chickens pecked on the ground, several hogs were in a pen.

"Not much of a place," Byrd said.

They dismounted at the front porch. Chloe Henderson, holding a double barrel shotgun, opened the door and stepped out. "What's your business here?" she said. "Speak up or I'll cut you in two."

"No need of that Greener, ma'am," Emmet said.

"I'll decide what I need," Chloe said.

"I'm a United States Marshal," Emmet said.

"I see your badge," Chloe said. "What do you want?"

"Talk to you about your brothers," Emmet said.

"What about them?" Chloe said.

"Can you put down the shotgun so we can talk?" Emmet said.

"My brothers ain't here," Chloe said.

"I know," Emmet said. "Look, can we just talk?"

"How do I know you won't pecker me

when you get me alone?" Chloe said.

"We're U. S. Marshals," Emmet said.

"You still got peckers," Chloe said.

Emmet removed his holster and hung it from his saddle horn. Byrd did the same.

"There, keep the shotgun," Emmet said. "All I want is a few minutes of your time."

"I just put on a pot of coffee," Chloe said. "I ain't got no chickery. Come on up."

Emmet and Byrd walked up to the porch. "Sit," Chloe said.

There were four chairs on the porch. Emmet and Byrd sat in two. Chloe went into her house and returned a minute later with a tray that held a pot of coffee and three cups. She left the shotgun inside. She filled three cups, took one and sat. Then she pulled a Walker Colt from a pocket of her skirt and set it on her lap.

"Say your piece," Chloe said.

"Your brothers, Mitch and Jonas, were they here recently?" Emmet said.

"My brothers is good for nothing scum," Chloe said. "Killers, thieves and rapers of women, but they are still my blood."

"Understood," Emmet said. "But they murdered a seventy-two-year-old man in cold blood after he offered them a meal."

"It sounds like them," Chloe said. "Is there reward money offered?"

"Yes," Emmet said. "Can you read?"

"I can read," Chloe said.

Emmet took out the warrant offering a ten-thousand-dollar reward for information that aids in the capture of the Henderson brothers and handed it to Chloe. She read it and handed it back to Emmet.

"They're my blood," Chloe said.

"They're no good, Mrs. Henderson and you know it," Emmet said.

"I was a young woman when I came here with my husband," Chloe said. "Why he thought he could make a go at it here is a mystery to me, but we gave it a shot. Renegade Apache's got him in seventy-one. Mitch and Jonas was here about six weeks ago. Said they came to see their sister, but I figure they needed a place to lay low for a while. They stayed a week and moved on."

"Do you know where?" Emmet said.

"Said they wanted to see Brud, the youngest brother," Chloe said. "I told them it wouldn't do no good, that Brud was reformed since he married that Mormon woman up to the Salt Lake, but they wouldn't listen."

"Does Brud send you money?" Emmet said.

"Every three months he sends me five gold eagles," Chloe said. "Otherwise I'd never make it out here alone."

"Alright, thank you for the information," Emmet said.

"I got three rabbits fresh killed I plan to make a stew with," Chloe said. "I get lonely for talk sometimes. Stay and lunch with me."

"Your firewood bin is nearly empty and your corral gate needs mending," Emmet said. "We'll keep ourselves busy while you cook."

"I'd be obliged," Chloe said.

Emmet and Byrd went outside. "I'll chop the wood," Emmet said.

Emmet chopped wood on the side of the house, while Byrd repaired the broken corral gate. By the time Chole called them to lunch, Emmet had chopped enough wood to last a week and the corral gate was as good as new.

Chole had three plates and coffee ready at the kitchen table. She filled the bowls and cups as Emmet and Byrd took chairs.

"Brud is a true believer of the Mormon faith," Chloe said. "I know Mitch and Jonas went to see him with the purpose in mind for him to join up with them again, but Brud would have turned them down."

"The three of them rode together?" Emmet said.

"For quite a spell," Chloe said. "Brud is youngest and he'd probably still be with them except he met his Mormon wife and took to religion."

"When he sends you money, do you save the letters?" Emmet said.

Chloe stood, went to a chest against the wall and returned with a stack of envelopes and set them on the table. Emmet picked up an envelope. The return address was Brian Henderson, Salt Lake City, Utah.

"You've been a great deal of help," Emmet said.

"Not because I want that reward money," Chloe said. "Because Brud is a good man with a wife and young'uns and I don't want Mitch and Jonas destroying his life."

"I understand," Emmet said. "One last question. Would you know where they might go after Salt Lake City?"

"Brud might know," Chloe said.

"You got what you came for, now what?" Byrd said.

"I'll go to Salt Lake City and talk to the brother," Emmet said.

"People are funny when it comes to kin," Byrd said. "He may have found religion, but that doesn't mean he'll turn his back on his brothers."

"No, it doesn't," Emmet said. "I got to send a telegram and then have dinner at my hotel around seven, if you care to join me."

Rose and Anna were about to leave for the evening when a messenger from the telegraph office arrived with a telegram.

"What is it?" Anna said.

"Emmet is going to Salt Lake City before coming home," Rose said.

"Want to work late and help James?"

"Why not?" Rose said. "He'll be gone for several more days, so no hurry getting home."

Emma, Josh, John, and Sarah ate supper at the table beside the Dutch oven so they could watch the sunset. It was a comfortable spring evening and the ladies used just a wrap around their shoulders to keep them warm.

"Pa, we need your help," Emma said. "Josh and me, we don't know where to go or who to talk with about Mr. Olson's will."

"It should be easy enough, honey," John said. "Monday morning, we'll go to town and see a lawyer and then get the funds released at the bank."

"He left a lot of money, Pa," Emma said.

"It sure is, honey and the both of you have

a responsibility to Mr. Olson to use it to make this the best ranch you can," John said.

"We know, sir," Josh said. "And we will do our best."

"Oh, we almost forgot," Emma said. "We finally decided on a name."

"We did," Josh said.

"It's about time," Sarah said. "What is it?"

"Jorn Frederickson Paden," Emma said.

"That's grand, Emma," Sarah said. "Mr. Olson would be very pleased."

The ten o'clock train out of Santa Fe got Emmet to Salt Lake City at nine o'clock the same night.

The ride was pleasant enough. He had lunch and finished reading the novel *The American*, with an hour to spare before the train arrived.

As he walked Blue through the streets, Emmet was struck by how much the city had grown since it first connected the railroad eight years ago. The welcome sign at the depot claimed a population of fifteen thousand residents, three times the number eight years ago.

Almost the entire city was Mormon, but the main church should be able to locate Brud Henderson and his wife.

On Main Street, a sheriff's deputy approached him. "Brother, firearms are not allowed inside the city limits," he said.

"Even by United States Marshals," Emmet said.

The deputy looked at Emmet's badge. "I beg your pardon, Marshal," he said.

"Could you recommend a good hotel and livery?" Emmet said.

"Yes. I'll take you to the best one in town," the deputy said.

The deputy and Emmet walked Blue several blocks through quiet, almost deserted streets. "A lot has changed since my last visit here in sixty-nine," Emmet said.

"One thing hasn't changed," the deputy said. "You won't find a saloon anywhere in the whole town."

"I didn't come here to drink," Emmet said.

"Here you go, Marshal," the deputy said. "The Hotel Salt Lake. Best in town and they'll livery your horse."

"Where can I find the Marshal's office in the morning?" Emmet said.

"On Brigham Boulevard, three blocks from here," the deputy said.

"Thanks and goodnight," Emmet said. He took his saddlebags, satchel and Winchester into the hotel and stopped at the desk.

"Good evening, Marshal," the desk clerk said. "Would you like a room?"

"I would," Emmet said. "And a shave and a bath in the morning and stable my horse."

"Very good, Marshal," the clerk said and handed Emmet the key to room 212.

Emmet went up to his room, tossed his gear on a chair and lit the lantern on the table. Beside the lantern was the Mormon Bible. He closed the door and looked at the notice on the door. *Alcohol prohibited anywhere in the hotel.*

"Even if I had some, I'm too damn tired to drink it," he said aloud.

Marshal Greg Thompson read the warrants at his desk, handed them back to Emmet and said, "Today is Sunday. You won't be able to see or speak to anyone until late afternoon."

"Why is that?" Emmet said.

"Obviously you don't understand Mormons," Thompson said.

"I was Chief of Railroad Police in sixty-nine," Emmet said. "I was here when they drove in the Golden Spike. I worked with and lived with them for months. I understand them. What I don't understand is a U.S. Marshal sitting on his ass when another U.S. Marshal shows him three warrants in his own town."

"I resent that," Thompson said.

"I don't care," Emmet said. "Services haven't started yet, I'll walk over to the church and see Brigham Young myself."

Thompson sighed. "Alright, let's go."

Brigham Young was changing in a large, private room behind the church. Voices from a choir filtered in through the door.

Young was close to eighty and appeared in poor health. A dozen members of his immediate circle assisted him.

Young turned to his second-in-command, John Tayler. "Brother John, would you help the Marshal with his request?" he said.

Tayler took Emmet and Thompson to a separate room.

"I need to speak with this man," Emmet said. "He is not in any trouble, but I need to speak to him about his brothers."

Tayler read the warrants. "Brother Brian is a fine, upstanding member of the community."

"No doubt," Emmet said.

Tayler sighed. "He and his wife are in the church. Wait here."

Ten minutes later, Brian Henderson and his wife June, along with Tayler, entered the room where Emmet and Thompson waited.

"Marshal, Brother Brian and his wife June," Tayler said.

"I've broken no laws," Brian said.

"No one said you did," Emmet said. "This is about your brothers."

"What about them," Brian said.

"Were they here recently?" Emmet said "

"Marshal, they're my brothers," Brian said. "You can't expect me to . . ."

"Brother Brian, your brothers are out-laws," Tayler said. "Murderers who will no doubt kill again. It's your bound duty by the laws of our church to tell what you know."

"They were here," Brian said. "Up to their sinful ways as usual. They wanted me to go with them, but I refused. They said they were going to Deadwood to find gold."

"Deadwood?" Emmet said. "In the Black Hills where Hickock was killed?"

"Yes sir, that's what they said," Brian said.

Rose took the turkey from the oven and carried it to the long dining room table and set it on the table. "John, you do the honors," she said.

Except for Emmet, the entire family was present. James sat beside Anna.

"Anna, help me bring out a few things," Rose said.

"I'll do it," Emma said. She went with Rose to the kitchen.

"The potatoes, carrots and gravy," Rose said.

"Rose, it's my fault Emmet isn't here," Emma said. "I made him promise."

Rose touched Emma's cheek. "I'm afraid Emmet would do this regardless," she said. "It's who he is and neither you nor I can change him anymore than we can change the weather."

"Would we?" Emma said. "Change him. If we could, I mean."

"No," Rose said.

"Do you know where he is?" Emma said.

"He was in Utah," Rose said. "He could be anywhere by now."

As the railroad had yet to reach western South Dakota, Emmet had to travel to eastern Wyoming to Casper and then ride to the Black Hills by horse.

He had sent a telegram before leaving Salt Lake City, explaining to Rose that he might as well finish the job rather than coming home only to set out again the next day.

Since discovering gold in the Black Hills, there were just three ways to reach the settlement of Deadwood, South Dakota. On horseback, by stagecoach, or walk. By horse, the journey would take five days. The same with the stage. Walking through the Black Hills was out of the question.

If gold wasn't enough to make Deadwood famous, Wild Bill Hickock getting shot in the back of the head by Jack McCall raised its legendary status to new heights. Almost overnight, the settlement grew tenfold. From a few dozen seeking gold to five thousand or more, and all of them anxious and willing to do anything to get rich overnight.

Some did, most didn't, but the real winners were the saloon keepers and shop owners.

The road was well marked and highly traveled by freight wagons, stage coaches and men on horseback. There were at least a dozen layover stations for the stage line in route and Emmet paid for a bed and livery for Blue the first three nights.

The fourth night, the way station was full with stagecoach passengers, but there was room in the barn for Emmet and Blue.

The afternoon of the fifth day, Emmet rode into Deadwood behind two stagecoaches and three freight wagons.

The main thoroughfare of Deadwood was crowded with what seemed like every citizen in the settlement. The streets were filled with mud and no one seemed to notice or care. Some buildings were made of wood, others were under construction and some were just large, wood-framed tents.

There were three saloons on opposite sides of the street. The Gem Variety Theatre, Nuttal and Mann's Saloon and the Belle Union saloon. All three featured gambling of every type and prostitution.

Emmet rode past the freight wagons and stage coaches and dismounted in front of the stage line office.

A beefy man of about fifty was checking off passengers on a clipboard.

"Excuse me," Emmet said.

The man ignored Emmet.

"I said, excuse me," Emmet said.

The man continued to ignore Emmet.

"Mister, if I have to ask again, you'll be face deep in mud," Emmet said.

The man looked at Emmet, then at the badge on Emmet's shirt. "Marshal, huh," the man said.

"You have any law in this town?" Emmet said.

"Across the street in the hardware store," the man said.

Emmet walked Blue across the street to the hardware store. He tied Blue to a post and ignored the two men fighting in the mud and entered the store.

A tall man wearing a suit was behind the counter. "Is the sheriff in here?" Emmet said.

"I'm the sheriff. Part time," the man said. "Name is Seth Bulloch."

"Well, Sheriff Bulloch, if you would oblige me, I'm here on official business," Emmet said.

"Sol, take over," Bulloch said to a thin man stacking supplies. "Come on, Marshal, I'll buy you a cup of coffee."

Emmet and Bulloch stepped out to the sidewalk where a man was attempting to steal Emmet's rifle. Emmet drew his Colt and smacked the man in the head with the barrel and the man fell unconscious in the mud.

"Across the street there, the cafeteria," Bulloch said.

Emmet walked Blue across the street and tied him to a post. A man was sitting on a wood crate on the sidewalk.

"Anybody touches my horse, you come get me pronto," Emmet said and tossed the man a dollar.

The cafeteria was crowded and Emmet and Bulloch had to get coffee at the long counter.

"So what brings a United States Marshal

to Deadwood?" Bulloch said.

"Two murderers," Emmet said.

"As half this town is a murderer in one fashion or another, could you be a bit more specific?" Bulloch said.

Emmer took out the warrants and handed them to Bulloch. "Henderson brothers," Bulloch said. "I can't say as I've heard the name, but a hundred men a day arrive here seeking gold and half use fake names."

"But how many brothers?" Emmet said.

"I admit I don't know," Bulloch said. "But I know someone who might."

Emmet and Bulloch left the cafeteria and Emmet gave the man on the crate another dollar. "You keep watching my horse and there will be two more in it for you," Emmet said.

Bulloch took Emmet to the Gem Variety Theatre, where a very large man sat on a stool beside the swinging doors. About thirty men were at tables and the bar. Several women, scantily clad were at tables with men. A tall, thin bartender was behind the bar.

"Johnny, where's Al?" Bulloch said.

"Office," Johnny said.

"Get him," Bulloch said.

Johnny left the bar and went to a back room. He returned a minute later with a short, stout man, wearing a suit minus a tie. Johnny returned to the bar, Al Swearengen walked to Bulloch and Emmet.

"Not guilty on all counts," Swearengen said.

"I haven't said anything yet," Bulloch said. "This is United States Marshal Emmet Boyd. He has a few questions."

"Should I be concerned?" Swearengen said. "Is this for public consumption or best behind closed doors?"

"Cut the shit, Al," Bulloch said.

"Closed doors," Emmet said.

"Office," Swearengen said. "Johnny, coffee for our guests."

Swearengen led Bulloch and Emmet to his office, followed by Johnny, who carried a tray with three cups of coffee on it.

After Johnny left the office, Swearengen sat behind his desk, Bulloch and Emmet took chairs.

"So what's on your mind, Marshal?" Swearengen said.

"Two brothers wanted for murder," Emmet said. "Name is Henderson."

"Brothers, you say," Swearengen said.

"They would have arrived here about a month ago," Emmet said. "Looking for gold."

"Everybody in the damn camp is looking

for gold," Swearengen said.

"But not you," Emmet said. "My guess is you make more money selling whiskey, women and dope than any gold claim could bring you."

"You do get to the point," Swearengen said. "Don't you, Marshal."

Emmet took a sip of coffee, then looked at Swearengen. "One of two things are going to be true by the end of this day," Emmet said. "The first is you are going to give me the Henderson brothers. The second is you don't and in that case I will ride out and return with twenty-five marshals and we will close this camp down tighter than an unopened can of peaches. Pick the outcome you prefer."

"I knew right off those two were walking under a black cloud," Swearengen said.

"Meaning what?" Emmet said.

"They got a claim, alright," Swearengen said. "Although I doubt they work it much."

"And what do they do when they're aren't working?" Emmet said.

"Now, Marshal, are you interested in say, things peripheral to this situation?" Swearengen said.

"I am not at this time," Emmet said.

"You'll leave things be if you leave here with the brothers?" Swearengen said.

"I will," Emmet said.

"Are you aware that General Custer discovered gold about thirty miles to the north in what is now known as Rapid City?" Swearengen said.

"I'm aware. Get to the damn point," Emmet said.

"When they aren't busy mining their claim, they pick up and deliver opium from Rapid City to Deadwood," Swearengen said.

"And into your hands," Emmet said.

"Peripheral, Marshal. Remember?" Swearengen said.

"Go on," Emmet said.

"They will arrive on the stage from Rapid City noon tomorrow," Swearengen said.

"No one interferes with my processing the warrants and peripheral business goes unnoticed," Emmet said.

"Fair enough," Swearengen said.

"Is there a hotel in camp?" Emmet said.

"Across the street, owned and run by E.B. Farnum," Swearengen said. "Tell him I said to give you the suite."

"Obliged," Emmet said.

Emmet and Bulloch left Swearengen and crossed the street and entered the two-story hotel.

"E.B., this is U.S. Marshal Emmet Boyd,"

Bulloch said. "Al says to give him the suite."

"I'd like a shave and a bath," Emmet said. "Sheriff, would you join me for dinner?"

"Seven o'clock at the cafeteria," Bulloch said.

"See you then," Emmet said.

After Bulloch left, Emmet signed the register.

"Would you like a woman sent to your room?" Farnum said.

"I would not," Emmet said.

Rip and Steve stood at the corral and watched as a few of the hands worked with a new mustang.

"Steve, if my mother left me this ranch, why can't I live here and run it?" Rip said.

"I guess because you're only fifteen," Steve said.

"I'm old enough to take care of myself and I have you as the foreman," Rip said. "We can make out just fine."

"Those kinds of decisions aren't up to me, Rip," Steve said.

"It should be my decision," Rip said.

"I'm afraid you're going to have to wait three more years," Steve said.

"I don't think so," Rip said.

John, Sarah, Ellis and Bettina helped Emma

and Josh with the freight delivery of their new furniture.

"I hope you didn't spend too much of Mr. Olson's money on all this," John said.

"No, sir," Josh said. "We have forty-five thousand left. We're going to buy fifty head of cattle for a thousand dollars and a dozen horses for another three thousand. We figure we're off to a really good start."

"I'd say you are," John said.

"Emma, let's get the first ever supper going in your new home," Sarah said.

John, Josh, and Ellis sat in new chairs on the new porch and drank coffee from new cups.

"So what are your plans for the cattle?" John said.

"Grow the herd until it's large enough to sell," Josh said.

"That will take time," John said.

"I know, but if I can bring a herd of horses to the Army the first year, we'll make a nice profit," Josh said.

Sarah came out to the porch with a cup of coffee and sat next to John. "I heard what you said about making a profit," she said. "That's good, because you're going to need it. Baby number two is on the way."

"What?" Josh said.

"Oh my God, James, what have we done," Anna said as she hurried and dressed.

"I believe the correct medical term is making love," James said.

"We're not supposed to, we're not married," Anna said. "It's my fault. I teased you too much."

"It's nobody's fault, it just happened," James said.

"Rose will know just by looking at me," Anna said. "And so will Emmet."

"Well we can't undo it," James said.

"Emmet has killed more people than the plague," Anna said.

"He's not going to kill me," James said. He looked at Anna. "Is he?"

Anna looked at James. "Oh boy," she said.

"That was a good steak," Emmet said.

"The Chinese butchers know their business," Bulloch said. "Can I buy you a drink?"

"One is my limit," Emmet said.

They left the cafeteria and went to the Gem Variety Theatre and found a vacant table by the wall. Swearengen and Johnny were behind the bar. Swearengen grabbed a bottle of whiskey and three shot glasses and went to Bulloch and Emmet's table.

"A drink is imminent," Swearengen said and took a chair.

Bulloch picked up the bottle and filled the three glasses.

"How long have you been a marshal, Marshal?" Swearengen said.

"I was Chief of Railroad Police on the Transcontinental," Emmet said. "I was appointed Marshal of Cheyenne in seventy."

"Appointed by whom?" Swearengen said.

"President Grant," Emmet said.

"Hear that, Bulloch?" Swearengen said. "We are in the presence of royalty."

"Knock it off, Al," Bulloch said.

"Mr. Swearengen, if the Henderson brothers don't get off that stage, you will get on," Emmet said, tossed back his drink, stood and walked out.

"Was it something I said?" Swearengen said.

"Al, that man is nobody to fool with," Bulloch said.

At the dinner table, John said, "Congratulations to both of you."

"This one better be a girl," Emma said. "Hear me, Josh?"

"Ellis, are you going to tell them or not?"

Bettina said.

"Tell us, what, son?" John said.

"I haven't decided yet," Ellis said.

"Decided what?" John said.

Bettina stood, went for her purse and returned with a letter and handed it to John. "I don't have my reading specs," he said and passed the letter to Sarah.

Sarah read the letter, lowered it and looked at John. "The Grange wants Ellis to run for the state senate," she said.

Emmet had breakfast in the cafeteria with Bulloch.

"The entire camp is talking about the Marshal and why he is here," Bulloch said.

"If it concerns any of them, I will let them know," Emmet said. "Do you have any deputies to speak of?"

"My partner Sol and Charlie Utter will wear a badge if I need them to," Bulloch said.

"Deputize them and clear the streets before the stage arrives," Emmet said.

"I'll back your play," Bulloch said.

"Not necessary," Emmet said.

"One lawman to another," Bulloch said.

"Alright," Emmet said. "But remember, it's my play."

■ ■ ■ ■

Rose looked across the breakfast table at Anna and said, "You're not eating."

"I'm not hungry," Anna said.

"I've seen the look of guilt before, but not like you're wearing it," Rose said.

"It shows?" Anna said.

"Like Hester Prynne," Rose said.

"Oh God," Anna said.

"Want to tell me about it?" Rose said.

"I don't know what happened," Anna said. "We were kissing and . . ."

"Say no more," Rose said. "It usually happens that way."

"What do I do? Emmet will . . ."

"Not find out," Rose said.

"How do I do that?"

"For one thing, stop looking like a cat that ate the family bird," Rose said. "And for God's sake, make sure James doesn't feel the need to confess to Emmet or we'll be looking for another doctor."

Anna nodded. "Yeah," she said.

Emmet waited in the street for the stage-coach to arrive. Bulloch stood beside him. Sol, Bulloch's partner at the hardware store and Charlie Utter stood on the sidewalk, each wearing deputy badges.

From the balcony of the Gem Variety Theatre Saloon, Al Swearengen watched as he drank a cup of coffee.

"Cigar, Marshal?" Bulloch said. "They come from Cuba."

"Thanks," Emmet said.

Bulloch handed Emmet a cigar and both men struck matches and lit up.

Emmet looked at his watch. "The stage is ten minutes late," he said.

"It's usually ten minutes late or ten minutes early," Bulloch said.

A few minutes later, proceeded by a cloud of dust, the stagecoach arrived and docked at the station.

Emmet watched as eight passengers got off the stage, two of which were Mitchel and Jonas Henderson. Each carried a satchel. Both wore Smith & Wesson, Schofield pistols. Both had the look of men who would kill in cold blood for no reason.

"Mitchel and Jonas Henderson, I have a warrant for your arrest," Emmet said.

The brothers turned and looked at Emmet as the main thoroughfare fell completely silent.

"Are you talking to us?" Mitchel said.

"I am if you're the Henderson brothers," Emmet said.

"Do we know you, Marshal?" Jonas said.

"Both of you men come with me right now," Emmet said.

"Now why would we do that?" Mitchel said.

"You'll answer for the seventy-two-year-old man you murdered in cold blood," Emmet said. "Here or at the end of a rope. At this point, I don't care which."

"What old man? What are you talking about?" Jonas said.

"His, name was Olson, and he was building a ranch south of Carson City," Emmet said. "You rode by and he offered you a meal and you shot and killed him in cold blood and robbed him. You were on your way south from Salt Lake City after visiting your brother. Any of this sound familiar?"

"You ain't taking us, Marshal," Jonas said. "Nobody is stretching our necks."

"You can't get us both, Marshal," Mitchel said.

"Can't I?" Emmet said. "Move for your guns and I'll kill you both."

For several seconds, it was as if the entire thoroughfare collectively held its breath.

Then, the brothers reached for their guns.

Emmet drew his Colt, cocked, and shot Mitchel in the chest, cocked, and shot Jonas in the chest and both hit the ground before anyone else even moved.

Bulloch looked at Emmet. "Damn," he said.

Emmet walked to the brothers. Jonas was still alive.

"I told you," Emmet said.

"It's better than a rope," Jonas said right before he closed his eyes and died.

Emmet walked back to Bulloch. "Sheriff, you and your deputies write what you saw for me to take back to Judge Briscoe in Carson City," Emmet said.

After breakfast with Bulloch the following morning, Emmet walked Blue along the main thoroughfare. They passed the Gem Variety Theatre Saloon, where Swearengen was on the balcony with a mug of coffee.

"I hope you come back and visit us again, Marshal," Swearengen said.

Emmet looked up. "Doubtful," he said.

At the edge of camp, Emmet shook hands with Bulloch. "Be seeing you, Sheriff," Emmet said, mounted the saddle and rode off.

Bulloch turned and walked back to his office. At the Gem Variety Theatre Saloon, he looked up at Swearengen.

"I told you he was nobody to fool with," Bulloch said.

■ ■ ■ ■

The entire family gathered at Emma and Josh's new house for Sunday dinner after church. The house was warm and Emma was feeling the need for some fresh air. She took a cold glass of lemonade to the porch and sat in the shade.

She spotted a tiny cloud in the distance and stood up for a better look. Then she ran off the porch and stood in the road. When she was sure it was Emmet, she ran down the road to meet him.

"Hey, little sister," Emmet said when she reached him.

"You got them?" Emma said.

"I got them," Emmet said.

He extended his hand, grabbed Emma and lifted her onto the back of the saddle.

"I'm having another baby," Emma said.

"Not today," Emmet said.

"No, of course not," Emma said.

"In that case, hold on," Emmet said and broke Blue into a flat out run.

ABOUT THE AUTHOR

Al Lamanda was born in the Bronx, New York, and lived most of his life in Manhattan. His debut novel *Dunston Falls* received high praise from *Kirkus* and *Publishers Weekly* and from there he was hooked, writing more than twenty novels and several screenplays.

He wrote the screenplay for *American Violence,* which starred Bruce Dern and Denise Richards. He was nominated for the Nero Award for *This Side of Midnight, First Light,* and *With Six You Get Wally.* He was nominated for the Edgar Award for best novel for *Sunset,* which was also voted the best crime novel by the Maine Writers and Publishers Alliance. In his spare time, Lamanda is an avid weight lifter and boxer, and housemaid to his Maine Coon cat. Under the pen name Ethan J. Wolfe, Lamanda has written a dozen historical western novels that are both popular and highly reviewed.

Printed in the USA
CPSIA information can be obtained
at www.ICGtesting.com
JSHW020429030524
62356JS00007B/9

9 798885 799713